Dear Santa

Also by
Nancy Naigle

*Christmas
Joy*

-

*Hope at
Christmas*

Visit www.NancyNaigle.com
for a full list of novels
by Nancy Naigle.

Nancy Naigle

Dear Santa

ST. MARTIN'S GRIFFIN
NEW YORK

DEAR SANTA. Copyright © 2018 by Nancy Naigle. All rights reserved. Printed in the United States of America. For information, address St. Martin's Press, 175 Fifth Avenue, New York, N.Y. 10010.

www.stmartins.com

The Library of Congress Cataloging-in-Publication Data

Names: Naigle, Nancy.
Title: Dear Santa / Nancy Naigle.
Description: First edition. | New York: St. Martin's Griffin, 2018.
Identifiers: LCCN 2018026426| ISBN 9781250185174 (trade pbk.) |
    ISBN 9781250185181 (ebook)
Subjects: LCSH: Christmas stories. | GSAFD: Love stories.
Classification: LCC PS3614.A545 D43 2018 | DDC 813/.6—dc23
LC record available at https://lccn.loc.gov/2018026426

Our books may be purchased in bulk for promotional, educational, or business use. Please contact your local bookseller or the Macmillan Corporate and Premium Sales Department at 1-800-221-7945, extension 5442, or by email at MacmillanSpecialMarkets@macmillan.com.

First Edition: October 2018

10 9 8 7 6 5 4 3 2 1

Let your traditions remain strong,
and may a bit of childhood innocence find its way
into your holiday this year.

Wishing you and your loved ones
a very Merry Christmas.

Acknowledgments

Special thanks to senior editor Eileen Rothschild for helping bring this fun story to the page. To the whole St. Martin's Press team . . . thank you for working so well together. You always come through at every stage of the process, from the beautiful cover and the amazing graphics to distribution, promotion, and marketing to make *Dear Santa* a success. I'm so excited about this book. It was such a fun one to write.

To Kevan Lyon, my amazing agent, thank you for your support, and for believing in me and the stories I write. This journey is so much more with you at my side. I appreciate all you do to enable me to live this dream.

Thank you to Lisa Coleman for her tireless support, and for extending her hand following my accident in the snow resulting in a ruptured Achilles tendon that required surgery, and helping me stay on track despite the crazy physical therapy schedule. Thank you for helping with the fun Dear Santa letters at the beginnings of the chapters. Your experience with children brought real life to those letters.

And to those who helped me daily behind the scenes: Andrew, Mom *aka Miss Bettie to my friends*, Dr. Teasdall and my PT Mark, Marie, Dana Beth, Dad and Greta, and my furry boys, Dakota and Sarge—thanks for the brainstorming, beta reads, for getting

Acknowledgments

me back on my feet before my book signings began, the snowy rescue, girl talk, cheerleading, being a sounding board, boosting me up when things went sideways, filling your little free library with my books, snuggles, giggles, and celebrations. Writing this novel would not have been nearly as satisfying without y'all's help and fellowship.

AND TO ALL OF YOU READING THIS ~ THANK YOU!

Dear Santa

Chapter One

Dear Santa,
It's me, Chrissy, again. I'm still being good. I'm going to
have a Christmas tree in my room. You can put my presents
there so I don't have to wait until Daddy wakes up Christmas
morning. He sleeps way too late. Be careful on the stairs.
                                                    Chrissy

Angela Carson prided herself on keeping things simple, like coffee, for example. She made her own. No K-cups or fancy electronic gadgets. Just a good old-fashioned automatic drip pot. The same one that she'd had in her college dorm days. No exotic flavored coffee either—just the local grocer's brand.

She used the same simplicity when it came to her store, Heart of Christmas, located in the old lighthouse at the edge of town where the road curved hard to the right, hugging the coastline near the jetty. And not just any lighthouse, but the one where her great-great-grandfather had worked until the day he died.

When her grandmother, affectionately called Momma Grace, died she'd left the family heirloom with all its charm to Angela, along with the beach house she'd grown up in, which was on the adjacent oceanfront property. And even though the lighthouse had been decommissioned long ago, it still sported its original daymark, a unique harlequin-like diamond pattern, adding a touch of whimsy among the sun-bleached pastel-colored beach houses in the surrounding area.

Beachcombers came in droves year-round to Pleasant Sands, North Carolina, because the jetty pumped up the ocean waves, allowing for huge deposits of shells. Shell seekers spent hours rooting through the piles and piles of colorful treasures.

Small prize shells, like the colorful coquinas, augers and tiny olive shells, could be found among larger shells such as clams, scallops, occasional whelks and Scotch bonnets, which were always a keeper.

The bounty brought people back again and again. And with that came a steady flow of customers.

Thankful was how Angela felt about all of those shell-seeking customers, and her dedicated staff. But today Heart of Christmas was closed so she and her staff could enjoy the holiday with their families, despite the fact that her competition had chosen to stay open on Thanksgiving Day.

Angela gulped a cup of coffee to chase the bitter taste in her mouth. Christmas Galore? There wasn't a single thing sincerely Christmassy about that store.

She opened the large glass 27-by-40-inch frame that protected her message-of-the-day board on the street side of Heart of Christmas. Locals said they enjoyed the local facts she posted there, which was nice because she loved posting them, and changed them at least weekly . . . more when the mood struck her.

With the canvas tool bucket next to her, she pulled out a few wet wipes and cleared yesterday's message, leaving a shiny black surface with just the words DID YOU KNOW? in bright red along the top.

She grabbed a wide chalk paint marker in royal blue and wrote out the message of the day, switching up colors to make it look festive.

DID YOU KNOW?

In 1710, Edward Teach, aka Blackbeard the Pirate,
spent Thanksgiving in Pleasant Sands as a guest of the
owners of the Topside Tavern, the Collins family, on
Checker Street. Thirty years old, his table manners weren't
the best, but he gave a gold coin to each child there.

HAPPY THANKSGIVING

She stepped back to proofread for spelling, squinting against the bright sun. Last year she'd had to break out her winter coat on Thanksgiving but today the sun shone as brilliantly as if it were an end-of-season summer day.

Angela's phone began playing "Jailhouse Rock," the ringtone for her lawyer sister, Marie. "Hey, Marie."

"Are you busy?"

"Just finished switching out my message at the shop."

"I can't believe I didn't think of this," Marie said, "but Brad is asking about Momma Grace's oyster dressing. I forgot to ask you to make it. Do you have time? Apparently it's more important to Brad than the turkey."

"I thought that was expected," Angela said. "I made it this morning."

"You're the best sister."

Angela heard the whoosh of relief. It wasn't until just a couple years before Momma Grace died that she'd finally trusted Angela with that recipe—sort of the official hand-off of the legacy. Just like the store had been.

"I have another favor to ask too. Can you zip over to the

Crabby Coffee Pot and pick up an order for me? It's already paid for. It'll save a trip out for Brad."

"Sure. I can do that." Not a fan of fancy brews, Angela hadn't been to the new coffee shop, even though it was practically across the street from Heart of Christmas. From the front door she could see their sign: a bright red crab with its open claw waving to the patrons below as he balanced on a blue speckled coffeepot. "As soon as I get your coffee, I'll get the stuff from the house and head your way."

"Have I told you lately that you're my favorite sister?"

"I'm your *only* sister." Angela laughed. "But that does make me feel a little better about letting you do all the work on these big holiday meals."

"You know I love doing it," Marie said.

Marie wouldn't stop at just dinner for the family either. Right after they ate she'd start welcoming guests for her Holiday Warm-up, an annual event with an open invitation to all of Angela's and Brad's customers and vendors, along with neighbors and friends. People would come and go for hours, noshing on delectable desserts and getting ready for the holiday season. Angela was exhausted just thinking about it.

"That I do. I'll see you in a while." Angela ended the call and tucked her phone into her back pocket.

She crossed the beach road and cut through the parking lot toward the small row of colorful storefronts, each a different shade of blue, peach, yellow and green.

To her surprise, the Crabby Coffee Pot was as busy today as any workday.

The front door had been propped open to take advantage of the mild weather. As she got closer to the bright yellow front door the aroma of fresh-brewed coffee wafted out into the parking lot and mingled with the smell of bacon from the diner down the way, making her hungry.

Bright blue nautical ropes herded the customers to the counter to place their orders in a line that wrapped around twice like a giant snake. She let herself be nudged along, thankful that at least the line was moving.

People stepped up to the register, recited their order and then left with a lift in their step before even taking the first sip of the caffeinated concoction. Some of those drinks were quite pretty, with their whipped cream, sprinkles and all.

She was tempted to treat herself to one.

Other customers were picking up orders too, some of them quite large. Angela suddenly found herself hoping Marie hadn't ordered so much that Angela wouldn't be able to walk home with it. It wouldn't surprise her one bit. Marie was her complete opposite, going whole hog on everything she did. No telling how many people would pass through her sister's house this afternoon and evening. Angela would stay just long enough to slip out when the house got crowded.

Across the way a dark-haired man reading *The Wall Street Journal* at a two-topper caught her attention. His watch glimmered beneath the edge of his perfectly tailored suit. Crisp ocean-blue cuffs peeked from beneath his sleeve a perfect half-inch. He looked the type to have money to spare. There were quite a few of his kind in Pleasant Sands since all those high-end condos had been built near the marina.

She'd take her weathered beach house any day, but these transplants were bringing new things to the area. Like this shop, for instance. Most of them were partial-year residents who closed the doors of their condos at the end of the season and disappeared until spring.

Her eyes followed the line of the man's sharply creased dress pants to his leather loafers. Nice shoes said a lot about a man. So many of the beach guys around here opted for sneakers or flip-flops year-round. That drove her nuts. Didn't they know grown-ups were supposed to wear real shoes?

She lifted her gaze, to see him looking directly at her. Their eyes locked. Even from here she could tell his were blue. As blue as the starched button-down dress shirt he wore. And for a moment she felt unable to look away.

Please tell me he didn't notice that I was checking him out.

But the slight lift at the corner of his mouth said he'd definitely noticed. She managed a smile, certain her cheeks were red.

Her phone rang. Thankful for the distraction, she dug for her phone and answered. "Hi, Marie. I'm in line to pick up your order. It's really busy."

"I appreciate you picking that up for me," Marie said.

Angela could tell she was on speaker. She could just picture Marie multitasking in her kitchen. "I don't mind. What's up?"

"Can I borrow that gravy carafe I gave you for Christmas last year too?"

"Sure, I'll pick up the carafe when I go home to get the dressing. I'll see you in a little while."

"Good. I've got all of our favorites. I love tradition."

"Me too. I wouldn't miss it." Heart of Christmas had been tradition too. Only, that might not be the case for long. Angela's gut ached at the thought.

"What would I do without you?" Marie said. "You're an angel."

"Aren't all sisters angels-in-waiting?" Angela remembered those words of comfort from their mom. It was the only thing about her mother she still remembered.

"Oh great, like that's not pressure," Marie said with a heavy sigh.

6

"I'll talk to you in a little bit." Angela ran her hand through her hair, trying not to give into the temptation to look back at that guy again. But by the time the next customer had walked away with their coffee and pastries, she found herself drawn back in his direction. *Nothing nonchalant about that.*

Thankfully, his newspaper seemed to have his full attention. As she looked closer, she realized he didn't really have that fancy-condo boat-guy look. Didn't have the weathered skin, or remnants of the sun lightning his hair, the way those guys did. Maybe he wasn't from around here at all.

"Next!" a brisk shout came from across the counter.

Angela felt a thump on her shoulder.

"That's you," the teenage girl behind her said as she almost pushed Angela off balance.

"Sorry." Angela lunged toward the counter, glancing back at Blue-eyes one last time. He was smiling at her.

She managed an awkward finger wave then turned before he saw the hot rush of embarrassment racing up her chest.

"May I help you?" The barista's words carried an edge that didn't even require a finger snap to get her attention.

Angela cleared her throat to place her order, then managed another quick glance, but he'd already moved on.

"Um, yes. Sorry." Somehow a plain coffee seemed way too ordinary after the long wait. "I'll have what she just ordered."

In a flash there was a sparkly paper cup with a peppermint-striped sleeve in front of her. Steam rising from the top, which reminded her of the other reason she preferred to make her own coffee: so she could sip it without burning the first layer of skin off of her lips.

"Whipped cream?" It was almost a threat the way the barista waved the shiny silver can.

"Why not? Go wild." Angela watched the sugary sweet confection stack into a swirly peak, followed by a toss of chocolate sprinkles and a cherry right in the middle. At least the whipped cream should cool down the coffee a little.

"Pretty." Angela handed over a ten-dollar bill.

As the woman counted back her change, Angela remembered the reason she was even here in the first place. "I'm sorry. I'm here to pick up an order for Marie Watterman too."

"Of course you are." The girl standing behind Angela propped a hand on her hip and cocked her head, checking her watch as if she were late for something.

The barista shoved a fancy blue sack toward her. "Already paid for."

Angela wrangled the bag, trying to maneuver it and not spill her coffee. The bag was so large it wouldn't even fit in the overhead compartment of an airplane. And it was heavy.

The barista craned her neck past Angela. "Next."

Angela left with barely enough change to satisfy the bell ringer standing on the sidewalk, but she dropped the coins and dollars into the kettle anyway. "Merry Christmas."

"You too. Thank you."

Despite his snow-white beard, Santa's hands looked strong, and even this late in November he had a tan. Probably a young surfer earning a few extra bucks to make it to the next big waves. Lots of locals, especially the fishermen and surfers, had tans late into the year. Angela's brother-in-law, Brad, was like that too, from being out on construction sites. He was successful enough now that he could sit in the office and never swing a hammer again, but he loved the physical part of the job, and his crews loved him for that.

The growth spurt in Pleasant Sands had been very good for his business.

Not so much for hers. Quite the opposite, in fact.

She stopped to get a better grip on the heavy bag, and then took another sip of her coffee. She had to admit it was pretty good coffee. She could see how people got hooked on it.

As she walked to the end of the strip mall heading home, she noticed the handsome stranger on his phone leaning against the open door of a shiny red sports car.

She smiled and waved, her stomach whirling, but he didn't seem to notice her. Too bad; she wouldn't have minded a quick conversation with him.

She crossed the street. Her old beach house could use a new coat of paint this spring. The once beachy, deep grayish-blue called Nantucket Fog had faded to more of a rainy-day gray, making the pewter shutters almost disappear. She knew she should've gone with the brick-red shutters even though Brad said it wasn't a beachy combination; at least the house wouldn't be fading into the backdrop right now.

She wondered where the stranger would be eating dinner tonight. She wished she'd thought to look at his license plate. Was he one of the new condo residents who had moved into the area, or was he only passing through on his way somewhere else?

Wouldn't it be funny if he ended up being one of the guests at her sister's Holiday Warm-up tonight? she thought. It could happen. This big old world had a way of seeming small most of the time, with everyone intersecting in one way or another.

What was it people said about that small-world experiment? That whole six-degrees-of-separation theory? That we're all connected in an average of just six hops among family, acquaintances or friends.

When Angela got back to her beach house, she stopped and

put the bag in the front seat of her car, and then ran up the stairs to her front door.

She straightened its beachy wreath. A ring of artificial fern looked soft beneath the bevy of starfish, sand dollars and assorted shells she'd collected on the beach.

As soon as she opened the door, parsley, sage and thyme from the dressing filled the air. She gathered the casserole dish and the carafe for Marie.

She loved spending Thanksgiving with Marie's family, and now that there was an itsy-bitsy chance she might run into the handsome stranger there, it was even more exciting.

It wasn't a stretch that she might run into the dark-haired man from the Crabby Coffee Pot again—as soon as tonight—with all of the guests her sister always entertained at her Holiday Warm-up party. Angela might even stay for the whole party this year. She put the covered dish down and ran back into her room to change into something a little dressier.

Chapter Two

Dear Santa,
I'm sorry I told you to put my presents under the tree in my
room this year. Daddy said that was bossy. I didn't mean to
be bossy.
You can do whatever you want and it's okay with me.
Happy Thanksgiving,
Chrissy

At eleven o'clock Angela stood at the front door of her sister's house carrying Momma Grace's large casserole dish. The aqua Pyrex with the gold starburst was as precious as the recipe itself. She gave the door a one-two knock then balanced the dish against her hip as she opened the door to let herself in.

The huge wreath flopped against the door as she nudged it open with her knee. "Happy Thanksgiving." Angela kicked the door closed behind her and headed straight for the kitchen. A baritone woof sounded from somewhere in her wake.

"Aunt Angela!" Chrissy squealed as she came flying across the room, wrapping her arms around Angela's hips.

"Hey, Chrissy," Angela said. "Let me put this down so I can get a real hug."

The tiny five-year-old bounced on tiptoes. Fat orange-and-brown rickrack ribbons bobbed from her ponytail, just like the ones Momma Grace used to put in Angela's and Marie's hair when they were kids.

Angela put the dish on the kitchen counter, then swept her niece into her arms. "Chrissy, you look bee-yooo-tiful." Chrissy clung to her like a koala bear as Angela twirled around.

"More, Auntie Angela. More!" Chrissy cried out between fits of giggles with her hands reaching toward the ceiling.

Marie stepped up beside them, shaking her head. "Put her down before you make her toss her cookies. Literally. She's been sampling treats all morning." Marie had a way of losing her patience when she was busy, leaving Angela feeling like a scolded child.

Angela put Chrissy back down, and then gave her niece a boop with her fingertip right on the end of her nose. "Mommy is just no fun."

"You're always fun," Chrissy squealed.

Marie's voice was steady. "Mommy is worried your auntie forgot to bring the coffee."

"Did not," Angela said. "It's in the car. I couldn't carry everything in all at once. That bag was heavy."

Chrissy sped off to the living room. "Daddy, Auntie Angela didn't blow off. She's here."

Marie's face went red.

Angela grabbed a cookie and leaned against the center island. Brad's success as a contractor had blessed her sister with a kitchen any television chef would drool over. Not that Marie did all that much cooking, but she sure did love to entertain.

Angela lifted a brow, waiting for Marie to explain Chrissy's comment. But she didn't. "So, was it you or Brad who thought I'd be a no-show? We just talked this morning."

"I didn't think you'd completely blow us off."

"Really?" Angela knew that tone. Her sister had an opinion about everything.

Marie said, "Okay, so I might be a little surprised you didn't decide to open the store today."

"Why would you even think that?"

"Because you said there was a chance you might have to close the store for good, and Christmas Galore is open."

Angela felt her blood pressure rise. It wasn't like she hadn't considered it. "I don't care if every other store in the nation is open. We've never done it, and I never will. Thanksgiving is a day for families to spend together." She unclenched her fists. She was angry. Not so much at Marie as she was the situation. "You're the one always saying I do nothing but work. So I make a decision that is about family and you judge me for that too. I can't win with you."

"Fine. I'm sorry. You're right." Marie walked over and hugged her. "I'm glad you're here. If you hadn't shown, I'd never have lived it down." Marie stepped back, swung her dish towel over her shoulder and folded her arms. "But in Brad's defense, it's not like you haven't been dodging us since the store's been in trouble. And I still say it's not a bad thing if you do close."

"You're right. I'm guilty of not wanting to talk about that stuff with you, but it's my problem. Not yours. And I've never missed a Thanksgiving." Angela took another cookie from the tray and rearranged the others to hide the open spot. "I know you don't understand my commitment to the store, but this isn't easy."

"I didn't say it was. I just said it wasn't a bad thing."

"I don't want to let the store go under." Angela swallowed, the lump in her throat making it hard to get that last cookie down.

"Of course you don't. Heart of Christmas is your whole

existence," Marie said. "Except for one serious relationship, you've given that store one hundred percent of your heart and time."

Marie hadn't even used his name, yet Angela felt that familiar pang of hurt. She and Jimmy had had their whole lives planned here in Pleasant Sands until he got that job offer in Texas. Her family had just buried Momma Grace, and there was no way she could leave Heart of Christmas behind. But he'd already made up his mind to take the job. Sometimes she still wondered what would have happened had she gone with him. But she hadn't, and when he'd shown up the following summer with his new bride and baby she'd chalked it up to "not meant to be."

"At least the store has always been there for me. Can't say that about Jimmy," Angela replied.

"And now the store is going to break your heart too."

Those words hurt like a slap to the face.

"You've got to quit dragging this out, sis. You're going to end up losing everything you've got trying to keep that place open."

Angela knew Marie meant well, and she was right. Angela had taken a loan against the beach house, a risky move.

"If it makes you feel any better, I've decided to make my final decision this weekend. Black Friday sales are always an indicator of how the rest of the season is going to play out. If we don't pull off a great day, I'm going to close."

Marie stood there. Blinking.

"Why are you looking at me like that? Isn't this what you've wanted?"

Marie's brows pulled together. "Oh, Angela. I'm sorry, I'm glad to hear you're finally dealing with facts and reality, but I know this is killing you. That being said, they say there's magic in Christmas. If anyone deserves it, it's you." Marie slid Angela's dressing into the oven. "Something new is going to come your way. Something even better."

Angela didn't dare say it out loud, but she was praying for magic too—a lot of it. She'd give anything to not have to close, but that didn't change the fact that Heart of Christmas was in trouble— serious like might-have-to-lock-the-doors-at-the-end-of-the-month trouble. At least Marie hadn't chosen this moment to give her another speech about how Angela didn't have a legal obligation to keep Heart of Christmas up and running. Marie was never going to understand her connection to the store.

She'd never been as close with Momma Grace as Angela had been.

And for the seven years since Momma Grace had died, Heart of Christmas had afforded her a comfortable lifestyle, even if it hadn't left her much time for anything else.

"I'll go get the coffee," Angela offered, happy for the escape and a moment to pull herself together.

Rover, the 150-pound Newfoundland who still thought he was a twenty-pound pup, trotted behind her out to the car and back. That dog had as much education as some people. Puppy school. Obedience school three times. A private trainer. He'd even been shipped off to boarding school twice. He'd been a slow learner, but now he was a well-behaved, and giant, part of the family.

He nudged Angela from behind as she walked inside.

Making her way to the kitchen, Rover was at her heels. "It's just coffee beans, boy." She placed the bag on the end of the long island, the only spot that wasn't lined with cookies, cakes, pastries and pies.

Angela patted Rover on the head absently as she watched Marie hustle through the kitchen, moving pots from the big stainless steel commercial range to the quartz countertop.

"What can I do to help?" Angela asked. "Want me to start the coffee?" She eyed the huge commercial brewer. It didn't look too complicated.

"That would be great. The water's already in it. Just put five of those scoops in the thingamabob on top. Then press *start*. It's ready to go."

Angela turned her back on the huge Sub-Zero glass-front refrigerator, which just reiterated the differences between herself and her sister. If Angela owned that refrigerator it would be so cluttered it would probably autodial Molly Maid to come clean itself. Marie's was as orderly as the local high-end market, and not one fingerprint on the thing. With a five-year-old in the house, how was that even possible?

Angela opened the coffee and began scooping out heaping doses. The grounds were dark and moist, and the aroma so fresh that just the smell gave her a burst of energy.

After their quiet little turkey dinner, the dishes would be cleared and things would quickly shift to Holiday Warm-up mode and the doorbell would start ringing.

Angela was exhausted just thinking about all the work her sister put into these holiday parties. From flower arrangements and door wreaths to a table setting that Martha Stewart would *ooh* and *ah* over, even the most pretentious people in this town wouldn't find a thing to complain about.

At least for the next hour it would be just Marie, Brad and Chrissy. And Rover.

Marie wiped her hands on her apron. "Would you tell Brad and Chrissy that dinner will be ready in ten minutes? We're just waiting on the rolls."

Angela knew Marie well enough to know that she just wanted her out of the way so she walked down the hall to the great room, where Brad was reclined in front of the big-screen television with Chrissy playing on the floor quietly with a Christmas book.

"About ten more minutes," Angela said.

"Good. I'm ready." Chrissy rubbed her tummy. "I've been hungry for turkey all year."

"Me too," Brad said. "Only I've been hungry for turkey *and* stuffing."

Angela loved that Brad was as crazy about the family recipe as they were, even if he did call it stuffing. Momma Grace had always said stuffing was the cornbread mixture you stuffed in the bird while it baked. Dressing was for the good stuff and deserved its own pan.

Oyster dressing wasn't everyone's thing, but fresh oysters from here off the coast made all the difference. "I made an extra-big batch, just for you."

"Thanks. How've you been, Angela?"

"Good. Busy with the store."

"You've been scarce around here lately." He nodded, as if waiting for more.

She shrugged. "You know me. Work. Work. Work."

Brad laid down the remote. "I saw you did some advertising in the local paper for Black Friday. I've never known you to advertise. It looked good."

"Yes. Well, I've never done the Snow Valley before. I wanted to be sure the word got out."

"But you're not opening early on Black Friday?"

"No. Our regular store hours give everyone plenty of time to shop. And now they can play in the snow too."

"Hope it works out for you. Your sister's been worried." He looked a little worried too.

"I'll be fine."

"I have no doubt about that. If it's one thing I know firsthand, it's that you Carson girls are smart and tough."

Marie walked into the room. "You've got that right. We're tough as they come." She glanced toward her sister. "A little hard-headed too."

Brad got out of his chair. "You're not going to trick me into agreeing with you." He put his hand out to Chrissy. "I'm pretty smart too. Come on, baby girl. I bet dinner is ready."

"It is. I was just coming to get you." They all walked into the dining room and sat down to eat. Chrissy said grace and then Brad passed the tray of perfectly sliced turkey around the table.

Angela had seen Brad with the electric knife before; she was certain this was not his doing, and Marie never could carve a turkey. She had a sneaky suspicion her sister had bought a pre-cooked, pre-sliced bird. Probably paid a pretty penny for it too. Actually, the way everything was set in pretty chafing dishes, Angela wasn't sure that the whole meal hadn't been catered, except for the oyster dressing she'd brought. Momma Grace's old Pyrex looked so out of place in the lineup.

Not that she'd complain.

She'd never baked a turkey in her life and she was perfectly fine letting her sister run with the big holiday hosting duties. That was just one more thing to be thankful for today.

With a small spoonful of everything on her plate, plus a good-size dollop of the oyster dressing, she wasn't halfway through eating before she was feeling full. "We could've fed four more families with all of this food. We've barely put a dent in this extravagant spread."

"Everything is so good, babe," Brad said to Marie.

"I think we're going to be eating turkey for a lot of days," Chrissy said, putting her palm against her forehead. "Forever, maybe."

"There's not one of these things that we could do without."

"Definitely not without the stuffing," Brad said with a big smile toward Angela. "Or the yeast rolls. Or gravy."

"Collards," Angela interjected.

Marie surveyed the table. "And you have to have mashed potatoes, even though there is dressing and sweet potato casserole. It's just the way it's supposed to be."

"I know, and it's all so good," Angela said.

"And cranberry sauce," Chrissy said, raising her fork in the air like a scepter.

"On the bright side," Marie said, "you're taking leftovers home to eat."

"Fine by me," Angela said.

Brad stuffed another forkful of turkey into his mouth.

Marie cleared her throat, and reached for another roll. "Brad was telling me that he saw Jeremy yesterday."

Angela stopped chewing. Jeremy worked for her at Heart of Christmas. She had no idea where this conversation was headed, but she was pretty sure she was getting ready to lose her appetite.

"He said," Marie continued, "that even your Saturday holiday craft classes aren't filling up anymore."

"They've been smaller. That's true." She sipped her water, hoping Marie would let it go.

"Used to be the locals counted on your year-round classes. It was something affordable and fun to do with the kids on the weekend," Marie said.

"People get busy," Angela said. "You haven't brought Chrissy to one in months." The words came out more like a bite. She hadn't meant to say that out loud.

"Well. I . . ." Marie struggled for an excuse. "Yes. You're right. People get busy."

That had shut her sister up, but she knew what the point of the conversation was and her sister was right. There'd been a time when Angela had to turn people away because the classes were full. This Saturday she was offering a class to make reindeer ornaments from reclaimed corks donated by the vineyard two towns over that produced the best darn muscadine wine around.

Brad looked amused by the conversation, like he enjoyed seeing Marie get put in her place. For once. "You and Chrissy should go to that class, Marie."

Angela could teach it with her eyes closed. It was a kid favorite so she'd scheduled the class expecting a full house. Plus, parents filled their buggies with holiday gifts while the kids crafted. But she only had six people sign up for the class this time. The past year there'd been a steady decline in sales and the classes that used to supplement them.

Marie glared at him. Clearly she had other things to do.

"No," Angela said. "It's fine. It'll be what it's meant to be. Besides, how many ornaments does a person need?" Marie had thrown that in her face the last time they'd talked about this. Angela really hoped it was the last time they'd discuss it.

She picked up the basket of still-warm rolls and passed them toward Brad. "Roll?"

"Definitely." He grabbed one and passed the basket to Marie.

Marie reached for his hand, and then Chrissy's. "I'm so thankful for our family."

They ate quietly until Chrissy piped up and asked to be excused.

"Yes, you may." Brad folded his napkin and placed it on the table. "I'm pretty much done too. Why don't you girls catch up? I'll clear all the dishes."

"Thanks, babe," Marie said.

Angela wished she'd offered to clear the table. That would've been better than getting the third-degree from Marie, because she could feel it coming.

Marie said, "Sis, what do you think the odds are that things will be okay for the store?"

"We'll know tomorrow."

"I know. You said that, but what's your gut telling you?"

Angela heard Brad clanging around in the kitchen. She lowered her voice. "You know it's been struggling."

"Are you behind financially?"

"Things are tight since Christmas Galore opened. We've definitely seen a decline in sales. I didn't expect them to be competition for us since the only real thing Christmas about their store is the name of it. It's a stretch to call it a Christmas store at all, but—"

"Well, they might not be just Christmas, but they do have a lot of Christmas stuff," Marie said.

"It's just a clever marketing ploy riding on Christmas's coat-tails. From what I understand they have sand chairs to sunscreen and every other beach whim under the sun." Angela shrugged.

"You haven't been over to Christmas Galore to check it out?" Marie asked.

"No. I have *not*." Angela snapped her head around. Did her sister really think she'd step foot in that place? "Have *you*?"

"Sure."

Why did that feel like such a betrayal? "Please tell me you didn't buy anything."

"Some deals you just can't pass by. You said yourself the stores are completely different."

"Seriously? Marie? How could you do that?"

"It wasn't like I bought Christmas stuff," Marie said.

"What about the wreath and the little fake Christmas tree for my room?" Chrissy stood wide-eyed and innocent in the doorway. "It's so pretty."

"I bet it is," Angela tried to say sweetly to Chrissy, but her heart was sinking. "I can't believe you would do that, Marie."

"You don't even sell fake trees."

"For. A. Reason." Angela wanted to scream. "You really bought one?"

"So?"

Angela stood and turned to face her sister straight on. "So you're my sister. You're supposed to be on my side."

"I am on your side, but Christmas Galore is a cool store, and they have great sales. Nothing like Heart of Christmas."

"My store isn't cool?" Angela practically choked on the words. Holding back tears, she squeezed her hands together.

Chrissy bounced at her side. "They have cherry sno-cones in paper cones that look like Santa hats."

Angela stooped next to Chrissy and tried to hide the bite she felt in the words she was about to say. "That sounds like so much fun, Chrissy."

"It was. And it looked like I had red lipstick on when I was done." Chrissy kissed the air. "I was so pretty."

Brad came in to clear the rest of the dishes. A fork fell from the top plate and fell in front of Angela.

She picked it up, squeezing it in her hand and hammering it into the air as she spoke. "Not only haven't you come to any of the classes at Heart of Christmas this year with Chrissy, but you haven't even bothered to come see how Snow Valley turned out. I worked hard pulling that together."

Marie's mouth dropped open, but she held whatever it was she was going to say.

Chapter Three

Dear Santa,
You can text my mom at (555) 432-1314 for my list. I used
her phone to take pictures of everything I want this year so
you don't mess up.

Thanks,
Reggie

Brad took the fork out of Angela's shaking hand and disappeared into the kitchen with the dirty dishes.

Marie lifted her chin. "You have to admit, snow at the beach is just a little out there. We never have snow in Pleasant Sands."

"Well, we have it this year," Angela said.

"I don't see how that's going to help sales."

Angela hated fighting with Marie. Usually she could let Marie's opinions roll right off of her, but this time it was personal. "Christmas Galore is sucking the last life out of Heart of Christmas, and I'm brokenhearted at the thought of having to close. I couldn't go down without a fight. Why can't you at least understand that?"

"But an indoor snow town?"

"Snow *Valley*." Angela sucked in a breath.

Marie held up her hand. "Valley. I stand corrected. Look, I'm sorry. I didn't mean to sound judgmental or uncaring. I know how much that place means to you."

Angela wasn't so sure she did.

"You were so little when Momma died, and then when Daddy left." Marie grew quiet. "While I was in school, you were stuck in that store every day with Momma Grace."

"I wasn't stuck. It's what I wanted to do. Where I wanted to be."

"It's all you knew. And then after school, summers, and holidays you were always at the store with her, while I was off with friends."

"I really loved being a part of Heart of Christmas with Momma Grace." Tears slipped down her cheeks. "You act like it was the worst childhood ever. It wasn't. I treasure every memory."

"But Angela, you've never done anything else. That store isn't your dream. You're living our grandmother and her mother's dream."

"Just because I didn't want to be a lawyer like you doesn't mean that I'm not doing what I want."

"You don't do a single thing that isn't somehow tied to Heart of Christmas."

Angela pulled her arms across her chest.

Marie glared at Brad, who now stood at the door.

"All I'm saying, sis, is that it's probably not the worst thing in the world if you have to close that store. You need to live your life. Whatever that ends up looking like. Right now you're all work. You're living like some kind of spinster keeping up that place." Marie passed Angela a cloth napkin with a colorful cornucopia embroidered on the corner.

Angela dabbed at her eyes, and the tears on her cheeks.

"I picked those out," Chrissy said. "Are you crying?"

Chrissy's face was etched with worry. "I'm okay, Chrissy." Angela turned the cloth napkin over in her hand. It was pretty, but not the quality linen her sister usually was drawn to. She looked to her sister. "I don't even want to know, do I?" Angela was certain these had also come from her competitor. No. Napkins weren't putting her out of business, but it was the principle of the thing. "All I've ever wanted to do was run that store."

"There's got to be something else you've wanted to do." Marie let out a breath, looking as if she were one of those holiday inflatables losing its boost of air. "You were always the smart one."

"Says the lawyer sister? Really?"

"You went to college too."

"I have a business degree. I'm running a business. Seems like a perfect fit to me. And yet I've failed."

"Remember when you wanted to rescue turtles? You could work at the aquarium."

Angela shook her head. "I'd hate that. I'd cry every time one came in hurt. I'd end up with a herd of turtles in my backyard."

"I think they're referred to as a dole."

Angela felt ready to dole out a little piece of her mind. "Herd. Dole. Whatever. It wouldn't be good."

"Turtles are so cute. I can help name them," Chrissy offered. "Pete is a good turtle name. Or Tina if it's a girl turtle."

"Thank you, Chrissy." Angela cupped Chrissy's chin. At the rate she was working Angela knew she would never have a family of her own, although she'd always dreamed of having children. Two. A boy and a girl, but she hadn't had a relationship since Jimmy. Sure, some women took it upon themselves to have kids on their own, but that wasn't her style either. She rolled her eyes. "I won't be working with turtles."

Reacting to Angela's eye roll, Marie quickly added, "Or you

could write that book about the history of Pleasant Sands. You know more about this town than anyone."

Brad cleared his voice as if clearing the way for his return to the kitchen. "It's a holiday, maybe we need a new tradition. Like not talking about anything work related?"

Marie turned and glared at him.

Angela appreciated his attempt to throw her a lifeline.

"After all this amazing food, with my amazing girls, I can't wait to do nothing but eat turkey sandwiches all day tomorrow," Brad said.

"Speaking of tomorrow," Marie said. "Christmas Galore is opening at one o'clock in the morning for their Black Friday sale."

Brad shrugged, then left for the living room. He'd tried, but Marie was tenacious when she had a point she wanted to make. A trait that was very helpful in her career as a lawyer, but exhausting as a sister. "I sell Christmas décor, not the hot toy of the season or cheap TVs. I don't understand that whole Black Friday hype anyway. I'd never get up in the middle of the night to go shopping."

Marie said, "I couldn't shop right now no matter what the deal was." She rubbed her stomach. "But by one in the morning I might be up for it to work off some of these calories."

"I could have another sno-cone," Chrissy said.

"How about pumpkin pie instead." Marie grabbed plates from the island and began slicing pie. "I have whipped topping too."

"Thought you were stuffed," Angela said.

Chrissy clapped her hands, then tugged on the sleeve of Angela's shirt. "I hope your heart doesn't break, Aunt Angela."

"Me too, sweetie."

"You're lucky this is happening right now," Chrissy said.

Great. Now her niece was going to echo her sister's thoughts? "Lucky, huh? Why do you think that?"

"Very lucky. Because Santa is around. He can help you." Chrissy folded her arms tightly across her white pinafore dress. "He'll give you anything you want if you've been good."

Angela's mood softened. Wouldn't it be nice to have that blind faith again? "I don't think he can fix this, but thank you. That was really sweet."

"No. He can!" Chrissy stabbed a finger in the air. "He does it all the time. We can write him a letter. I know how."

"I gave up on Santa answering my letters a long time ago," she said, remembering her last letter to Santa. She hadn't been much older than Chrissy at the time.

Marie lowered her voice. "Bringing Daddy back home wasn't something Santa or anyone else could do. I can't believe you're still angry about that."

Angela pushed her hair back over her shoulder. It might be stupid, and childish, but yes, she still had a little angst with Santa over that one.

Chrissy pursed her lips. "You might not have been a good girl that year. Sometimes I'm bad and kind of forget too. You've been good this year, though. Right?"

"Very good," Angela said. For whatever good it did her.

"I can help you write the letter. I have the app on my iPad." Chrissy ran out of the room, her patent leather shoes slapping against the terrazzo tile.

Marie nodded. "She does."

"I'm so behind the times," Angela admitted.

"Don't get me started," Marie said. "I'll get you some pie. Pie cures everything. Momma Grace always said so."

"That's true. Her pumpkin pie was the best. Remember the year we grew pumpkins?"

"I do. She made us weed that garden every day."

"I remember helping Momma Grace prepare the fresh pumpkin to be used in those pies. What a mess, but so much fun."

Marie's face screwed up. "It was gross."

Chrissy returned, holding up her iPad. "See!" She shoved the tablet toward Angela. "I've got the app all ready for you. Isn't it pretty?"

"We're going to eat some pie. Don't you want some?" Angela said, trying to change the subject. She had no intention of writing a letter to Santa.

"I'm kind of full," Chrissy said. "Can I just have bites of yours?"

"Sure." This wasn't the first time Angela had shared pie with Chrissy. "You'd better make mine a double," she said with a wink to Marie.

Marie cut a large slice of pie and put it on a plate.

"Whipped cream too!" Chrissy insisted.

Angela took the can of whipped cream out of the refrigerator and squirted three dollops into a smiley face on the slice, then slid her plate toward Chrissy.

"Here. You carry the iPad." Chrissy handed it to Angela. "I'll carry the pie." Chrissy carried the plate with both hands, one foot in front of the other, never taking her eyes off the plate.

"It's easier to not spill it if you just look ahead," her mom said.

But Chrissy was on a mission to get to the table without incident.

Angela set the iPad on the kitchen counter and started for the table.

Marie caught her by the arm. "Would it kill you to play along with your niece?" She bumped her shoulder. "Might even be fun."

Angela picked up the iPad with a huff, then joined Chrissy at the table. Darn iPad was daunting. She turned it over, hiding the screen.

Chrissy wiggled into the chair next to Angela. "You have to know exactly what you want to say to Santa. He only lets you have so many words."

"How do you know that?"

"I've sent him lots of letters. Mommy taught me how to dictate like she does."

"You didn't." Angela looked at Marie. "Why would you do that?"

"It gives her the freedom to type her thoughts even though she doesn't know how to write yet. Believe me, this is a good thing. She's recognizing words already. I think this is going to really prepare her for school."

"Great. She's more skilled than I am."

"What's 'skilled' mean?"

"That you're very smart," Angela explained. "I'm proud of you."

"Want me to show you how to talk-type?"

"I can just type."

Marie sat back, looking pleased. "It'll be fun."

Chrissy turned the iPad face-up and slid it toward Angela. "You're going to need this."

Angela looked at the screen. The words "Dear Santa" sparkled in a swirly green-glitter script across an inky-blue sky, with white snowflakes falling softly across the screen.

As soon as Angela tapped the *Dear Santa* button, a bright red-and-white candy-cane-striped envelope soared into the center of the screen, spun around and opened, displaying the fields to be filled in.

Angela typed in her email address and name then tabbed down to the note section and let out a sigh.

"You've got to be kidding me." Angela turned the iPad toward her sister. "Can I even catch one tiny break?"

Chapter Four

Dear Santa,
I have been a very good girl. I want a rabbit for Christmas.
My brother wants a skateboard but he's been very bad so
don't bring him anything no matter how many letters he
sends you.

Thank you,
Victoria

"Look at this!" Angela tilted the iPad toward Marie, waving her finger in an accusing circle. "Down at the very bottom. See that? It says, 'Sponsored by Christmas Galore.'"

"Oh?" Marie leaned in for a closer look. "I'm sorry. I honestly didn't notice that before." She clicked back and refreshed the screen. "See. Now it shows the hammock company as a sponsor. Christmas Galore is probably just one of fifty sponsors that rotate through. No big deal."

"I'm not going to get sucked into the Christmas Galore infatuation. They're putting me out of business." Angela pushed the iPad away.

"Christmas Galore is not putting you out of business," Marie said. "Time, technology and cheap products are putting you out of business. It's the age of online ordering and disposable holiday stuff. I don't know how you've made it this long without an on-line presence. You're lucky you've lasted as long as you have."

"Is that supposed to be some kind of compliment, because it does not feel like one." Angela took pride in knowing she was still doing business in the way Momma Grace and the generation before her had. It might be the old-fashioned way, but it suited her just fine.

"You know what I'm saying." Marie reached for her sister's hand. "I'm sorry. I didn't intend to sound mean. I'm just trying to be realistic."

"I'm not playing into Christmas Galore's superstore, one-stop shop using Christmas to get people in the door. It's like bait and switch, and now they're pretending they're . . ." she glanced over at Chrissy, then spoke in a whisper, ". . . the big guy." No matter how mad she was she couldn't blow the magic of Santa for her niece.

"It's just an app. Write the letter. For your niece."

"I'm the niece, right, Mommy?"

"Yes." Marie stacked the empty pie plates one on top of the other. "You know they don't answer those things. It's an auto-responder."

"Santa answers every single letter," Chrissy insisted before running out of the room, and calling, "Dad, doesn't Santa answer all of his letters?"

"See," Marie said to Angela. "He answers them personally. All twelve of them that she's sent. It's an app. Like picking your fake stripper name. Seriously, just do it. What do you have to lose? This is your chance to vent. No one is going to read your letter any-way, and maybe you'll feel better. It'll be like therapy."

Chrissy came back into the room and raced to Angela's side. "Please, Aunt Angela. I know he can help you."

"You're right. What's the harm? Santa is the best. He can fix any-thing." Angela hugged Chrissy close. "Will you help me write it?"

Chrissy hitched herself up into Angela's lap with a wide grin pasted on her face. Leaning on one chubby arm she pointed to the spot where Angela was to type. "Put your cursor there and type words."

Angela finger-pecked the keys, quickly and succinctly. Had it been a real keyboard those keys would have been bruised.

"Read it to us," Chrissy demanded.

> *"Dear Santa,*
> *I think old-fashioned Christmas is going out of style. Sadly,*
> *if sales don't pick up I will have to close the doors on my*
> *store, Heart of Christmas. My great-great-grandmother*
> *opened this store. It's been an important part of our family*
> *for generations now. I worked side-by-side with my grand-*
> *mother running it until her death. She left me the business.*
> *I can't let her down. Please help.*
>
> > *Respectfully,*
> > *Angela"*

"That's what you're writing to Santa?" Marie said. "Pitiful."

She'd said that last part under her breath, but Angela felt the full force of it.

Chrissy pulled her little hands to her hips. "You didn't even tell him you were on the 'nice' list. You have to tell him you've been good." Chrissy tossed her curls. "Everyone knows you have to tell Santa that you're on the 'good' list."

"I thought Santa knew who was on the 'good' list and the 'naughty' list," Angela reasoned.

"He does. He writes the list, but he's busy, and you have to help him so he has time to do other things. It's almost Christmas. He's very, very busy."

"I see."

Marie leaned forward. "Momma Grace is gone, and your life has stood still the past seven years. Heart of Christmas has had a great run, but now it's time for you to figure out what your own dreams are and quit living Momma Grace's. Heck, ask Santa for a pony. That would be better than what you wrote."

Angela sighed. A pony might be the only thing that would make her feel better right now. "Things were fine until Christmas Galore came to town."

"That's not true and you know it."

"Well, things have been a lot worse since they opened."

She loved Heart of Christmas. The building. The business. The place in the town's history that it held. Every single thing about it . . . even the hard work. Being in that store kept Momma Grace alive and present in her heart, and still all these years later she wasn't sure she could let that go. Unfortunately, she'd run through quite a bit of her savings waiting for a big summer that hadn't happened, and now with Christmas Galore in the neighborhood her Christmas holiday season might even be worse.

"Fine. How about this." She backspaced and began typing.

Marie clapped her forearms together like one of those director's clapboards, making Chrissy laugh. "'Dear Santa. Take two.'"

Angela read out loud as she typed,

"Dear Santa,
There's a bully in town threatening the Heart of Christmas,
and he's using your good reputation to do it.
I've been a very, very good girl, but he's ruining everything,
and Christmas may never be the same. I don't know what

to do. How can I fight back? I love Christmas, and Chrissy
says you can fix anything. I sure hope she's right. If not,
I'm going to need a year's supply of tissues to get through all
the changes to come. A pony might make me feel better too.

Merry Christmas to you, Mrs. Claus, the elves and all of
the reindeer.

Yours truly,
Anita C. Miracle"

"Anita C. Miracle?" Marie's eyebrow danced.

"I-need-a. *C* for 'Christmas.' Miracle."

Marie laughed so loud that Chrissy started laughing too even though she didn't understand the joke.

"What are you girls up to?" Brad asked from the doorway.

"Nothing," Marie and Angela said in unison.

"Like I believe that."

"We're writing letters to Santa," Chrissy blabbed.

"How many letters are you going to write to Santa, Chrissy? I just helped her with one yesterday."

Chrissy bounced up. "I didn—"

Marie slapped her hand over Chrissy's mouth. "We had a little special request. For someone special."

Brad beamed. "That's my princess. Come hug me."

Chrissy ran across the room and into his arms. "I love you, Daddy."

He ruffled Chrissy's hair. "Think you could talk Mommy into letting me have another piece of that pumpkin pie?"

"Pleeeease, Mom, can Daddy have more pie?"

"Of course, babe." Marie got up and cut another slice of pie for him.

Angela closed the app on the iPad, then walked over and gave Brad a hug. "I'm gonna head on out."

Marie handed Brad the plate. "No. Don't leave. I'm sorry. I shouldn't have brought up all the bad-news stuff." Marie frowned. "It's my fault. I just worry, and we haven't had any time to talk. Please stay."

Angela felt drained. "Everything you said is true. I just wasn't ready to admit it." And saying it out loud made it feel more than real.

"Stay. You'll have fun," Brad said. "You'll know most of the people coming, and might meet some new friends."

"And we're going to sing Christmas carols," Chrissy said. "I've been practicing with the radio."

"I bet you're wonderful," Angela said, picking Chrissy up and giving her a hug. "Thanks for having me over. I'm just going to go home. Tomorrow is a big workday for me. Y'all don't have to worry over me."

"You're family." Brad hugged her. "It's our job to worry about you."

"I'm going to be okay."

Marie held up a finger. "Hang on." She disappeared into the kitchen then came back and handed Angela a stack of containers that looked like a four-layer wedding cake. Apparently her sister had even planned the leftovers and put this together before Angela had arrived, because no one could put together a stack of left-overs that quickly. "Here's some to take home. And I'm going to try to not worry so much. I know in my heart you'll be fine. Always a beacon in the fog."

Momma Grace used to say that. And darn, if things didn't feel foggy now. The moral of that story was that the light came from within. Angela needed to quit looking for the light elsewhere and be a beacon in the fog.

"You're right." Angela hugged Marie. "Words to live by."

As she walked down the driveway to her car, Angela felt relief. She wasn't sure if it was Marie's reminder of Momma Grace's wisdom, or that she'd just dumped her worries on Santa, but either way it was good. She felt better. Not like things were going to be okay, but she was more relaxed about them.

Let Christmas Galore serve up the deals today to try to entice people out of their turkey comas to shop. That just wasn't her style.

To each his own.

Hopefully those same customers would go home, get some sleep and still have enough money to roll in to her store at a decent hour and buy something special that could be shared from generation to generation.

As she drove home with the pile of leftovers in the passenger seat, she remembered how Momma Grace used to get up extra early and bake her famous gingerbread cookies to give away in the store on Black Friday. Cut into intricate snowflake designs and sprinkled with sifted powdered sugar, the delectable ginger treats had always been a hit.

She hadn't thought about those in years. The smell of gingerbread was like a Christmas kickoff. The glass case they'd used to keep the cookies warm was still in the back room. She'd seen it just the other day.

Excited with the idea, she hoped she had the ingredients she needed.

It would be her Christmas gift to her customers, reviving memories of all the good years they'd spent together.

The recipe was a secret, and it was just as well, because no one would believe her if she told them it called for boiled black pepper, ginger, cloves and cinnamon in honey to get the most from the flavors. Someday she'd pass this recipe down to the next generation, but for now she'd make this the best Christmas ever for her customers and hold the recipe close to her heart.

She wouldn't have time to do the fancy snowflakes from the whisper-thin sheets of dough like Momma Grace had, but the cookies would taste just as good in rectangles. As her own little personal touch she could use powdered sugar to make a little rectangular stamp in the corner of each one, like a letter to Santa. Easy-peasy.

Finally home. Angela's beach house wasn't fancy like her sister's. She and Marie lived here as kids with Momma Grace, and other than going off to college this was the only house she'd lived in since.

Angela climbed the weathered wooden steps to the second-floor entrance. Inside, the whitewashed cabinets seemed bright this afternoon. Many meals and treats had been baked in this kitchen over the years. With any luck the cookies would taste just like Momma Grace's.

The old red-and-white-checkered cookbook was on the bookshelf at the end of the counter. The gingerbread-cookie recipe wasn't part of the book, but Momma Grace had handwritten each of her secret recipes on fancy cards and tucked them in the front of it. Angela shuffled through them until she found what she was looking for.

Momma Grace had the handwriting of an engineer. Neat and precise.

Angela made a quick pass through the kitchen checking for ingredients. Thankfully, she had everything she needed.

With the ingredients lined up across the kitchen island, she took the old Sunbeam Mixmaster out from the pantry and plugged it in.

She started the honey spice boiling. After gathering the measuring cups, she went to work mixing the wet ingredients together in the glossy white mixing bowl. The beaters twisted and spun the goop into a light, fluffy heap.

Then, slowly she mixed the whisked dry ingredients into the batter until it was time to add the molasses, which turned the dough a rich dark brown.

She dipped a spoon into the mixture and tasted it.

"Perfect." For a moment she was back in the kitchen tippy-toeing at her grandmother's side. "I miss our time together, Momma Grace."

She blinked back salty tears then lined several mini–loaf pans with plastic wrap. Pressing the dough into each pan as tightly as possible, she smoothed the top, covered the dough and tucked it into the freezer. In the morning, she'd slice and bake the loaves fresh.

"Marie might think it's time to throw in the towel, but I still have a trick or two up my sleeve. This is my journey just like it was yours, Momma Grace. Marie never did get us, did she?" Momma Grace would've smiled at that. *We're two of a kind,* she'd always say. "Momma Grace, please help me be strong. Is there any way to keep this store going?"

And in that smug moment, she could clearly hear Momma Grace say, *Don't presume you know the next step to take. Only He knows your path. Trust the journey, my dear.*

Chapter Five

Dear Santa,
I've tried to be good, but my sister makes it hard. Have you
thought about grading on a curve?
  I really want a bike.

                              Fingers crossed,
                              Bob

Geoff Paisley walked up the stairs to the second floor of Christmas Galore. Just as he reached for the door, Virgil, the operations director, walked out.

"Happy Thanksgiving." Virgil's deep commanding voice carried. Dressed in his customary denim button-down shirt with the sleeves turned back, the gray-haired man looked more like a visitor than an executive. Not only was he a key member of the store's team, but also Geoff's mom's best friend.

"I need to talk to you about a couple locations I found," Geoff said. "Do you have time?"

"Thought we were going to hold off for two years."

"We are. Maybe. Couldn't hurt to run numbers, though, right?"

"Things change. Could be a waste of time," Virgil said pragmatically.

"Or we could make sure we're not missing an opportunity. Where's Mom?"

"She's working on the Dear Santa letters."

"Already? It's Thanksgiving Day."

"They've been pouring in ever since she launched that new app." Virgil's grin was more of a smirk, and even in his late sixties he had an impish troublemaker's glint in his eyes.

The only thing Geoff liked about Christmas was that it made money roll into his bank account like a tsunami. Letters to Santa were the lowest priority on his list.

"You might take a minute to check it out. That app is pretty slick. Hashtag DearSanta is even trending on Twitter." Virgil's bushy mustache wiggled with each word.

Geoff couldn't hold back the groan.

Virgil leveled a stare. Geoff knew that look.

"Make time to understand why some of those things are so important to Rebecca. You haven't learned all there is to learn yet, you know."

Virgil played the mentor role well, and although Geoff had welcomed that as a kid, sometimes he wished Virgil would mind his own business when it came to his business. "I'll take a look at it as soon as we get through Black Friday."

"Sure you will." Virgil cuffed his shoulder. "Slow down and make the time to see what your mom and her team have accomplished. I think you'll be impressed." Virgil's thumb pushed down with pressure on Geoff's clavicle, causing him to buckle under the pressure. "*I'm* impressed." Virgil's statement was more like a challenge.

Geoff held his tongue. He found it ironic that this man who talked slower than maple syrup dripping from a tree in the winter was judging the pace of *his* life. But if Virgil was impressed with the Dear Santa app, that was saying something.

"Your mom knows little things matter. Just remember that you didn't get to fifteen stores up and down the coast by chance. Every step she's planned over the years has positioned you for the next one. She's achieved some lofty goals, and I know success when I see it." Virgil had once owned one of the biggest tech companies in the nation. He'd sold that company just to free up his time to help his dearest friend, Geoff's mom, when she decided to open her first store. He'd made a small fortune on the sale of his company too, so it wasn't a huge sacrifice. But they did owe Virgil. That much Geoff knew, and appreciated. "Thanks, Virgil. Noted."

Virgil dipped his head, as a cowboy would tip his hat, then walked down the stairs to the retail floor.

Those Dear Santa letters drove Geoff crazy. Every year they were such a time suck. He'd be less irritated if Rebecca just took the time off to go on a swanky vacation. Spending good money and resources on a project that didn't even carry their brand? That made no sense at all. She'd insisted the Christmas Galore brand would rotate among other vendors an equal amount of time on the Dear Santa portal. What was the use of funding the project if he couldn't get something directly out of it?

But Mom still held the controlling interest in Christmas Galore, so he could say only so much about it.

Sure, one day this would all be his, but until then, he respected his mother's and Virgil's positions, and the three each had decision-making power that made it all work. And it had been one heck of a ride.

For the past ten years he and his mom had relocated with each new store opening.

He hadn't put down roots, and that was fine by him. Moving every year had made for an easy excuse to keep women from trying to tie him down. *Sorry, babe, I'm only here for a short time.* If he'd used that line once, he'd used it a hundred times. That usually nipped any nesting in the bud. He didn't have time for all of that.

His focus was on Christmas Galore. There was no way he'd ever be in the position that his mom was when he was growing up. The luxurious lifestyle appealed to him, and he didn't mind having to work hard to guarantee it.

Today he was in their newest store, in Pleasant Sands, North Carolina, and for the first time in ten years they'd made a decision to stay put for at least two years, before opening the next store. He kind of liked moving every year, but it might be good for Mom to have a bit of a break. They'd built the chain from the ground up at an exhausting pace and he'd noticed this newest start-up was wearing harder on her.

They'd intentionally kept Christmas Galore small enough that they knew everyone on its management team, and the people that came to work for them stayed. Everyone that held a corporate position had worked their way through the ranks. That's how Geoff had earned his position too, and that was something he was proud of. But the store had really been Mom's vision. He looked forward to the day when he could advance the company into something even bigger. Meanwhile, he was making sure everything they did positioned them for that growth.

Geoff hadn't been convinced Pleasant Sands was the right location for Christmas Galore. The town was a bit smaller than the ones where they'd opened their other stores, and that model had never let them down. Only Mom was determined to have a store in this town, and that wasn't a battle worth fighting even though he'd had his concerns.

Good thing he hadn't argued too, else he'd be eating crow right now. Not only did the new store already hold bragging rights for the biggest grand opening of any of their stores, but Halloween had been a door buster too. All that was very promising for the holiday season.

He walked into the conference room. There was no meeting in here today, though. Not on Thanksgiving Day. Instead, in all fifteen store locations, the conference rooms had been transformed into dining rooms. Elegantly so, with festive tablecloths in brown, orange and cranberry and the best catered Thanksgiving dinner available.

The aroma of turkey and sage dressing filled the air. His stomach growled.

The same menu was being served in every one of the locations at this very moment. A buffet catered by the nicest restaurant in the area and another table with delectable desserts shipped in from Mom's favorite bakery in Delaware: pumpkin pie, sweet potato pie, pecan pie, chocolate pecan pie and maple seven-layer cake.

This was another of Mom's ideas. She believed if they took care of their people, their employees would in turn raise the bar on how customers were treated. And he'd continue to let her have her way as long as it didn't impact their profit.

She'd felt it was the least they could do for their employees since they were expected to work on the holiday. But to make it more palatable, Christmas Galore allowed them to bring along up to eight guests. And with all the employees and their guests rotating through the buffet, this room would stay busy all day long.

"Happy Thanksgiving," Geoff said as he entered the dining room.

A round of "Happy Thanksgiving"s echoed back in response.

People balanced heaping plates of food, while others were just starting to dig in. For the next six hours, staff would come and go like wrestling tag teams between shifts.

A woman dressed in black slacks and a sweater with a turkey embroidered on the front of it slid to his side. "Thank you so much for this lovely dinner."

"You're welcome," he said with a genuine smile. He really did like seeing his employees enjoy the holiday and the chance to meet their families.

Because Geoff had never married or had children of his own, the Christmas Galore family was his family. He wanted to spend time with them through the holidays—even if that family had changed every year as he and Mom moved to a new city when they opened a new store. He liked being sort of a nomad. No connections to anywhere, except for employees he'd see a few times a year on site visits.

He extended his hand. "I'm glad you joined us. I'm Geoff."

"It's so nice to meet you, Mr. Paisley. I'm Dana Beth Martin. Danny's momma. My husband and I are so happy we get to spend Thanksgiving with Danny. Thank you for making this possible."

"Nice to meet you."

"My son just loves working for you. This company is like a family. It's been so good for him. For this town," she gushed.

"Hey, boss." Chandler swept in before Mrs. Martin had the chance to start bragging on her son, like moms were known to do. "When you get a moment can I have a word?"

"I'll let you two talk," Mrs. Martin said. "Time for dessert, and thank you again, Mr. Paisley."

"Try the chocolate pecan pie. It's my favorite," he said with a wave, as he turned to his buddy, and VP of sales, only half paying attention as Chandler recited the latest sales numbers.

Finally Chandler stopped and waved a hand in front of Geoff's face. "What's up with you today?"

"What?" Geoff asked.

"My point exactly. Did you hear a thing I just said?"

"Yes. I was listening. Sales are good."

"The last thing I said was we've sold a thousand units of pickled peppers."

"Do we sell pickled peppers?"

"Exactly my point."

"Oh. Maybe I wasn't clinging to your every word."

"Everything okay?"

"Yeah. Yeah. Fine. I was just thinking about something I saw this morning."

"In the paper? I thought our ad looked great."

"More like something I saw while I was looking around the paper." He leaned forward, feeling that same rush as at the café. "I was in the coffee shop and as I turned the page I caught sight of this woman."

"A woman, huh." Chandler's lips curled into a smirk. "As long as I've known you I've never seen you sidetracked by a woman. Look at that grin. This one must be special?"

"Don't know her, but she's . . . different."

"And you could tell that across a crowded room?"

Geoff punched Chandler in the arm. "Funny. But yes. I could tell."

"She must be pretty?" Chandler said.

"Oh, very pretty with this big smile . . . and her eyes. Even across the room her eyes were as dark as chocolate. Melted chocolate, the way they sparkled." He licked his lips. She probably tasted sweet too.

"Okay, don't you ever say something like that again. You sound like a romance novel."

"Stop it."

"You're smitten," Chandler teased.

"Smitten? Now who's talking like a romance novel?"

"Yep. You're eat up with it." Chandler slapped his shoulder. "About time you did something for yourself. What's her name?"

"Didn't talk to her."

"What? You didn't talk to her?" Chandler took a step back. "You're this distracted by someone you didn't even talk to?"

"I know." Geoff inadvertently hunched his shoulders as he put a slice of pie on his plate. It had made a lot more sense before he said it out loud. He should've kept his mouth shut. "Crazy, isn't it? But there was something about her. Something that kept my attention. I've never had that happen before." And even right now he could picture her clear as day.

"You should have invited her over for dinner." Chandler grabbed a plate and heaped a large wedge of pumpkin pie onto it, then squirted a dollop of whipped cream on top. "Or at least dessert."

Should have, Geoff thought. "She's probably married with children."

"Was she wearing a ring?"

"No."

Chandler tossed his head back with a hearty laugh. "So you looked."

"Stop it." Geoff pushed past him. "Yes. I noticed. Now give me those numbers again."

An hour later Geoff had finished running through the numbers at all of the stores, and sent Chandler to communicate a couple of red-light-special sale items in two of the lagging locations to help boost their figures. All in all, they were on track to beat today's goal already. Best of all, he'd been able to finish that meeting and get away from Chandler without any more talk about the woman in the coffee shop.

He didn't even know her name, and she was already causing unpleasant moments.

He'd been down this road before. He didn't have time for this kind of distraction. What was he thinking?

Time to get back to the conference room and meet the next shift of diners.

He stopped by his mother's office and gave a quick double-knock before poking his head in the door. "Hello?"

She lifted her head and smiled. "Happy Thanksgiving."

"It's been a day to be thankful for. That's for sure. You coming to eat?"

"Yes, I am. Are you headed there now?"

"I am. Shall we?" He hooked his arm and waited for her at the door.

She pushed her chair back from her desk and made her way to him, graciously taking his arm. "Why, thank you. Thought you'd never ask."

"We know that's not true. We've spent every Thanksgiving since the day I was born together. It wouldn't be the same without you." He patted her arm. "So why is it you've been holed up in your office so much these days?"

"Taking care of business, son. Things are marvelous. We have paid sponsors on the Dear Santa app, and so much traffic they are already renewing their spots. Two have asked to reserve spots for next year already."

"Wow, now that's an update. All that happened since our meeting on Monday?"

"Indeed. I guess the kiddies are getting geared up now that Thanksgiving is upon us, because the letters are flooding in."

He stopped. "Wait a minute. You're not trying to answer all the letters yourself, are you? We talked—"

"No, son. I am not. I took your suggestions for the algorithm and my adorable blue-Mohawked computer programmer, Billy, not only built it, but he created it in a way that I can tweak the settings to adjust the flow of letters coming to the personal box."

"That's a great long-term strategy."

"It is, and the letters coming to me are truly the letters worth responding to personally. The rest are getting the computer-generated responses."

"And that's working well?"

She smiled brightly "Very well. We are a trending hashtag on Twitter."

"So I heard." How was it that suddenly his non-technical mother was speaking the language of social media? "And you know all this . . . how?"

"Billy taught me. I can tweet and even pin on Pinterest these days. Did you know that you can find great recipes on Pinterest?"

"But you don't cook."

"If I did, it would be my favorite place to browse. I'm quite good at it."

"You are tweeting and pinning?"

"Mmm-hmm. And answering the letters that come my way."

"I'm impressed," Geoff said. She seemed very pleased with herself. Why did he suddenly feel like he needed to tell her not to hang around with Billy?

"It's all very doable. You should be impressed."

"I am. I am." He stopped at the doorway to the conference room and let his mother make her entrance. Gracious and approachable, she never disappointed. He couldn't be prouder to be her son.

Chapter Six

Hey Santa,
My name is Grayson and I am 7 years old. I think I should
be on the nice list, because I have been very good this year.
I would like a football, a soccer ball, a baseball and baseball
bat, a Frisbee and a scooter. My mom says to please bring
me anything that will keep me busy!

Thanks,
Grayson

"Happy Thanksgiving to you all. We're so thankful you are part of our team." Rebecca Paisley had entered the room like a Thanksgiving princess. Her golden sweater shimmered against her maroon turtleneck as she opened her arms, making her look like the cornucopia of good cheer.

Geoff followed her inside, and they made their plates and chatted with the others before joining the Christmas Galore employee's families for dinner.

During the conversation, Mrs. Baxter mentioned that she was working on the spring fund-raiser for the Ruritan Club.

His mother seemed intrigued by the idea. "I have been really wanting to do something to give back to this community. Do you think I could be on your committee?"

Mrs. Baxter sat there dumbfounded until her husband nudged her in the ribs. "Yes. Are you serious? I . . . we'd . . . be honored to have your help, Mrs. Paisley."

"Call me Rebecca. I insist."

"Thank you, Rebecca."

"Excellent. I'm good at some things, especially ideas," she said with a laugh. "I'm sure I'll find a way to be helpful."

Mrs. Baxter could barely contain her excitement, all but forgetting about the plate of food in front of her. "You just being there will be a huge help. Thank you so much."

Geoff sat there stunned. Had his mother really just volunteered to help with a fund-raiser? Give to one, absolutely. All the time. She was a very generous woman. But giving her time? This was new.

"My pleasure, dear. Did you know I was on the tree lighting committee this year? It's part of the Pleasant Sands Christmas Giving Project."

"News to *me*," Geoff mumbled.

"I hadn't heard," Mrs. Baxter said. "My dear friend Joan Ewell is on that committee. You must have met."

"My goodness. What a small world. She's a lovely, lovely woman. Sure knows how to get things done," Rebecca said.

"Yes. She is quite a gal." Mrs. Baxter beamed.

"We should all do lunch sometime."

"That would be wonderful. I'll plan something for once we get past the holidays."

"Fabulous. You know, Geoff, you should look into getting on some kind of board or committee. It's really quite rewarding." Rebecca turned to the Baxters. "We've been on the move the last ten years. A new city every year. Moving to wherever the newest store would be opening, but we've decided to put some roots down here. I love Pleasant Sands."

"That's great news," Mr. Baxter said. "It really is a great place to live."

"Have you lived here all your life?" Geoff asked.

"No. I was in the military. We lived in Norfolk, Virginia, for quite a while," Mr. Baxter explained.

His wife interjected, "We moved here when he got out of the navy. We vacationed here once, and we knew right then this would be a wonderful place to retire. When Danny turned sixteen it seemed like the perfect time. And wasn't it great timing that you were opening up just as the school year was beginning? He loves working here."

"And we love having him as part of the Christmas Galore family."

Geoff saw the affection and respect the Baxter family had for one another. The kid was the spitting image of his dad. A tweak of jealousy caught Geoff a little off guard. He could hardly feel bad about not having a family when he'd never even given himself the time to build a relationship with someone.

His mother was donating her time to help the community, and making friends too, it sounded like. She was taking this two-year hiatus in Pleasant Sands seriously.

Was he working so much that he hadn't even noticed? Maybe he did need to take a breather from the office once in a while. He'd tried the whole golf thing but the problem was when he wasn't at work, all he thought about was . . . work.

The six-hour catered event, as always, went by quickly. It really was one of his favorite occasions of the year, sharing time with the people who made the dream of Christmas Galore a reality.

Business had been steady all day, and that was great news on Thanksgiving. The store had taken some early heat from the locals for being open on the holiday. He'd been worried, but by the looks of the sales numbers those complainers had been in the minority.

By eight o'clock the last of the leftovers had been packed up and distributed among the families. It didn't take much for the rest of the stuff to be cleaned up and carted out to the Dumpsters.

His mother gathered her things to go home just as Virgil and Chandler brought the late-shift team together to get things started for the big Black Friday event. By 12:59 the next morning, all of the sale signs and purchase limits had to be clearly marked. Bargain merchandise had to be moved to end caps to keep the flow of customers moving down the aisles. Splitting the team into groups of two, they divvied up the tasks and went to work.

"Thanks for all your hard work," Mom called as she left through the front door. "Happy Thanksgiving. I'm so thankful for you all."

Geoff stood in his office overlooking the sales floor. The one-way mirrored glass allowed him an eagle-eye's view of everything going on below. Employees ascended, hanging signs in Christmas reds and greens for the big specials. Others rearranged merchandise on the end caps according to the Planogram.

At 12:55 a group of customers was already waiting outside Christmas Galore.

Geoff did a quick walk-through on his way to unlock the doors for the official Black Friday opening.

Just a few hours ago all of the sale signs were in fall colors: bright orange, yellow and sage green. Tonight the inside of his store had shed its autumnal colors, and was now graced with the colors of Christmas by way of red and green signs in the shape of Christmas ornaments.

Outside, people anxiously pushed toward the front door as he approached.

Last year when they'd opened the store in Massachusetts, customers had been bundled up like snowmen, blowing clouds of freezing condensation as they spoke to one another. The weather here in Pleasant Sands was . . . well, pleasant.

Yes, opening a new store in the South in the fourth quarter of the fiscal year had its advantages.

A lump formed in his throat, and his mouth went dry as he noticed a woman standing near the edge of the sidewalk wearing a black sweater. She looked like . . . almost had the same coloring as . . . the woman at the coffee shop. Her dark hair fell in waves past her shoulders.

He stood straighter to get a better look. This time he'd get her name. He silently recited a greeting as he waited for her to enter.

Chandler stepped to his side. "Man? Couldn't you have worn something a little less formal for Black Friday in the middle of the night?"

Geoff glanced down at his suit. "I always dress like this."

"My point exactly." Chandler stepped in front of Geoff. "You're going to scare off our customers looking like a lawyer."

Geoff tugged on his shirt collar. So maybe he could have lost the jacket. "Fine."

"You're living at the beach. You need to get your beach vibe on. Relax. Good thing I'm here to help you." Chandler twisted the locks and pulled the doors open. "Here we go."

Geoff stepped to the side as the people flowed in like high tide on a full moon. Normally he'd be feeling that familiar whir of excitement, because Black Friday sales translated into dedicated customers that kept coming back to Christmas Galore even when Santa was hibernating for the summer. But what he was feeling right now had nothing to do with sales, and everything to do with a short gal in a black sweater.

With a smile on his face he welcomed customers into the store like an airline attendant. "Merry Christmas. Welcome. Good evening, or should I say good morning? Hello. Thanks for coming in. Merry Christmas."

But when the dark-haired woman in the black sweater came through the door, his heart dropped. It wasn't her. This woman was probably only in her early twenties.

It would have been a lucky accident if she had been here. Only, his disappointment made him realize something. He wanted to see her again. Even more than a big number on the final report, he wanted the chance to meet that gal.

Geoff went back upstairs and monitored the real-time sales from all locations. By two o'clock it was clear Black Friday was going to be a success.

All the preparation had paid off. Everyone knew what to do, and the sales were outperforming their projections. He got up and locked his office door behind him to leave. Rather than go out the back door where his car was parked, he chose to go downstairs and out through the store. It was a hive of activity. A better buzz than caffeine, any day.

Chandler held the door for a customer struggling with three huge bags. "Thanks for shopping with us tonight. We'll see you soon."

Geoff made a beeline for the door. "I'm outta here. Make it a good one, Chandler."

"Where are you going, boss?"

"Home."

Chandler froze. "I've worked with you through what? Ten years opening these stores. I know you, man. You've never left a new store on Black Friday." He shrugged his shoulders and wagged his hands about like a nervous Tyrannosaurus rex. "What? Really?" Chandler cocked his head slightly, his eyes narrowing.

"Need my rest so I can come up with the next big plan."

Chandler shook his head. "This is about that girl, isn't it? What? Next you're going to tell me you believe in love at first sight? All that hocus-pocus, Hollywood-love-story stuff? No. That would just be crazy."

Geoff didn't bother trying to hold back the laugh as he stepped out into the parking lot. "Maybe it's time for a change."

Chapter Seven

DID YOU KNOW?

Fishing for both finfish and shellfish has long
been an important source of income along
the Pleasant Sands coast.

At one-thirty in the morning Angela called it quits on trying to get a good night's sleep. She wasn't doing much sleeping anyway. All she could think about was Christmas Galore being open all night.

There should be a law against it.

She might as well have stayed at her sister's for the Holiday Warm-up. But she hadn't been in the mood to smile and make new friends, and she certainly didn't want to catch up with old friends, only to tell them that her store was in trouble.

Lightning flashed in the distance, and the rumble of thunder followed a minute later. The storm was too far off to bother them tonight.

And what was so great about Christmas Galore that even her own sister was shopping there?

There was only one way to find out.

She pushed back the covers and climbed out of bed. Pulling on a pair of blue jeans and a red long-sleeve T-shirt, she then put on a pair of tennis shoes and fluffed her hair as she jogged outside to her car.

What was the harm in seeing how many cars were in the parking lot? One quick little drive-by and then she'd be back home in bed for some real rest.

She started her car and pulled out of her driveway. If the world was awake shopping, you sure couldn't tell it from here. Her neighborhood was dark. *As it should be.*

Maybe Christmas Galore had experienced a big flop tonight. That would serve them right.

No. How could I wish that on them?

A few cars passed by in the other direction.

That doesn't mean anything. She'd never perused the streets of Pleasant Sands in the middle of the night. It didn't necessarily mean everyone who was out tonight was shopping at Christmas Galore. That traffic could be a nightly occurrence. Night shift at the hospital, maybe? But as she got closer to Christmas Galore, more than just streetlights lit the sky.

The parking lot was full, and cars were even parked across the street in front of an ice cream shop that was closed for the season. She eased into the parking lot, watching people come and go. No one was coming out empty-handed either. A car backed out just a few spaces ahead of her. She swung into the vacated space and took her key from the ignition.

Her heart raced.

What the heck was she doing here? She could just hear the local gossip if anyone she knew saw her. And why put herself in the position to get her feelings hurt if she did see someone she knew?

But all the self-talk and warnings couldn't stop her from needing to know just what the big deal was. She stared in her rearview mirror. From here she could see how busy the store was. Even the grocery store before a hurricane wasn't this busy.

She opened her door and got out of the car.

The bright lights from the building beckoned her closer. The people passing her as they left seemed so pleased with their deals.

As she got closer the differences between her store and Christmas Galore were clear. She had subdued lighting to show off the twinkle lights, candles and lighted villages. Christmas Galore was as bright as an operating room. Her displays were all custom-quality furnishings, constantly dusted to a high shine. Christmas Galore used those metal shelving units and bins with huge fluorescent starbursts announcing discounts. Even the music was different. At Heart of Christmas the music was a backdrop—soft, soothing and inspirational. Here at Christmas Galore a rock-and-roll version of "Jingle Bells" played so loudly it had taken a moment for her to recognize the song.

One thing was certain: she'd been right about Christmas Galore being completely different from Heart of Christmas. This was bright and had a warehouse feel to it, where her store was homey and full of history and tradition.

She was about thirty feet from the front door when a man wearing a button-down shirt and carrying a sport coat over his arm walked out of the building.

Angela recognized him immediately. A smile played at her lips. She'd hoped she'd run into him again. She sucked in a breath and took a step closer. He didn't have a shopping bag. He probably had the same attitude about this kind of store that she did. Something in common.

I'll just say hello. She wiped her damp palms on the back pockets of her jeans and started his way, wishing she'd put a little bit of effort into what she'd worn.

He started walking toward her.

Just as she started to lift her hand to wave and say hello, a young man in a Christmas Galore vest came running to the parking lot. "Hey, boss. Chandler said you forgot this."

The man spun around.

Boss?

He was thanking the employee when he turned and saw her.

He works at Christmas Galore? She spun around and race-walked back to her car. She jumped in and started the engine, hoping he hadn't recognized her.

Serves me right for spying.

"Hey!"

The voice came from behind her. He *had* recognized her, but there was no way she could face him now. What would she even say to him?

He was still standing near the door. She threw her car into reverse and got out of that parking lot as quickly as she could. Maybe he'd think she'd been leaving all along. When she got home she was still shaking.

She'd almost befriended the enemy.

Back in bed, she crawled under the covers and closed her eyes, thankful that she hadn't already said hello when his employee walked out. Now, *that* would've been awkward.

She hugged her pillow close, wishing she'd stayed put when the temptation had struck to snoop.

When she woke up, it was still way before the time her alarm was supposed to go off, but she'd gotten a couple hours of decent sleep.

Angela climbed out of bed and went into the kitchen to get a cup of coffee and start the day. While sipping her first cup, she preheated the oven, then took the gingerbread cookie dough out of the freezer. She rolled the frozen blocks out onto her quartz countertop and began carefully slicing whisper-thin rectangles with a cheese slicer.

Like a one-woman assembly line, she slid cookie sheet after cookie sheet into the oven. With each ding of the timer she moved cookies from the tray to the cooling rack.

The whole kitchen suddenly smelled like the holidays, and it wasn't even sunrise yet.

She dusted the cookies with the powdered-sugar stamp in the corner, then started stacking them in a large storage container to take over to the store. She may have gone a little crazy. There were a lot of cookies to pack. Finally, she pulled out the huge metal pot she used to cook a bushel of blue crab in the summer. She lined it with a linen tablecloth then began stacking the cookies inside. She tucked the box of small plastic sandwich bags into the top of the pot so her staff could take home any leftovers.

Surrounded by the warm scent of gingerbread, she felt a burst of energy. Somewhere between realizing Blue-eyes was connected to Christmas Galore and baking cookies, she was finding peace in the decisions that she needed to make.

Opting for a short jog on the beach before work, Angela put on her running gear and pulled on a ball cap.

She used her back door and took the stairs two at a time down to the beach in her bare feet. The morning was mild, and the cool sand felt good between her toes. She stretched, then took off into a slow jog, taking the short route, only a mile round-trip. When she got back to her house, she sat down in the damp sand and pulled her knees to her chest, then wrapped her arms around them.

November was her favorite time of the year in Pleasant Sands. All of the tourists had finally drifted back to their hometowns, and at this early hour she was the only person on the beach for as far as she could see.

The power of the crashing waves got closer as the tide began to roll in. She wasn't sure if she was daring the water to reach her and sweep her away, or just feeling fearless.

Last night's storm had left the ocean angry. Growing up here she'd come to know the ocean and its emotions as if it were an old friend—a moody one, but wonderful all the same.

Sometimes the waves lapped the shore gently, like an invitation. Then there were the days when the waves were rounded, creating a playground for the porpoises along the shoreline. But today was different.

The ocean was aggressive and unforgiving today, almost like the ominous music in a movie when something bad was about to happen.

All she could do was get through the day. The sales would tell her whether to keep fighting to keep the store afloat, or close at the end of the season.

As she blinked away tears, the water seemed to take on a darker, more ominous hue, like it was sad too.

The salt air dampened her skin as the wind pushed through her hair. She grabbed the out-of-control strands into a bunch, twisted them and tucked them under her ball cap, ducking her head to protect her face from the sand that stung her arms with each gust of wind.

Finally, just a tiny sizzling slice of fluorescent orange peeked over the horizon.

It was getting close to seven. Time to pull herself together and start the day.

She'd get through this. It wasn't the first time she'd been dealt a difficult hand.

Her phone buzzed. It had to be her sister. No one else would ever call this early. She slid the phone from her pocket and put it to her ear. "Good morning."

"You home?" Marie asked.

"At the beach."

"Of course you are." Marie laughed. "I should've known you'd be there."

"Couldn't sleep anyway."

"Sorry, sis."

"Not your fault." Taking in long slow breaths, she thought back to the days when she was just a beach kid skimboarding the waves under her grandmother's watchful eye, without a care in the world. "Do you remember how relaxed Momma Grace always was? Why didn't we inherit that gene?"

"Because Momma Grace was either *a,* an excellent actress, or *b,* plum crazy and didn't know to worry."

"She might've been a little crazy, but she was happy." *Think positive thoughts.*

"You're not unhappy," Marie said. "You're just having business challenges."

"Well, that doesn't make me happy." Angela glanced across the water. The whole fiery ball of sun danced above the horizon, painting the clear sky with broad, bold strokes of pink, gold and orange. In a little while those vibrant colors would fade into blue. *Magic.* "Did you call for a reason?"

Another wave rolled in with a thunderous crash. Somehow it was peaceful the way that filtered out all other sound. She pushed her feet deeper into the sand, trying to warm them. If only she could push her troubles away so easily.

"Just checking on you, and wanted to let you know that if you need extra hands at the shop, Chrissy and I are home today. Just let us know. We'll be right over."

Angela wondered if that was her sister's way of saying she wouldn't be at Christmas Galore shopping today.

She felt stupid for getting bent out of shape just because Marie bought a few cheap decorations from another store.

"Thank you." Angela took a deep breath of salty air, then rose to her feet and walked over the dune toward her house. "I'll let you know." Marie always had taken her big-sister role seriously. Even though she had her own family, and Brad and Chrissy sure kept her busy, she wanted to be there for her little sister.

"Are you okay?" Marie asked. "You sound kind of down."

"Down" was an understatement. "After admitting the store will have to close unless there's some kind of miracle today, I'm feeling torn."

"Torn about closing?" Marie asked. "I can understand that. It's a part of who you are."

Angela walked up the stairs to her back deck, remembering the mornings she and Marie raced up them. She'd always left Marie trailing behind her.

"That too," Angela said, "but more about how to handle today. Do I slash prices even further than I'd planned to boost sales today and get rid of inventory, or hope for the best with a better margin of profit? At this point, loss leaders are out of the question."

"I see what you mean. That is a difficult decision. I wish I knew what to tell you. Angela, I'm sorry I was so hard on you yesterday. I'm just worried, and I don't like seeing you so unhappy and stressed. I didn't mean to ruin your day. I wish you'd stayed."

"Thanks, Marie. I know your motivation was sincere. I love you."

"Call me if you need me."

"Count on it." Angela ended the call, then sat in one of the Carolina-blue rockers on her porch. She brushed the sand from her feet, then retrieved the big bottle of baby powder out of the deck box that sat next to the rocker. She shook some across both of her feet. She wasn't even in school yet when Momma Grace had taught her that a little baby powder was the best way to get damp sand off of your feet and keep from tracking it into the house. Pawpaw hated sand in the house, so Angela and Marie had learned quickly how to minimize it. Using the towel hanging by the door, she twisted it into a rope and gave her feet a good brushing side to side, like the shoeshine man, and then she was ready to go inside to shower and get ready for work.

A half-hour later, dressed in a festive Christmas cardigan over her favorite black slacks and a white blouse, she carried the big crab pot out to the porch and set it down so she could lock the door behind her. She took the steps slowly, peering over one side of the pot as she did, then made the short commute to Heart of Christmas over her personal boardwalk, which connected her beach house property to the parking lot of Heart of Christmas.

Down the beach road things were still quiet. Some of the houses had been battened down for the season for a well-deserved winter rest after the hot summer.

The year-rounders would soon be decorating with lights and holiday flags. But today you couldn't tell one house from the other, except that there weren't many cars in driveways.

There was a bustle in the air and cars were already moving down the beach highway. People were on the move this Black Friday. Tonight the six and eleven o'clock news would tell of people behaving badly to nab limited-supply deals, and show shelves in disarray from frantic customers.

People never behaved badly in her store, and that was the way she liked it. If good manners were out of style, then maybe it really was for the best that Heart of Christmas should close.

Walking the boardwalk was like a walk down memory lane, especially with the batch of cookies in her arms.

Her great-great-grandfather had walked that wooden path to work every day. Every night. Proud to be the lighthouse keeper until the day he died. Her great-great-grandmother took his place as the keeper after he died, but it wasn't long after that the light-house had been decommissioned.

Last year, Brad had sent his crew over to take a look at the boardwalk and rather than patch it, they tore it out and put in a fancy path that was as nice as a real boardwalk in a fancy tourist city, and even added a bridge to help preserve the dune line. It was so well built, she wouldn't hesitate to drive her car over it had it been just a little wider.

Momma Grace would've loved the updated version. Especially now that it had electricity. Not only to light her way home, but because it meant she could now add holiday lights to it too.

Angela counted off her steps to guesstimate how many strands of lights and pine roping she'd need to decorate the handrail. It seemed a fitting tribute to light a path to Heart of Christmas on what might be its last Christmas.

As Angela crossed the parking lot, Emma tooted her horn and waved as she swung her car into a space farthest from the store.

Across the way Jeremy and Stephanie, her other employees, stood chatting by the door, ready to get the day started.

At ten o'clock, if all went her way, this lot would be as full as Christmas Galore's had been last night, and customers would make joyous noise among the holiday music inside as they noticed their favorite holiday items on sale.

Angela's best customers had been eyeing their favorite things all year, just waiting and hoping they'd be on sale on Black Friday.

She'd be lying if she didn't admit that sometimes those coveted items only went on sale because she knew they were a splurge at the regular price for her favorite customers. She loved making them happy.

As she made her way across the parking lot toward Jeremy, Stephanie and Emma, she felt so blessed. She couldn't ask for three more faithful employees.

Chapter Eight

"Good morning, y'all!" Angela called out as she got closer.

Jeremy rushed over and took the crab pot from her. "I'm guessing these aren't crabs?"

"Nope. Momma Grace's famous gingerbread cookies."

"They smell so good." Jeremy lifted the lid and sucked in a breath. "You're lucky I'm still stuffed from Thanksgiving dinner."

"Good morning," Stephanie and Emma sang out as they too gathered around the crab pot.

Angela slid her key into the stiff lock. There wasn't enough graphite in the world to keep these old locks working smoothly in the salt air. She worked the key to the left and to the right, then one good push and the heavy oak door finally creaked open.

There were years of history in every groaning board, drafty window, and this door too.

"Did everyone have a nice Thanksgiving?" Angela asked.

Jeremy squeezed past her to put the pot of cookies down on the counter. "I brought a turkey sandwich for lunch, but I'm not even sure I'll be able to eat it. And now cookies?"

"We know you better than that." Stephanie grabbed a sale diagram and a handful of discount signs, and began placing them on the clips on the edges of the shelves. "You're always hungry."

Emma climbed on the step stool to switch on the steam engine that chugged around the room with happy horn blasts. "You might not have time to eat all day anyway if this year is anything like the past few."

"Jeremy, can you help me get the warming box out of the back room?" Angela asked. "I thought we'd channel my grandmother today with her famous gingerbread cookie recipe." Angela paused and made a slow, sweeping glance around the room. "Momma Grace will always be the heart of this place."

Emma stepped off the ladder and placed a hand on Angela's shoulder. "You are the heart of this place, my friend."

Angela pressed her hand to Emma's. "Best compliment ever."

Jeremy went back to the storage room and walked out carrying the glass-paneled warming box. He hoisted the heavy glass cube to the checkout counter. "Over here?"

"That'll work perfectly." Angela clapped her hands and then ran behind the counter to plug it in. The light came on, and there was still a ribbon with a gingerbread cookie pattern hot-glued around the edge. "Why haven't I done this the last couple of years?"

"Because some traditions are hard to carry on," Emma said,

patting Angela's heart then wrapping an arm around her shoulder. "It already smells like Momma Grace is here again." The aromas of cinnamon, clove and sugar filled the space.

Jeremy pushed his hair behind his ear. "Know where the key is to this thing?"

"Is it locked?" Angela walked over and tried the door herself. "I always wondered why there was a key lock on this thing. Never did make sense to me."

"A massive rush of cookie thieves could come in," Jeremy teased with a laugh.

"Let me check the office." Angela swerved around the counter and went back into the office. Momma Grace had spent countless hours in here.

The old desk was chipped and worn along the front edge, probably from the charm bracelet she always wore. It was kind of Momma Grace's signature. You could hear her coming down the hall, like a cat wearing a bell.

Angela shuffled through the random clips and ink pens in the top drawer. All the keys there were labeled.

Tugging open the file drawer, she flipped through the old manila folders. Warranty cards for things that were as old as she was were still filed there. One of these days she'd have to clean this mess out.

A folder labeled SWEET STUFF caught her attention. Right inside it was the manual for the cookie warmer, with the original receipt taped to it along with the key.

"Found it," she called out. As she leaned over to shove the folder back into the drawer a red envelope fell to the floor. She picked it up, then paused. The familiar block print read, DEAR SANTA.

She sat back in the chair and laid the folder on the desk. Turning the envelope over in her hands, she saw the words "Angela, Age 6" written in cursive in Momma Grace's handwriting under DEAR SANTA.

Angela slid the notepaper out of the envelope.

Dear Santa,
My sister is sad. Mommy went to heaven. Daddy took us
to the beach to see Momma Grace and PawPaw, but he left
and never came back. Marie says he went to heaven too, but
I heard PawPaw talking to him on the phone. I think he's
coming back. Please bring Daddy home for Christmas, and
bring me a sno-cone machine with cherry flavor. It's my
sister's favorite. It makes her smile.

I've been very good helping Momma Grace work in the
Christmas shop.

Angela

Angela still remembered writing the letter. She'd hated Santa for ignoring her. Opening the folder, among the booklets and receipts there were two more envelopes tucked inside.

Angela, Age 7

Dear Santa,
Momma was really sick and went to heaven. I miss her.
For Christmas can you tell her that I miss her?

Marie and I can share presents if you get something for
Dad. Momma always helped us buy him T-shirts for
Christmas. We don't know where he is, but I think he
would like a present from us, and maybe he'd come home.

Thank you,
Angela

Angela, Age 8

Dear Santa,
My name is Angela. I'm writing to remind you that my
sister and I have been really good. Momma Grace and
PawPaw said so. We are staying here until my daddy comes
back to get us. He's been gone a very long time.
I've been asking and asking for your help. Can you
please bring Daddy to our house for Christmas?
I want my own step stool so I can help Momma Grace at
the store. Blue is my favorite color. I don't need any presents
if you'll just bring Daddy back.

Pretty please,
Angela

Angela clutched her heart. Momma Grace had kept these letters all of these years. Angela had been so disenchanted with Santa after this. She did get a blue step stool that Christmas, but that had been like getting second place.

Daddy never did call or come back for them.

She closed her eyes, tipping her chin toward the lighthouse tower. "I'm so sorry I'm letting you down, Momma Grace. I can't believe I might have to close this store. You were always, always there for me." She took in a deep breath. "If there's anything you can do from up there as an angel, I sure could use your help now."

She opened her eyes. Through misty tears the festive twinkle lights looked more like rain against the fogged glass window of the office door. The soft holiday music filled the air and her heart. How she wished she could turn back time.

This place was as much her home as was the beach house. Not only did she spend more time here than there, but her family was in every part of this store. Her grandfather had built the wooden displays, and Momma Grace had taught her the business from the time Angela was old enough to say "Welcome" and "Thank you for shopping with us" to customers.

She'd never imagined that it would end one day.

Feeling adrift, she forced herself to get up and get back on the sales floor.

Once Angela got the warming box open, Stephanie transferred the cookies to it from the huge pot.

The four of them worked quickly, transforming the store for the official start of the Christmas holiday. It was tradition that Heart of Christmas look extra-special starting the day after Thanksgiving until New Year's Day.

It was no easy task Christmas-ing up a Christmas store! But they had some decorations that came out only in December.

And today the area behind the building that they'd once used as a live-tree lot would open as Snow Valley. With so many of the local clubs and churches selling trees it hadn't been practical to sell them at the store anymore, so Angela had worked a trade with an old friend who owned a ski lodge in the mountains for use of his snow machine for the weeks prior to Christmas Eve, rather than leave the space empty.

For the past three weeks, her team had worked tirelessly decorating Snow Valley. It had taken shape, a wintery village complete with a different-themed live Christmas tree in each corner. Jeremy had crafted fresh wreaths out of the trimmings from the trees to adorn the backs of the benches scattered throughout.

Now families could play together in frigid temperatures for an hour or two then warm back up inside the store. Angela had hoped and prayed these tweaks would breathe new life into the store.

It was her last hope.

Jeremy exploded through the Snow Valley entrance. "Are you ready for this?" He pulled a snowball from behind his back and raised it in the air.

"Are we *ready*?" Angela exclaimed. His excitement was contagious. "We're dying to experience the finished product."

"Come see!" Jeremy waved them out into the big-tented area.

Emma grabbed Angela's hand, and Stephanie ran ahead and held the door so Jeremy could go in first.

When the girls walked inside the tent, soft snow floated around them to the ground.

"It's so real," Angela said. She'd had high hopes, but this truly looked like the real thing.

A snowball flew by her arm and landed square between the slats of one of the benches.

"Perfect!" Emma exclaimed, then squatted down and packed a snowball of her own, throwing it at Jeremy and landing it right in his chest. "Gotcha."

Jeremy had made the snow in the perfect ratio of powdery to wet for a good snowball. He'd turned out to be a genius when it came to making snow. Who knew a beach guy who'd only seen snow a handful of times could be so good at making it? Unlike most guys, he'd even read the directions.

"Do you know the last snow that we had on Black Friday in Pleasant Sands was in 1941?" Angela asked.

"No," all three of her employees said at once.

"Well, it was, and it was a big one. A whopping three inches. One of the biggest snowstorms on our beach ever."

She saw the three of them exchange a glance. They teased her all the time about knowing so much trivia about the town. Whatever. Strangers enjoyed it, and so did she.

"People are going to love this snow," Jeremy said.

Emma smacked him in the leg with another snowball. "I already do!"

"Careful, Emma," Jeremy said. "I'm a good shot. Don't start something you don't want to really be a part of."

Emma laughed nervously, wiping her hands on her Mrs. Claus apron. "Sorry. You're right. I don't like it when I get hit." She turned to Angela. "My brothers were relentless. This is nothing compared to the snows we had back home in Pennsylvania, but it really is like real snow."

Angela lifted her hand and crossed her fingers. "Here's hoping it's a hit."

"It's new. That has to be good, right?" Emma said.

"I guess. I mean, we've always counted on keeping things the same. That's just not working anymore." Angela's great-great-grandmother had started selling handcrafted ornaments from the store to earn enough money to make ends meet. The first ornaments ever sold were made from the excessive inventory of wicks stored from the old days when oil lamps were an important part of how lighthouses lit the sky as a navigational aid, and for this one in particular, to warn ships of the rocks off the coast. Great-grandma braided, wove and painted wicks into beautiful stars, and people loved them so much the store quickly became the place to visit.

It wasn't until Momma Grace was a little girl that she and her mom, Great-grandma Mackey, started making the holiday mason jar oil lamps that the store was known for now.

The first year, the town of Pleasant Sands bought two hundred of them to dress up every store window on Main Street. That went on for years. The oil lamps were so pretty, but of course nowadays everyone used electric lights.

Monday night the outline of every building would be lit with white lights. Not much work for Angela since she kept hers that way year-round, a bonus of being in the Christmas business.

"Are we ready?" she asked the team.

"The biggest retail day of the year," Emma said.

"I need the biggest sales day in this store's history," she said. In the past they'd done very little in the way of promotion for the holiday, and always fared well. This year, she'd broken down and advertised specials and the Black Friday grand opening of Snow Valley in the paper.

To keep to the old tradition of family focus, Angela had decided to make the attraction free. One area had been fenced off for a snow castle competition. People could come in during store hours to work on them all month long, and the winner would receive a trophy and a hand-carved nativity worth over five hundred dollars.

"I think we're ready, team." Angela walked over to the register and checked the money drawer and credit card machine. Brightly colored stacks of tissue paper to protect the fragile ornaments were stacked next to the shopping bags with the store's gold lighthouse logo on them. Everything was ready to go.

"Ten more minutes," Emma announced. "And I just looked out front. There are at least twenty cars out there waiting."

"A good sign." Angela's stomach did a flip. She opened the top of the cookie warmer and let the sugary-sweet smell from the cookies fill the room.

"Our secret weapon," Emma said with wink.

A girl could hope.

"Let's go ahead and open. No sense making people sit in their cars on such a pretty day."

Chapter Nine

Dear Santa,
I'm so excited for you to come see me and my sisters!!
I am 4 years old, and I can't write yet, so my sister Sara is
writing this. Sara says she wants a bike for Christmas.
I would really like a Barbie house and car. Playing with
Barbies is my most favorite thing!

I love you Santa!!
Aimee

Normally Geoff parked in the back employee lot at Christmas Galore and took that entrance up to his office, but today he came right in the front door with the customers because there really was nothing like the buzz of Black Friday shoppers.

"Pardon me." He sidestepped a woman carrying a pile of striped beach towels at least ten high. Then skipped aisle four, usually his shortcut, due to the number of shoppers blocking it, only to help another customer negotiate an air fryer from a top shelf to her basket. "Merry Christmas."

"Thank you for your help. Isn't this the best store around?"

"I like to think so," he said with a smile. She had no idea it was his store. That made it all that much more of a compliment.

He made one sweep across the row of registers to make sure

everything was moving along. Pleased with the number of customers, and how quickly his employees were taking care of them,
he breathed a sigh of relief.

On his way to the elevator that led to the offices, someone
tapped him on the shoulder.

"Nine-thirty? Really?" Chandler gave him one of those what-
the-heck looks, head cocked.

"My schedule is not up for discussion with you."

"True," Chandler said with a touch of humility, "but I've never
known you to come in this late. Everything okay?"

"Yeah. Everything's good."

"Good for *you*. Me? Not so fine, thanks to those doggone sno-
cones," Chandler said. "The floors are already sticky."

"Well, those sno-cones are our signature."

"I know. I know. But those sno-cones are a disaster when we
have this many customers at one time."

"Be thankful for that. All those customers contribute to your
bonus, if you recall."

Chandler pulled his phone out of his pocket. "Trust me. I do.
Right now our sales are twenty-one percent over any other location's. And since we didn't mark down the beach stuff, we're
seeing a spike in profit in that department that we've never seen
this time of year."

Geoff wasn't surprised. "Told you it would work."

"Doesn't hurt that we don't have any competition in this town,"
Chandler said. "In every other beach town there's been at least
one other place with beach stuff on sale over the holidays, but not
here. All these beach shops are seasonal. Shuttered up. The only
competition is that little Christmas store, but their price points
put them in a whole other bracket. Not our demographic at all."

"The shop in the lighthouse, right?" Geoff remembered it from their original location reports.

"Yes. It's been in their family for years. Mostly high-dollar decorations, and one-of-a-kind holiday gifts with a focus on family and tradition. Heirloom stuff. Totally different kind of store from us."

"Good," Geoff said. "I'd hate to be responsible for making their little landmark store have to close its doors." Geoff held a sincere pose, but only for a half a second. "Okay, that's a big fat lie."

"Don't let Santa hear you. You'll get coal in your stocking," Chandler said.

"Doubtful," Geoff said. "I just saw the inventory alert that we're almost out of bags of coal. Row seventeen, bin twenty-two."

"That stuff is flying off the shelves. What we're not selling is the personalized ornaments. What's with that? We always sell out of those. Tess is down there doodling on cardboard boxes waiting for a customer."

Geoff's brows knit closer. "That's usually one of our most active areas. What's the problem?"

"I don't know," Chandler said. "I told the team in the last huddle to recommend the personalized ornaments as keepsakes to steer folks toward them. Maybe they're just not seeing them."

"Push the ones with this year already printed on them. We don't want to get stuck with those ornaments. Once they're out of date you can't give them away no matter how cool they are." He wasn't telling Chandler anything he didn't already know.

"I hear ya." Chandler turned toward the door. "Don't worry. I've got this."

"I know you do. I'm headed upstairs."

"Hey, are you feeling okay today?"

"Yeah. I'm fine." Distracted is what he was. Ever since he saw that girl at the coffee shop.

"You know I've got this place under control. If you're not feeling okay you don't have to stick around."

"Yeah. Yeah, Chandler. I know." He didn't need to be here, but working was his favorite pastime. "I'm not sick."

"You just seem off."

"I'm fine." He caught himself sounding short-tempered.

"Whatever you say." Chandler put his hands up and backed off. "Not to poke the bear, but you've been a little off ever since you got your mind wrapped around that girl you saw."

They'd been working together a long time. Chandler knew him pretty well. "Thought I saw her again last night too."

"Then she's in town. You're bound to run across her soon. It's not that big of a place."

He had a point. Geoff turned and went upstairs to his office. He closed the door behind him and walked over to the mirrored window that gave him a complete view of the store. Shoppers filled every single aisle. Business was good.

He turned to his computer and flagged the annual ornaments. He'd rather break even and get rid of them then get stuck with them. Easy enough. He reduced the price, and sent the sale stickers down to the printer on the floor. The team would take action on them immediately.

Virgil poked his head in the door. "I was looking for your mother."

"She's doing something with some women she met on the Pleasant Sands Christmas Giving Project committee today. She's consumed with that stuff all of the sudden."

"Not surprised." Virgil crossed one leg over the other, leaning against the doorjamb.

"Really? I am. She's never gotten involved like this in any of the other towns we've opened in."

"Pleasant Sands is different." Virgil ran a hand through his mop of thick gray hair. "Always has been."

Geoff closed the top of his laptop and looked up at Virgil. "Always?"

"You know your mom and I met here."

"In Pleasant Sands?"

"Yep. Like a hundred years ago," he said with a snicker. "Or forty. Whatever."

"She never said a thing." Geoff thought back to how his mother had fought for this specific location. "That explains her tenacity to open a store here even though it didn't fit our business model. The population in Pleasant Sands is way below our target market, and the average income much higher. We had better options."

"She had her reasons."

"I wish she'd shared them." He sat back in his chair. "Is she getting sentimental in her old age?"

"I didn't call her old," Virgil said, straightening.

"Yeah, don't tell her I did either." A *ho-ho-ho* echoed from Geoff's pocket. Mom's ringtone. "Great. She must know that I'm talking about her," he said. "Let me get this."

"Before you do, we're having problems in the Cape Cod store."

Geoff answered the phone. "Hey, Mom. You're on speaker. Virgil's with me."

"Happy Black Friday to you both."

"I was just telling Geoff that we're having a problem up in the Cape Cod store. I was going to see if you wanted to go with me. I'm flying out in about an hour. I'll buy you dinner at Lefty's."

"You know that's my favorite restaurant, but I'm afraid I've already made plans," Rebecca said. "Besides, there's really no need to be flying off for dinner in another town when we have so many charming places to try right here. So, what's this about a problem in the Cape Cod store?"

"The water main broke and the city has shut down water to the whole street."

"That shouldn't slow down sales," Geoff said, relieved.

Virgil shook his head. "The part of the story where the water main break is right in front of our entrance and will block our parking lot will. Not to mention that it flooded part of the front of the store, but I've already got a team on that."

Geoff slung back in his chair. "Man, and things were going so well."

"Yeah. We had a great night there. Thank goodness we were open when the main broke. The team was able to move things out of the way. No damage to merchandise."

"Hallelujah!" his mom sang out.

"I'll get things going as quickly as I can," Virgil said. "Hopefully we'll just lose a couple of hours."

"A couple of critical hours on Black Friday." Geoff pulled up the store sales and started calculating the potential loss.

"If we're not back online in a couple of hours I'll get some signs made up extending the special sales through the weekend."

"Thanks for handling it, Virgil," his mom said. "Now, Geoff, the reason I called is to let you know that I've just committed to donating two hundred Christmas stockings, candy canes and coloring books to the Pleasant Sands Christmas Giving Project. We should probably add some type of goody. Don't we have those chocolate marshmallow Santas?"

"We do, and why not add those ornaments with the year on them?" He'd rather write them off as a donation than have to clearance them anyway.

"Perfect. Can you get that pulled together for me? They'll pick them up next Thursday. We'll be putting the stockings together at the church that evening. You might get Chandler to post something in the store in case anyone would like to volunteer to help."

Geoff shot off an email to Chandler while they were on the phone. "Done."

"Perfect!" she exclaimed. "I'm enjoying being an active part of this community. Isn't Pleasant Sands enchanting?"

"I suppose it is." The only thing he cared about was that the town was proving to be a moneymaking location for the store.

"Now, bring me up to date. What do the numbers look like? I haven't had a chance to look."

"All of the stores are tracking to forecast. Would you like to place a wager on which store is leading sales at this moment?"

"No way," she said emphatically. "It's always the one you are standing in."

"Yes. Yes, it is." He took that as a compliment. Not something she lavished on him often.

"I'm going to do a little holiday shopping with some of the gals from the Christmas Giving Project committee this afternoon. I'll see you tomorrow morning at the store. I have an idea I want to run by you."

"You know I'll be wondering all day what it is you have on your mind."

"That's what makes it so fun."

It made it fun for his mother. It drove him absolutely crazy. If there was one thing he couldn't stand, it was being out of the loop.

Chapter Ten

DID YOU KNOW?
Heart of Christmas has been serving customers on
Black Fridays since before it had that nickname.

Heart of Christmas opened in 1925.
The term Black Friday was coined in 1961.

Thank you for being a part of our legacy.

Black Friday shoppers mingled in front of the tall arched doorway of Heart of Christmas waiting for the store to open.

Jeremy jogged to the front door and flipped the sign to OPEN, then flung open the door and threw out his arms. "Merry Christmas, everybody. Come on in!"

He was just a big kid. Angela couldn't be luckier to have these three on her team.

The shoppers rolled in. Angela's heart leapt when she saw Marie and Chrissy among them, both dressed in festive red.

"What are you two doing here?" Angela held her arms out and Chrissy ran into them.

"Mommy said if you say it's okay we can help today. She said I can say, 'Thank you for coming, and Merry Christmas,' to the customers, just like you did when you were little like me." She extended a white-stockinged leg. "Look. I even got to wear my good shoes."

"Beautiful." Angela had bought Chrissy those black patent leather Mary Janes. She knew how much she loved them.

"You were her age the first time you worked Black Friday," Marie said.

"I was." Angela stooped over and tapped Chrissy on the nose. "I'd love to have your help."

"And I'll hang out and help run herd over her. Really, sis, we want to help."

She hugged Marie. "Thank you. You're my angel-in-waiting."

"Always," Marie said.

"And forever." Angela held Marie tight, and for so long that Chrissy ended up wrapping herself around the two of them.

"It looks like it's going to be a busy day. We'd better get to work," Angela said, finally breaking the hug. "How about you help at the counter, Chrissy? You can welcome people when they first come in, and after they buy their stuff, you can thank them."

"I'll be very good at that," Chrissy said with a curtsey and skipped to the register, where Stephanie was already ringing someone up.

"Merry Christmas," Chrissy said cheerfully.

Marie made herself busy at the counter, removing price stickers and helping wrap ornaments in the pretty tissue paper.

The shoppers sounded like Fourth of July fireworks spectators, the way they *ooh*ed and *ah*ed as they walked by the gorgeous displays, and children discovered the train in motion above their heads.

"Let me help you with that," Angela said to a customer eyeing one of the hand-carved Santas. "He's so lifelike." She handed the customer the piece, and just as she looked up, one of her favorite customers race-walked by. "Jean? Hello! Merry Christmas."

"Hi, Angela. I promised the kids some time in Snow Valley," Jean said, herding her kids into a line like little ducklings and counting to be sure they were all there. "And their personalized ornaments. It's tradition, after all."

"You brought the whole crew." Angela wondered how any woman managed seven children all so close in age all by herself. "They're going to love Snow Valley. Jeremy has done an amazing job with the snow. It's like the real thing."

The woman Angela was helping piped in. "My grandchildren will be here in two weeks. I'll have to bring them."

"It's a winter wonderland out there." Angela was proud of the end result.

"This is wonderful too." The woman handed the Santa back to Angela. "I'll take it."

"Excellent choice. I'll get the box for him." She walked her customer to the register. "I'll be right back with the box. Stephanie will ring you up. Thank you for shopping with us today. We look forward to seeing you and your grandchildren soon."

"Thank you, dear." The woman already had her credit card out.

Jean came over to Angela, half out of breath. "They wear me out."

Angela laughed. "Well, maybe they'll tire themselves out. By the way, I have a surprise for you."

"Really?"

Angela led Jean over to the cherry cabinet that her grandfather had built for the Christmas village display. Each shelf was terraced, giving the illusion of a town against the backdrop of a mountainside. Buildings, people, pets, even tiny wrapped presents under

Christmas trees and ice skaters filled the levels, each one hand carved and painted. These figures were truly the type of craftsmanship that you handed down generation to generation.

Just this morning she'd put out several new pieces. It had been so hard to keep them in the back until today, but Angela had to have something special for Black Friday.

She watched as Jean ogled the detail of all the new pieces. But they weren't what she'd wanted to show her.

"The carousel is on sale. Your favorite piece." She turned the tag so Jean could see the marked-down price.

Jean's smiling face fell. She'd almost bought the intricate piece last week, and now it was discounted 40 percent. She was probably relieved that she'd waited to make the purchase now.

The woman shook her head, and then wrapped her hand around Angela's forearm. "You're not going to believe this. I just bought one. Not nearly as pretty. Or nice. But cute. I was over at Christmas Galore and they had one for just nineteen ninety-nine. I mean, it's plastic or resin or something, but it's just for a few weeks anyway, right?"

"Nineteen?" Angela's heart fell. "Um, yeah. Gosh, too bad."

"I'm sick about it."

So was Angela. She waited for Jean to gather her senses. For twenty bucks she could stick that bargain bin item in one of the kids' rooms. This one was a real piece of art. Not some disposable trinket.

Jean had practically drooled over the artistry of the hand-carved wooden piece. The painted details made it uniquely different.

"Carved right here in the U.S.A," Angela reminded her. But Jean seemed happy with her $19.99 Christmas Galore purchase.

"More money to spend on other things, right?" Jean looked embarrassed. "Christmas is really for the kids anyway."

A little girl tugged on Jean's purse. "Mom, can we have cookies?"

Angela turned to get cookies for the kids, more to hide the feeling in her gut than to be helpful.

"Thanks! These are so good, Mom."

"They'll be on a sugar high all day. They just had sno-cones over at Christmas Galore. That place is so much fun."

The thought of that made Angela's eye twitch.

The whole warehouse concept, stock to the ceiling and gaudy sale stickers, was everything Christmas was not supposed to be.

"Come see Snow Valley, Mom!" Jean let her children drag her toward the back, leaving a trail of their half-eaten cookies on the display tables along the way. Their high-pitched squeals could be heard all the way at the front of the store. No way did they have that much fun at Christmas Galore.

When Jean led her whole tribe out of Heart of Christmas an hour later without spending a dime, Angela's knees threatened to buckle. Jean hadn't even bought the ornaments that she'd mentioned getting.

Emma rushed over. "Was that Jean? I bet she was so excited about the carousel being on sale."

"No."

"What?"

Angela's mouth went dry. "No. She didn't buy a thing."

"Nothing?" Emma looked totally perplexed.

"I know. I'm as surprised as you are. That carousel is a steal at a hundred and fifty."

"Of course it is. Those are made one by one," Emma agreed. "So why? I don't get it. She almost bought it at twice that price last week."

"She bought one for twenty bucks at—"

"At Christmas Galore. Oh no." Emma grabbed Angela's hand. "I was afraid of that. I saw their ad, but those are nothing like what we sell."

"Apparently, that's not the point."

"What if people come in to play in our snow, but don't buy anything?" Emma bit her lower lip.

Angela stroked the pricey hand-carved carousel. It was her favorite piece in the Christmas village too. She thought for sure Jean would be walking out with it today. She'd pretty much mentally deposited the check for it.

Christmas Galore was gobbling up her Christmas spirit, right along with her customers.

Angela tried to look at the bright side. "Christmas Galore is new and that will wear off. Things will soon be back to normal."

"Do you really think so?" Emma asked.

"No." She shook her head. "I really don't." She suddenly felt light-headed. "I need to sit down for a second."

"Are you okay? Do you want me to get Marie?"

"No. Definitely don't get Marie." She blew out a loud breath. "I just need a minute."

Emma laid her hand on Angela's shoulder. "With all the online shopping and warehouse-type stores, there are so many choices. But with Christmas Galore right up the street? How do we compete with that?"

"That's just it. I never wanted to compete. I wanted to carry on tradition. Quality products. Fair prices. Family values. Hard work. I guess it's just not enough anymore."

Emma spoke slowly. "You know what else is not enough?"

"What?"

"You. In this store. All the time. Angela, you need to get out and do some things for you. When was the last time you went on a date, or did something fun?"

"It's been a while."

"A while? I don't think you've been on a date in the two years we've worked together. How do you do that? Do you even notice men anymore?"

"I noticed a handsome man yesterday. At the Crabby Coffee Pot." She didn't bother to tell Emma the rest of the story. It was too embarrassing.

"Wait a second. You were at Crabby's? You never get coffee out."

"I know. I was being adventurous. See. You don't know everything."

"Well, I do know that you worrying about this place isn't going to save it. We've done everything we can do."

Emma's words weren't comforting.

Angela had a hunch that the sales were not going to be up to par tonight. "Thanks for being my right hand around here."

"It's like getting paid to hang out with my bestie." Emma hugged her. "Things will be okay no matter what happens with the store. You'll see. Hey, we should have a snowball fight after we close tonight."

"I call Jeremy on my team." Angela knew Jeremy had pre-made snowballs stockpiled out there for the kids.

Emma laughed. "Fine by me. Guess you didn't know that Stephanie is the pitcher on her softball team."

"Just my luck," Angela said. "Snowball fight at closing. Be there!"

"I'll tell them."

Angela walked over and relieved Stephanie at the register. "I've got this for a while. Why don't you take a break?"

Things were so busy that when Stephanie came back it seemed like she'd just left.

When Brad walked in Angela couldn't believe it was already four o'clock.

"I'm here to see if my girls can get away for some pizza," Brad said.

"Yes!" Chrissy screamed. "I love pizza!"

"Come with us, sis," Marie said.

Angela shook her head. "No. Y'all go and have some family time. Thanks for your help today. It's been so fun having you here."

Brad held up a finger. "But before we go, we need to visit the famous Snow Valley! I even brought jackets. They're in the truck." He swung Chrissy up onto his hip. "Come on! You ready?"

"Yee-ees!" Chrissy sang out as he swung her around and made a dash for the truck.

Marie laughed and nudged Angela. "If that man thinks I'm having a snowball fight, he's got another think coming."

"Oh, I'm pretty sure you're going to be in a snowball fight. There's no stopping him. So you'd better just make your mind up to it." Angela had to laugh. She knew Marie was not going to be a good sport about this. She had half a mind to join them just so she could see her reaction.

Brad came inside with Chrissy already wrapped up in her winter coat with fur-edged hood, and gloves. He'd tied a blue and black scarf around his neck, and had Marie's winter coat over his arm.

Marie let Brad help her slip into her heavy wool pea coat, then drag her toward the door to Snow Valley.

"Help!" Marie waved her arms, pretending to resist.

Almost an hour later, Angela realized she hadn't seen Marie,

Brad and Chrissy come back through so she went out to Snow Valley to check on them. They were all three huddled around what looked like a two-foot Santa's sleigh made out of snow. In the back of it were individual boxes and toys.

Marie's back was to her and there was a big snowball splat right in the middle of her coat. It was good to know that Brad had lived through that.

She backed out without bothering them. If her sister and her family enjoyed Snow Valley, that was reason enough to have brought the project to life.

Seeing them had lifted Angela's spirits like those man-made snowflakes drifting around in the blower as she walked back into the store.

"I was just looking for you," Emma said. "Someone is asking about the music box. They want to know if it's for sale."

"Oh. Well. It's always been just for display, but I can talk to them."

"It's that older couple over there. They just spent Thanksgiving with their daughter down the coast. She told them about the store," Emma explained.

"Got it. Thanks." Angela greeted the couple with a smile. "Hi. I'm Angela Carson. What can I help you with?"

The woman jumped right in. "Our daughter told us about this place. We're on our way home, and she said we had to stop."

"I'm so glad you did," Angela said.

The music box was the size of an old record player, but made of a unique wood with beautiful grain. It had been in the store for as long as Angela could remember, just as decoration and a conversation starter.

She remembered Momma Grace being asked lots of times over

the years if it were for sale, but she'd always declined. But this time . . . Angela knew she should let it go if the price was right.

"My husband has been looking for a piece like this for as long as I've known him." The woman's white hair was perfectly coiffed and she wore an outfit that was pretty snazzy for a car ride home.

"It's true," he said. "Years. This is a Porter Swan Elite Music Box." He ran his fingers gently across the grain of the highly polished wood. "Gorgeous."

The woman hugged her husband's arm.

"Yes, it is," Angela said. "Made in Randolf, Vermont. It's been in my family for years."

"Please don't say it's not for sale," his wife begged.

Angela paused. "Actually . . ."

The man closed his eyes, listening to the perfect pitch of the Christmas tune. "Fifty-four teeth on each comb make the distinctive sweet sound and full range of four octaves. Remarkable. Before you say anything, let me just make you an offer."

"You know a lot more about this music box than I do," Angela said. "I just love the sound."

"Do you have a piece of paper?" he asked.

Angela dug into the pocket of her apron. "Sure." She handed it to him.

He snatched a pen from his shirt pocket. "Thank you." He scribbled something on the slip of paper and handed it back to her. "Go ahead. Look at it," he said.

She glanced over at the man's wife, who gave Angela a zealous smile.

Angela looked at the paper. On it was written *$7000.00*. She looked back in his direction and then back at the number, trying to not look too stunned.

"You can't be serious," she said. There was no way he meant to write seven thousand dollars. Sure, it was an amazing piece, but that was a crazy price. She'd thought she might get one thousand for it and had been pretty excited about that.

"Fine. I can go another five hundred." He pulled his checkbook out of his pocket. "I can write you a check right now, and if you're not comfortable with a check, you can ship me the music box once it clears."

"Or we can put it on a credit card," his wife offered, hope hanging to each word.

Seventy-five hundred dollars? That would surely come in handy.

"Whatever works for you," his wife said. "This would be the best Christmas present ever. I can never find something special enough for him."

Angela heard Chrissy yell goodbye near the door. She raised her hand and waved as she and her parents left, then glanced between the husband and wife.

"Yes. Sold." Angela's heart pounded. "Check or credit card is fine."

The poised woman let out a wild whoop then leapt into the air. "I'm so happy for you, honey!"

He kissed her full on the mouth. "Never would have found this had you not insisted on stopping here on the way home."

Angela rang up the sale personally. "I think I can find a box for you, and Jeremy can carry it out to the car."

"Not necessary," the man said. "I can carry it. We're driving straight home from here and I know exactly where I'm putting it. We don't need a box." His enthusiasm was contagious. "Thank you so much. You've made our Christmas."

"You're welcome. It couldn't have gone to a better home." Angela would've never gotten that kind of money for it locally, even if it was worth it. She looked toward heaven. *Thanks, Momma Grace.* There's no way she hadn't had a little something to do with those people happening into the store today.

At the end of the night the store was in a total state of disarray. Some of the shelves looked bare, and it had been a good day, even not including the sale of the music box.

Angela called her team out to Snow Valley. "Thanks for an awesome day. There's only one last thing we need to do today." She paused. "Snowball fight!" And she was the first one to throw a snowball.

"You're on my team, Stephanie," Emma yelled.

They burned off the stress and weariness through a flurry of snowballs and laughter until they were all breathless.

"Man, I haven't had this much fun in years," Jeremy said. "This is my dream job."

Stephanie's nose was bright red. "I should have brought a coat!"

"You guys are the best team ever," Angela said. "Thank you for everything."

They walked back into the store, stomping the snow from their shoes on the carpet mats as they did.

"Snow Valley was a big hit. People loved it," Angela said. "I'm not sure Snow Valley really helped with sales, but at least it was a memorable day for a lot of people. Including me. And that's something we can be proud of."

"Sure is," Emma agreed.

"How do y'all feel about putting off straightening up the store until tomorrow morning before we open?"

"Don't have to ask me twice," Jeremy said. "I'm beat."

"Yeah, me too," Angela said. "Y'all head on out."

As soon as Stephanie and Jeremy left, Emma and Angela closed out the register and carried the till back to her office.

"Here we go." Emma reached across the desk and placed her hand on top of Angela's. "No matter what happens, this store is a landmark in this town. Heart of Christmas will always be remembered."

Angela's lips quivered. She stared out her office door into the store. The lights still twinkled brightly, and beautiful holiday ornaments and decorations showed their festive colors next to framed black-and-white photos of Pleasant Sands' history, including those of the lighthouse in its working days.

Her throat tightened, making it difficult to swallow, much less talk, so she just nodded her thanks.

Together she and Emma counted out the money and balanced the tape.

Angela pulled out her ledger from last year to compare sales numbers, but when Emma slid the final numbers across the table to her, Angela didn't even have to look.

"It's not enough." Angela dropped her chin to her chest.

Emma lowered her head. "I'm sorry."

"Me too." Angela balled her hands in her lap. "But I kind of already knew it wouldn't be."

"If only Christmas Galore had never come to this town," Emma said.

"If only." Angela swallowed hard. "Emma, I'm closing the store. New Year's Eve will be the last day Heart of Christmas will be open."

She had no idea what she would do now. Liquidating the inventory would buy her some time, but she wasn't sure how she'd get through December with a smile on her face, much less in her heart. Letting go of Heart of Christmas would be just like losing Momma Grace all over again.

Chapter Eleven

DID YOU KNOW?
In 1970, Pleasant Sands' year-round population was 414.
Today, the year-round population hovers around 2,800,
making it one of the most populated beach towns
along the Outer Banks.

With Black Friday behind her, Angela decided to get an early start cleaning up and restocking before the others got to work.

As Angela put her key in the lock, Emma opened the door. "Good morning, my dear friend."

Angela stumbled back. "You scared me to death. What are you doing here so early?"

"I wanted to help, not give you a heart attack. Sorry."

Angela let a nervous giggle escape. "I'm fine."

"I remember you telling me how you and your grandmother would come extra early to the store in the mornings and the two of you would drink chocolate coffee."

"We did. Momma Grace made the best chocolate coffee."

Emma counted off the ingredients. "A scoop of cocoa, a splash of vanilla, a teaspoon of sugar and black coffee? Did I remember that correctly?"

"You did. What was Momma Grace thinking? I bet I was a maniac on those days. Chocolate *and* coffee. Talk about winding a kid up."

"But you loved it." Emma walked inside toward the counter, and Angela followed.

"I did," Angela said. "More than anything."

"I made you some." Emma turned and picked up two dainty bone china cups.

Angela's eyes teared. "In the pretty dishes?"

"Yes. I thought you might need some cheering up this morning."

"This is really thoughtful. Thank you so much." She raised the teacup to her lips.

"I know this is hard, but you should think of this as a shift in your life, not an end to the store. We're best friends. I know you are so much more than this store. Let this be an opportunity to spread your wings and try something new. Let it be a blessing."

Angela took a sip of the chocolate coffee. "It tastes just like Momma Grace used to make. Thank you."

"You're welcome." Emma approached the table set with fine china, and a Christmas bear in each chair. She moved one of the bears and sat down. "Come sit."

Angela took her cup and set it down on the table. She lowered herself onto the chair, and put her folded hands between her knees. "This is nice."

"Did you get any sleep last night?"

"Some." Angela ran her fingers under her eyes. Did she look that tired? "I kept thinking about how I flat turned down that offer from Sheetz to build a gas station and restaurant here last year. That almost-too-good-to-turn-down offer. I didn't even consider it. Did you know that my sister didn't speak to me for a week after that?"

"Why was she so mad?"

"She said I was living my life by my heart instead of using my business sense."

"Well, there's really nothing wrong with going with your heart."

Angela wasn't so sure about that anymore. "You know, my great-great-grandmother bought this place and the land for less than we'd pay for a car these days."

Emma nodded. "That was still a lot of money back then."

"True. I should've at least considered that offer last year. I was thinking about the memories this place holds for Momma Grace and me, but I'll always have those memories. I wouldn't be worrying about what I was going to do for a job next year if I'd made a different decision back then."

"That's easy to say now, Angela. Don't beat yourself up over it. Besides, would you really want a gas station right in front of your house?"

"You've got a point."

"Exactly, and closing the business is one thing, but the lighthouse is still yours. You could do something else with it. Rent it out for office space, maybe?"

She'd never really thought of doing something else here. "It's only ever been Heart of Christmas for as long as I've lived."

"But it was a lighthouse first. So it's not like you'd be doing anything different than what your great-great-grandmother did. You told me yourself she started Heart of Christmas to make ends meet."

"True." Angela hadn't really considered that. "After she bought the lighthouse, she had all this junk that had been stored in it. Wicks and lanterns. That's what became the first ornaments and decorations she sold. It hadn't been out of artistry or a big love for the holiday. It had been out of necessity."

"She was smart."

"Very. Momma Grace used to say she wished she'd been crafty like that. She wasn't, but she loved this town as much as she loved Christmas. That's how I learned so much about it. Marie used to hate it when Momma Grace started one of her stories. Kind of like on *The Golden Girls* when Blanche and Dorothy cringe when Rose starts one of those 'back in St. Olaf' stories. Only it was always here in Pleasant Sands . . ." Angela loved hearing those stories. "It was like story hour at the library for me. I didn't even care that I'd heard them all a hundred times."

"I love it when I hear you telling our customers stories about the old photos in the store. You come alive. It's like you were there."

"Hearing my grandmother tell those stories was just like being there. She was a wonderful storyteller." Angela sipped her chocolate coffee. "Thank you for doing this."

"It was nothing really." Emma smiled gently. "It was the best thing I could think of."

"It's perfect." Angela took the last sip from her cup. "I'm going to tell the others that I'll be closing the store. I figure I should do it this morning. Any closer to Christmas just seems wrong."

"Let me know how I can help."

"I think we'll start with an extra thirty percent off this week. Then we'll work on putting together an exclusive, by-invitation-only shopping day for our regular customers. They should be rewarded for being so dedicated all of these years."

"That's a great idea."

"Enough reminiscing. Let's get these shelves restocked." Stephanie and Jeremy would be there in about an hour, but she and Emma worked well together. Emma moved things that had been laid around in random spots back to their places while Angela pulled stock from the back room.

By the time Jeremy and Stephanie got there, things were in pretty good shape.

"Did y'all ever leave last night?" Jeremy asked.

"We did," Angela said. "But I do have something I need to discuss with you both before we get our day started."

Jeremy looked worried.

"Look, I've been putting this off. Hoping something would change, but it hasn't and I don't want to leave you hanging." Angela's hands unconsciously twisted together. "I'm going to have to close the store after Christmas."

"No." Jeremy slumped and shoved his hands into his pockets. "I love working here."

"I'm sorry." Not only was she failing Momma Grace, and dropping the ball on generations of hard work, but she was letting down three dedicated employees.

Stephanie *tsk*ed. "This is because of Christmas Galore, isn't it?"

Jeremy cracked his knuckles. "You can't tell me that billboard a block up the road wasn't a deliberate attempt to steal our customers. People new to town will think Christmas Galore is the local Christmas shop."

"Their Christmas stuff is cheap. My mom went. She said

everything she picked up was made overseas, and will probably break before it makes it home," Stephanie said. "Totally different from us."

"Completely," agreed Emma.

"They have crazy deals, though," Stephanie said. "Appliqued stockings two for five bucks. Mom bought enough for all the ladies in her book club. I hope Christmas Galore lost money on them."

Angela glanced at the mantel that displayed intricately cross-stitched stockings, some adorned with Swarovski crystals, and even a Western-themed boot made from real cowhide. Not a one was under forty dollars. She was determined to take the high road. "We sell quality. They sell quantity."

"They discount," Jeremy said. "For a hundred bucks you can get a whole lighted winter town scene, and people. Here, you can't even get one building for that."

"Not true," Angela said. "You can get the carolers, and they are quality heirloom pieces. They even have legible sheet music in their hands."

Emma added, "The Christmas carol booklets are affordable, and we have a lot of ornaments under ten dollars."

Angela understood how they felt. She'd rather be in bed with the covers over her head right now, but that was just not how a good Carson girl behaved. "Quality products are what we sell, and top-notch service is our way."

"I don't know what other job I'll like as much as this one," Jeremy said, sounding a bit beaten.

"I'll give you all glowing recommendations elsewhere. I hope you'll be able to work through the season with me. Jeremy, I wouldn't be surprised if the ski lodge wants to hire you, the way you have that snow machine mastered."

"That would be amazing. Summer at the beach. Winter in the mountains." Jeremy looked delighted at the prospect. Little did he know she had the contacts to make that happen, especially with her recommendation.

"After we close there will be a few weeks of work to shut down everything."

Emma piped up. "You know, we could move excess inventory over the internet. I know you were against it as a business model, but it's a good way to get our products into the right hands. People that appreciate quality and art."

"I wish I'd explored your idea sooner," Angela said quietly. "But yes, your help on that would be great."

"Count me in," Jeremy said. "I'll be here with you as long as you need me."

"I'm in until the end too," Stephanie said.

Emma placed her hand on Angela's shoulder. "I'm in too."

"Thank you." Angela clapped her hands together. "Now, there will be no pouting. We're proud of the work we do here. We have no apologies to make. We will do this with style and grace."

"Right," they said.

"Great. Emma, how many people do we have signed up for the reindeer cork ornament session this afternoon?"

Emma opened the scheduling book. "We had a couple of cancellations earlier in the week. That leaves the Madison twins, and Reva is bringing her daughter. Janice Johnson is down for three."

"Six," Angela said, trying not to show her disappointment. "Okay, well, we'll be able to give lots of hands-on attention, then. A good thing."

"Right!" Emma exclaimed. "I'll get everything set up for you in the craft room."

"Great. Well, it's time to open the doors. Are we ready for a wonderful day?" Angela raised her hands in the air. "Let's do this."

Angela unlocked the front door and turned the sign to OPEN.

Emma turned on the twinkle lights and Jeremy started the train as Stephanie straightened the money in the till and turned on the credit card machine, before hitting the button for the music.

Angela turned around, taking in the store as if she were a stranger coming in for the first time. The old building had charm. Every display sparkled, and the cheerful colors of Christmas brought warmth to the place.

Jeremy grabbed his jacket. "Off to get the fresh snow going."

"Thanks, Jeremy!" Angela went to the back and grabbed a stack of eight-inch starburst sale signs that had been sitting on a shelf in the storage room for years and a fat marker and carried them to the front counter. She took the cap off of the marker and the strong odor flooded the room. She'd better be quick about it before the smell drowned out the cinnamon and pine they were known for. The marker squeaked against the shiny cardboard stock as she printed 30 % OFF on each one. Great. Now her store was going to look just like Christmas Galore, with all these sale signs.

By the time the craft class was to begin, only the Madison twins had shown up.

She wondered if something was going on in town. Was the triathlon this weekend? The Christmas parade wasn't until next Thursday night. That always impacted store traffic for a while, but today was unusually slow.

Emma joined Angela at the front counter. "I don't think we've ever had a class with just two people in it."

"Can I teach it?" Stephanie had made the cork ornaments before. "Please?"

"Sure." That was the least Angela could do. "Everything is

already set up in the craft room. If anyone else shows up, we'll send them back."

"Awesome! I'm going to get them started."

"Have fun."

Jeremy came up front—a wisp of cool air following him from Snow Valley. "I love that snow machine. It's cold as heck, but it's a blast." He grabbed his coffee mug and went back into the break room, and returned with hot chocolate.

"I love Snow Valley," Angela said. "It's more fun than I'd ever imagined." Unfortunately, it was a little too late to make a difference.

He slurped his hot chocolate as he read the newspaper over Emma's shoulder. "What the heck? No way!"

"What?" Emma turned around.

"Right there." He pointed a finger to the bottom of the page.

"Oh dear." Emma's voice held concern.

"What is it?" Angela moved in closer.

Christmas Galore had a large ad inviting families to come play in the snow in their parking lot.

"Snow is our gig!" Jeremy muttered under his breath. "They are copying us."

"Imitation is the sincerest form of flattery." But the words caught in Angela's throat. Who was she kidding? This was flat-out wrong. She smiled through clenched teeth. "Excuse me, I just remembered I need to check on something." She excused herself.

Safely behind closed doors she flopped into the chair behind her desk.

Putting on a brave face didn't make it any easier to take a hit like this. She slipped out the back door and got in her car.

At this point, she didn't even care if anyone saw her. Christmas

Galore had already done her in; now they were just stealing customers and her ideas . . . for sport.

Was there any way humanly possible that Christmas Galore could have snow even half as good as what they'd perfected for Snow Valley? They'd worked a solid month on it.

And why was she feeling so competitive about it?

She pressed her foot on the accelerator. She drove over to Christmas Galore with the intention of seeing firsthand what the fuss was all about, but when she got to the block where the store was located there were cars backed up out to the street. The place was packed.

It seemed so unfair that her store would be so empty, only to have practically everyone in town, and their out-of-town neighbors, spending time at the new store in town.

She parked around the corner and walked over, shoving her hands in her pockets, trying to blend in with the other shoppers. One of her neighbors was just in front of her, so Angela slowed down and ducked behind a man and his family, putting some space between them.

There was as much foot traffic heading toward Christmas Galore as there was at the county fair. It was crazy.

Finally, she rounded the front of the building. What she saw was in no way, shape or form like her Snow Valley.

Christmas Galore definitely had snow, but they didn't have snowflakes from a snow machine like Jeremy had perfected for Heart of Christmas. Nor was it a place at all. There wasn't a pile of fresh snow where families could make a snowman together, or build a snow sculpture.

What they had was an arsenal of pre-formed snowballs.

An all-out snow war.

Complete chaos right there in the parking lot. Red paper sno-cone cups littered the man-made snow like little dead soldiers.

The sight made her feel a little sick, because no matter how appalled she was, people were having fun. Lots of it.

Across the way the guy from the coffee shop stood off to the side, laughing.

Her heart betrayed her, doing a flip when his eyes met hers. He wore a suit and a very nice smile, but that didn't make him a nice guy. Looks could be deceiving.

Chapter Twelve

Dear Santa,
I'm sorry. I lied when you asked me if I'd been a good boy.
I'd tell you who I am, but then I'd be on the naughty list.
                                                    D. L.

Geoff and Chandler stood among the crowd of their first-ever outdoor Snow Throw at Christmas Galore. People had piled into the parking lot to see how they'd pull it off, and it looked like they had.

With sno-cone equipment in every store already, it was no big stretch to churn up a pile of snowballs and it was the cheapest promotional tactic they'd come up with in a long time. The store was as busy today as it had been on Black Friday. A definite win.

Geoff scanned the crowd, feeling on top of the world. He couldn't believe his luck. He grabbed Chandler by the sleeve, gesturing with a dip of his forehead in Angela's direction. "She's here."

"Who?" Chandler turned to look.

"Don't look."

"Then how am I supposed to see who you're talking about?" Chandler tried to look again.

Geoff rammed his elbow into Chandler's gut.

"Ouch. What was that for?" Chandler choked out.

"Shhh. Don't be so obvious." Geoff nodded subtly toward the left.

Chandler eased his attention in that direction. "What's she doing here?"

What was Chandler talking about? "No, man. I'm talking about the woman I saw at the coffee shop. She's right over there."

Chandler looked again. "The woman you thought was so pretty?"

"Yes. She is." Geoff turned and checked her out again. "She's very pretty. You have to agree."

"Wait a minute." Chandler leaned around casually. "The one overdressed for the event, wearing the black dress slacks and Christmas sweater?"

"Yes."

"That's the woman who has had you so distracted?"

"I haven't been *that* distracted." Geoff saw the look on Chandler's face. "Fine. A little distracted."

Chandler raised his brow.

"Fine. I've been thinking about her. She's . . . interesting." Chandler looked like he had an opinion. "What?"

"It'll never work." Chandler shook his head.

"What do you mean? What do you know?"

"Besides the fact that things never work out for you with the ladies?"

Chandler wasn't wrong. In all the years they'd known each other while opening stores in ten different towns, it had been the same old story. But that had been by choice. Even so Geoff felt compelled to fight for his own honor. "I've had a couple good relationships."

"Monica?" Chandler challenged.

"Monica was meteorically eccentric. Never saw it coming."

Chandler curled his lips. "That's putting it nicely. How about Louise?"

"She wanted a herd of children. I don't want six kids. I barely have time for me. That was not my fault. It was an impossible situation."

"Maybe you need to get to know these ladies a little better, *before* you start dating them."

"Thanks for the advice, Casanova. All my relationships haven't been that bad."

"You're right. There was Jenny."

"Well, that was my fault, but I won't make that mistake again. I should have spent more time with her. Put her before business once in a while."

"Or once."

"Whatever." His eyes darted across the way and then back at his friend. "There's something about her. She's pretty, yeah, but look at her sitting there alone. She's confident. Nice. I'd definitely like to get to know her."

"How can you tell someone is nice by just looking at their smile? Looks can be deceiving. Look at you. You have a nice smile. I know you're not nice."

"I'm *very* nice," Geoff said.

Chandler busted out with a loud laugh.

"Shh." Geoff raised a finger.

Surprise registered on Chandler's face. "Wait a second. You're not kidding around. You really don't know who that is, do you?"

"No. I don't know her," Geoff said. "Trust me, if I'd met her I'd remember."

Chandler let out a low laugh. "You know more about her than you think. Geoff, that's Angela Carson."

"You know her? Well, introduce me. Let's go"

Chandler stepped over in front of Geoff to keep him from heading that way. "Angela Carson who owns the little Christmas store in the lighthouse. Heart of Christmas. The one that is going to go out of business because of *you*."

"Me?" The breath caught in his throat. She was the owner of Heart of Christmas? Well, this time Chandler was right. There's no way this would ever work. "I'm not . . . It's not my fault that people are seduced by discount prices and sno-cones."

"I hate those sno-cones," Chandler said for the tenth time in two days. "Well, folks say her store has been struggling awhile, but our store is pushing her over the edge. Word on the street is she might not stay open past New Year's."

"I hadn't heard." But still he couldn't help wanting to look her way again. "We've only been open a couple of months. Certainly she can't blame us for her business failure. She sure has a nice smile."

"I bet her smile won't be nearly as chipper when she realizes who you are."

"Only one way to find out." He pasted a smile on his face and started toward her.

She locked eyes with him and threw her hand in the air.

His smile broadened. Chandler was overreacting.

Angela didn't return the smile. *This is not a social call.* A few days ago she'd swooned over his nice suit and baby-blue eyes. That was before she knew just exactly who he was. That was not the case today.

He made his way across the parking lot toward her, edging between the throng of onlookers.

She took in a deep breath and stepped away from the crowd closer to the building.

He followed her moves, and with each step closer her heart beat faster. Ready for battle, she stopped, widened her stance and raised her chin.

"I've been looking for you," he said, a little out of breath.

"Why?" His warm greeting threw her off her game for a second. Fueled by anger she squared up to him.

He paused, looking into her eyes, then smiled. "Since Thanksgiving in the coffee shop. I'm Geoff Paisley, by the way. You remember? At the Crabby Coffee Pot? We saw each other. You waved."

"You were there spying on me, weren't you?" Her eyes narrowed as she sucked in a trembling breath and tried to keep her knees from buckling under her.

He stepped back, momentarily rebuffed. "Spy on you?" He cocked his head, as if waiting for her to explain.

"It's crystal clear now," she said. "You had a perfect view of Heart of Christmas from your seat at the Crabby Coffee Pot, didn't you? Oh yeah, you gave me that handsome blue-eyed gaze like it was an unexpected meeting."

"But we haven't met." He had a weird look on his face, like he was confused or thought she was crazy.

Every fiber in her body warned her. That smooth act wasn't going to work with her.

"We may not have been introduced officially, but that didn't keep you from stealing my idea." She leaned in toward him, her words cutting as her jaw tightened along with every muscle in her body. "The billboard one block from my shop?" She flung her arms in the air. "Then this one day after I opened Snow Valley?"

"*This?*" His look was incredulous. "You didn't invent snow. And this . . . is what we do. Give our customers what they want."

"Oh yeah. Like trinkets that'll break before the holiday is over."

"And who really cares anyway? They don't make anything like they used to."

That was his rebuttal?

"Christmas is just one day out of the year," he said. "You can buy ten of my holiday decorations for the price of one of yours. What's so wrong with that?"

"Don't belittle the importance of Christmas," she said. "I sell quality products. One of a kind. Traditions that hold family memories together made by artists from all over the world. You can't put a price on that."

"But you do, don't you?" His eyebrow cocked. "A quite high price too."

"And you don't care about the value you're offering to your customers." She rocked on her heels. "I do."

"Are you saying price is the only guide to value?"

"Maybe it is." She'd made her point. *Score!*

"So, let me be sure I understand." He spread his stance, getting down to her eye level. "You're saying a four-year-old enjoying a ten-cent sno-cone has no value?"

She searched for a response.

But he wasn't finished. "If making memories is so valuable, I'd argue my sno-cones will be fond memories for lots of kids, and I don't care if their parents spend half their paycheck on cheap trinkets that may or may not make it through the holiday while their kids slurp cheap sticky syrup . . . then so what?"

"That's just the kind of thinking I'd expect from you. You're only interested in filling your pockets. You are nothing but a money-hungry . . ." She couldn't even complete the sentence. "You don't care about the people of this town at all."

"Look at this crowd. They look pretty happy to me. No one is making them *buy* anything. But I see a lot of Christmas Galore shopping bags." He raised a finger and started counting. "One. Two. Three. Four. There have to be eighty just in plain sight."

"Flimsy plastic bags that can fill a bird's stomach until it ultimately starves to death, or chokes marine life, and if they survive that, the plastic breaks down and passes toxic chemicals through the food chain right to our dinner plates. Yeah. Thanks so much for that." She pulled her lips into a tight line. "You!" She stabbed a finger in his direction. "You are an irresponsible oceanfront merchant, and you are a thief. You stole my idea for snow at the beach. And you are just riding on Christmas's coattails for a buck." Her eyes began to tear. She could not—would not—cry in front of him.

"Well." He was flustered. "Business is about bucks. Or is that news to you?"

She growled in frustration. "No." She thrust her hands to her sides. "You . . . you are nothing but a suit. All you care about is money. There is much more to Christmas and this town than money."

"I will not apologize for focusing on my bottom line. Something, truth be told, that you probably should have done a better job of."

She gasped. *How could he?* "You don't know anything about me or my business."

"Au contraire, my dear. I've done my homework."

"Do not call me 'dear.'"

"I know that little shop of yours has been in your family since the early 1900s and still pretty much operates that way. Do I need to recite your revenue too? Or how about that I know you pride yourself in being a part of the fabric of this community? Well, my dear, your fabric is as outdated as wool underwear."

A hundred things reeled through her mind, but before any of them passed her lips, *SPLAT!*

She screamed, gasping and reaching for her face, where an icy snowball had just smashed into her shoulder and ricocheted off of her cheek.

She worked her jaw. Nothing seemed to be hurt except for her pride.

Geoff stood there staring at her with his mouth agape.

She spun around and hightailed it out of the crowd to her car. She didn't slow down until she hit the red light at the intersection two blocks up the road.

She stretched to see her cheek and chin in the rearview mirror. That snowball had left a bright red mark on her cheek. She couldn't very well go back to work looking like she'd been in a fight.

As soon as she got home she texted Emma to let her know she was at the house in case she needed anything, then put a compress on her cheek, hoping it wouldn't end up bruising.

Not ten minutes later there was a knock at the door. She took the warm rag from her cheek, stopping at the hall mirror to see if the red had gone away yet. No such luck.

She turned and answered the door. "Emma? Is everything okay?"

"The store's fine. Jeremy and Stephanie have everything under control."

"Oh good. You scared me for a second there."

"Are you okay?" Emma let herself in. "Oh my gosh. What happened to your cheek?"

"Oh. That." Angela turned away and walked to the living room. "I'm fine."

"You don't look fine. Did someone hit you?"

"A snowball. It was stupid."

"Snow?" Emma pulled her hands to her hips. "You went over to Christmas Galore, didn't you?"

Angela tucked her feet under her on the couch, then fell over into the fetal position. "I did." She covered her face. "I'm so embarrassed."

"Who hit you?"

"I don't know. Some kid, I guess."

"You didn't see it coming?"

"No. I was looking at . . ." She closed her eyes. "Remember that guy that I saw at the Crabby Coffee Pot? He was there."

"At Christmas Galore?"

"Right there in the parking lot." She got lost in the moment, recalling him standing there so at ease like he'd done nothing wrong.

"The one with the nice smile and blue eyes?"

Feeling miserable, she uttered, "That's the one."

"Well, then, it wasn't all bad. Maybe he's your consolation prize for closing the store."

"He's the boss," she said.

"I don't get it. What do you mean?"

"On Black Friday I drove over to Christmas Galore, just to see how many people were there at one-thirty in the morning."

"Angela! You didn't."

"I did. And I saw him, and I almost went inside the store just because he was standing there."

"What stopped you?"

"One of the employees ran out to catch up with him. He called him 'boss.'"

Emma fell silent. "That doesn't necessarily mean he's the boss of Christmas Galore. It could be a nickname."

"Oh, he's most definitely the boss. I was just there. He introduced himself."

"Wow." A nervous giggle escaped Emma. "I can honestly say this is the last thing I expected to hear when I came over."

"I'm so embarrassed. And mad. And . . . I don't know . . . humiliated, I guess." She pushed her hair from her face. "He said my store is as outdated as wool underwear."

"Well, that was just plain uncalled for." Emma threw a dismissive hand in the air. "It doesn't matter. Pleasant Sands will never award him or that store of his with the town's Landmark award. Do I need to pull out my copy of the article from the *PS News* to remind you of how much Heart of Christmas means to the people in this town? I've got it in my scrapbook."

It was true. The Pleasant Sands newspaper, *PS News,* had written up a glowing article about the store and its history just last season. Every paper in the state had picked it up, bringing new customers in from all over North Carolina. That had been so exciting. But now, things had taken a turn for the worse.

What was it that Christmas Galore had that she didn't?

Wait a minute. There's one important thing I have that Geoff from Christmas Galore doesn't! Connections in this town. "Hand me my phone."

Emma picked Angela's phone up from the coffee table and tossed it to her.

"Game on." Angela swiped her finger across the screen and typed in a number.

Chapter Thirteen

Dear Santa,
This app is the best thing ever.
Could you add a checklist so I don't have to write
everything down? It's hard to remember every commercial.
Kevin from the nice list

Geoff stared at the morning news in disbelief. "I can't believe I thought she was so pretty." He grabbed for the remote on his desk, swearing under his breath.

"Hey, boss." Chandler stood just outside of Geoff's office. "Are you still talking about your coffee shop hottie?"

"Pfft." Geoff shook his head. "She's crazy." He pointed the remote toward the television on the wall and turned up the volume. "Have you seen this?"

Chandler stepped in the office just in time to hear Angela Carson say, "He told me that he didn't care if parents spend half their paycheck on cheap trinkets that may or may not make it through the holiday while their kids slurp cheap sticky syrup." She tossed her head, dark hair swinging around her proud shoulders. He could see the beginnings of a bruise on her cheek where that snowball had hit her. He prayed the field reporter wouldn't mention that.

"You know how to pick 'em." Chandler snickered. "The owner of the only store on our competitive analysis. I don't think she's in to you, boss."

The news reporter held the mic back to Angela. "Oh yes, well, the snow at Christmas Galore is made out of the ice they use for those sno-cones. An icy snowball hit me." She touched her cheek with a flair of drama, including a wince as her fingers brushed her bruise. "The snow we have in Snow Valley is—"

Geoff turned off the TV and tossed the remote to the side. "Really?" At least she hadn't made it sound like he'd hit her with the snowball on purpose. He hung his head. "It's been on every local station."

"Did you really say that?"

Geoff nodded, but didn't lift his head. He could kick himself for letting loose on her. "She caught me off guard. She wasn't nice to me either."

Chandler's brows flickered. "Yeah, but no one is telling that side of the story."

"Who knew she was hiding a venomous arsenal under those pretty brown eyes?" The corner of Geoff's mouth twisted. "Hopefully this will fade away before Virgil gets back in town. He'll never let me live this down."

"She's like the town sweetheart. People say anything you want to know about this town . . . she knows. You'd better make nice with her, or the next two years in Pleasant Sands are going to be anything but pleasant for you."

"I don't know how she got this to the news so fast. And that snowball . . . that was an accident. She didn't say that."

Both Chandler and Geoff said at the same time, "She's the town's sweetheart."

"Maybe she'll be at the tree lighting. You could apologize to her there," Chandler suggested. "I hear everyone in town goes. People standing around waiting for a tree to light up seems like a pretty safe place to get a minute with her."

Geoff hated the thought of giving in to her after such a public display, but it wouldn't do to get on the wrong side of the townspeople this early in the game. "When is the Christmas-tree lighting?"

"It's on Christmas Eve."

"I can't wait that long!" Geoff's phone rang out with the familiar *ho-ho-ho*. "Great. Mom has probably already heard what happened. Hang on." He answered the phone sounding as lively as possible. "Hey, Mom. Good morning."

"Is this Geoff Paisley?"

"Um?" The man's voice caught him off guard. "Who's calling?"

"This is Garvy. I own the restaurant down at the pier. Is Geoff Paisley available?"

Geoff paused long enough to let that sink in. "Yeah. This is Geoff. Hey, Garvy. How are you? Did my mom leave her phone?"

"No. I'm sorry to call with bad news, but she was here for breakfast. I'm not sure what happened, but the ambulance just left with her. She was alert when they left."

"I'll go," Chandler whispered and turned to leave.

What the heck? Geoff grabbed Chandler's arm, motioning him to wait. "Did she fall? Is she okay?"

"They just took her to County General Hospital. Her phone was here on the counter. I wanted to be sure someone contacted you."

"Thank you so much. I'll head there now. Hang on to the phone. I'll send someone over to pick it up later. Thank you for calling." Geoff ended the call, still letting the details sink in.

"Your mom?"

"They're taking her to the hospital."

"What happened?"

"Not sure. She was having breakfast in the restaurant at the pier. The owner called me from her phone. I wonder if she tripped and fell. I'm always telling her not to wear those high heels. Especially on the pier. That's just an accident waiting to happen."

Chandler nodded. "You better go. Let me know if there's anything I can do once you find out what's going on."

"I will." He went straight out to the parking lot, gunned the engine of his car, and headed for County General Hospital, using every bit of horsepower under the hood of his Mercedes.

Luckily every single traffic light was green so he didn't have to slow, or run one. Something he'd paid more than his fair share of tickets for.

His mom was spry. She'd give women twenty-five years her junior a run, and she did not like to be slowed down.

Geoff was amused at the picture in his mind of Mom giving the doctors and nurses a hard time. They'd probably thank him for showing up.

He followed the blue hospital signs, then turned into the parking lot in front of the Emergency Room.

The shiny metal and green glass hospital looked starkly out of place around here, where most things had a cottagey look and pastel colors. He parked, and jogged across the lot.

Glass doors opened as he walked up. The huge waiting room was probably full during tourist season, but today there were just a few people scattered across the vast space. It was eerily quiet.

The check-in desk was clear across the ballroom-size waiting area. Who the heck thought that was a good idea for sick and hurt people?

His leather loafers tapped against the beige concrete epoxy

flooring. There was no way the lady behind the desk hadn't heard or seen him come in, but she didn't even lift her gaze from the computer.

"Excuse me. I understand my mother was just brought in by ambulance."

"Your name, sir?"

Seriously? The place is nearly empty. Seems like a simple deduction to me. He cleared his throat. "Geoff Paisley. My mother is Rebecca Paisley."

"Paisley?" The woman's eyes narrowed, then she smiled a toothy grin and propped her elbows on the desk. "Oh gosh, are you any relation to Brad? I love Brad Paisley. His songs just crack me up. Isn't he playing Raleigh soon?"

Wasn't the first time he'd gotten that, but this wasn't the place for that kind of dillydallying. "No relation. How's my mother?"

"Oh. Yes." The woman leaned closer to her screen. "I've got her right here. Let me get someone to update you."

"Can't you do that? There must be something on that little screen. How is she?" Why couldn't anyone answer a simple question these days?

"I don't have that information. Have a seat and someone will be right with you." She turned her back to him and made a call.

He began to insist on information, but then he shut his mouth. No sense making a scene. Especially after what happened after the last one.

The television was just loud enough that he couldn't make out the conversation the woman was having on the phone. On a bright note, if his mother were in any real danger certainly the woman would have had that information.

A steady stream of chatter about the latest drugs to help depression and erectile dysfunction and convincing arguments to quit smoking blasted from the televisions around the room. What he needed right now was a drug for patience, because his was running thin.

This hospital didn't have the sense of urgency he'd like to see from the people taking care of his mother in an emergency.

The woman finally put down the phone, but still didn't offer an update. Instead, she slipped out from behind her desk and down the hall.

"Seriously?" he said to the three other people still sitting in the waiting room. *What kind of customer service is that? If I ran this place I'd make a change to that, tout de suite.* But he didn't run it, so he'd just have to wait, just like he had to wait to make the changes he wanted to Christmas Galore. Not one of his strongest skill sets.

A door swung open across the way.

Geoff turned, anxious for an update about his mother.

Virgil strode into the room carrying a cup of coffee.

"Virgil?" Geoff pulled his phone from his pocket and tapped the screen. He hadn't missed any phone calls. "Were you with her? I didn't even know you were back."

"I got back late last night. They just took her to do some tests."

"How is she? What happened? And who called you?"

"Don't know. I'm just as worried as you are. She collapsed at the restaurant. I came as soon as I got the call." He put a hand on Geoff's shoulder.

"Well, somebody knows something." Geoff pounded on the desk hoping to get the receptionist's attention. "Miss, I need some answers."

"Slow down," Virgil said in an even tone.

"Why would they call you instead of me?"

"That's really not where our focus should be right now."

Geoff's jaw clenched.

"She probably didn't want to worry you."

"I don't like this." It was hard to control things if he didn't know what was going on. "Are we just supposed to sit around and wait?"

"Mr. Paisley?" An ER physician dressed in blue scrubs and a white coat approached him from across the room.

"Yes. Dr. Flagg," Geoff read his name on his jacket as he shook the doctor's hand. "I don't have any information except that she was brought in. How is she? What happened?"

"Hey, doc," Virgil said.

"Virgil," he said with a nod.

Geoff glanced between the two men.

"We're running some tests. With her history of heart problems and the medications she's taking, we want to check her out thoroughly after this episode."

"Her history?" What was this guy talking about? "Episode?"

"I've contacted her cardiologist. He's going to stop in later today. Meanwhile, we're going to get her moved to ICU, where we can keep her under careful watch. The next couple of days she'll need to rest."

"I think you've made a mistake. Are we talking about Rebecca Martin Paisley?"

"Yes," Dr. Flagg said, flashing a quick glance toward Virgil.

Geoff swiveled toward his friend. "Virgil?"

The doctor looked from one of them to the other. "I'll be back to give you an update as soon as we have more information."

Mom would give him a straight answer. "Before you go, can I see her?"

"Yes. Keep it short, please." The doctor waved toward one of the nurses. "Nurse Jones will take you back."

Geoff turned to Virgil. "Are you coming?"

"I've already been back. You go talk to her. I'll wait here."

Geoff shook the doctor's hand then fell into step behind the nurse to the curtained room where his mother was.

Looking an odd shade of gray against the blue-and-white hospital gown, his mother reached her hand toward him as he walked in.

"Sorry, son. I know you've got a million things on your plate this week."

"You have a heart problem?"

She squeezed his hand, but she didn't deny it. "Please be sure to stop down at the pier and pay Garvy for my breakfast. Goodness gracious, this is embarrassing." She smoothed her hand along the sheet.

"Garvy called me. You left your phone there. Good thing, else I may not have known at all." He tried to contain his anger. "Don't be embarrassed. I doubt Garvy thinks you pulled this stunt to get a free breakfast."

Virgil walked into the room.

Geoff was aggravated by it, but kept his attention on his mother. "Virgil knew. Were you not going to tell me?"

"Virgil knows a lot of things. He's my best friend. My confidante."

"I'm your son."

"And I'm still your mother. How is business? Is the new store keeping up with the chain goals?"

"It is," Geoff said. "And you couldn't even call me to tell me you were in the hospital?"

"I would have called you if there was anything to tell you."

"You're in the hospital. They are moving you to ICU. That's something to tell."

He turned on Virgil. "Were you there when it happened?"

Virgil shook his head. "Not this time."

"So you called Virgil instead of me?" Geoff's gut twisted. A bruise on his mother's cheek was already starting to color. "How did you hurt your cheek?"

She reached for her face, wincing when her fingers grazed her cheekbone. "I'm not quite certain. I felt a little nauseous, began to sweat. I must've passed out. Fell? The next thing I knew I was in an ambulance with a young man in white telling me to breathe easy."

Geoff glanced over his shoulder to see if the nurse had left them alone. She had, so he pulled a chair up next to the bed. "Mom, the doctor said you're on medication to treat a history of heart problems. Is this your first heart attack or episode?" He air quoted "episode." What did that even mean? "What is going on?"

"You worry too much."

"I'm not only your son, I'm your business partner. I deserve to know."

His mother didn't respond.

"How could you not have told me, Virgil?"

Virgil sucked in a loud breath, his mustache forming a fluffy line across his face. As close as they were, he knew that Virgil would never betray his mother. They'd been friends for as long as Geoff could remember.

"Geoff, son, calm down. I'll be fine until I'm not, and nothing you do or worry over is going to change that."

"Until you're not is what I'm worried about, Mom. Why would you keep something like this from me?"

"I'm the parent. It's my job to worry about you, and I choose to not let you worry about me."

"Mom. That's ridiculous. Dr. Flagg said they've called in your cardiologist. I didn't even know you *had* a cardiologist."

"It's the way I want it." Her voice was steady, but her chin quivered slightly. "I'm going to be fine. It's a teensy hospital. They put all heart patients in ICU here. It's not like I'm in dire straits, but in case something does happen there are a couple things I want to be sure we're clear on."

"I think this can wait," Geoff said. She always seemed invincible. It was unsettling to see her like this, although she didn't look fragile in the least. "You need to just relax."

"No. I won't be able to relax unless I know you and I are on the same page."

"With what?" He passed a glance between his mother and Virgil.

Virgil let out a little moan that made Geoff nervous. "I'll get some coffee. I'll be back, Rebecca."

"Thanks, Virg." She waited until he cleared the doorway. "When I'm dead and gone I know you're going to catapult our business into the technology age."

He laughed. She wasn't wrong. The only reason they weren't already there was because she still held 5 percent more power in the company than he did. "Stop it."

"Well, I'm no fool. I know you, and I'll admit . . . it's probably not an entirely bad thing." She lifted a finger in the air. "No gloating or I-told-you-so. So here's what I need you to promise me."

"You're being dramatic."

"I'm being pragmatic. Totally different. Hush. Put your listening ears on. I'm still your elder."

"Fine."

"Promise me that you'll personally handle my Dear Santa letters. Do not hand those over to anyone else for at least two years."

"Mom."

She raised a finger. "Promise me."

"Stop."

The beeping machine next to her did a giddy-up. She glanced toward it. "Don't upset me."

"You're going to ride this for all you can, aren't you?"

She grinned, and if her hair had been long like it had been when he was a kid, that smug little nod she just gave him would've been followed by a toss of that silvering hair. "Like a prizewinning pony. Now, promise me."

"You're not going anywhere."

"Promise me."

"Fine. I promise."

"Thank you. Now get to work. The stores need your undivided attention. And so do the Dear Santa letters."

"They'll hold a day until you're back. If you're really as fine as you're trying to let on."

"Don't sass me, but don't worry either. I'll be fine. I always am. How do the sales numbers look?"

Virgil stepped back into the room. "Didn't they tell you to relax?"

"I'm just listening. No effort at all."

"Better than ever," Geoff said. "The new store surpassed all of our forecasts. You were right."

"I had a feeling about this location."

"Virgil told me you have history in this town. Mom, I feel like I don't know you at all."

"You know me better than anyone. Now, stop that." She patted his hand. "I'm proud of you, Geoff. You know that, right?"

"You just like our big sales numbers," he teased, trying desperately to lighten the mood.

"It is our best time of year." She squeezed his hand tight. "I love you, Geoff. Get to work."

"Are you sure you're going to be okay?" She didn't even look like herself. Her color was wrong, and she looked so tired.

Her pause felt heavy on his chest.

"Virgil will be here with me."

That hurt Geoff's feelings, but insisting would only make her dig her heels in.

A short nurse scurried into the room and started pressing buttons then took his mother's wrist in her hand. "I'm going to have to ask you to leave. We're ready to move her to ICU."

"I'll wait with you until they get you settled in."

"No, son. You go on and get to work. You can't do anything here. I'm in good hands."

He shoved his right hand deep into his pocket. There was a lot to do, but this was the first time he'd ever seen his mother look fragile. How had she hidden her health problems from him? Sure, there were plenty of weeks that they didn't even see each other face-to-face with all there was to do. She did like to take off and check on other stores at the drop of a hat. Had she been lying to him? He'd always thought of himself as observant. How had he missed this?

"I can check back on you later tonight," he said.

"Please don't. I'm going to be fine. I'll probably sleep all day. I'll see you tomorrow morning. How about that?"

"You sure?"

"Positive. I'll tell you what you can do for me. Bring me a nightgown from my top dresser drawer tomorrow. This thing is not comfortable or very fashionable."

"You've got a deal." He leaned over and gave her a hug. "Please do what the doctor says. And rest."

"Get out of here," she said with a wink.

He stepped out of the room, but waited in the hall, unwilling to leave until he saw her safely wheeled out of the emergency room toward her ICU room. It was a small hospital, it was quite possible all heart patients did go to ICU here like she said, but that really didn't make him feel any better.

She didn't see him when they wheeled her out of the emergency room and through the set of double doors at the end of the hall. He watched until they turned the corner, then he made his way through the maze of corridors to the exit.

He walked through the parking lot trying to understand why his mother would have kept something like a heart condition from him. She had to know that he'd eventually find out.

By the time he unlocked his car, Virgil was taking long strides toward him.

"You okay?" Virgil asked.

Geoff threw the words at him like stones. "Why didn't you tell me?"

"She asked me not to."

"But—"

Virgil clasped his hand on Geoff's right shoulder. "You'd have done the same thing."

"You're probably right, but I have a right to know."

"I've been telling her that. Especially since she's had some concerns recently. It's part of the reason why she was so insistent you open the store here in Pleasant Sands."

"Why? Because she's sick? Seems like she could've picked a place with better hospitals."

"She surely could have done that, but she picked Pleasant Sands for a whole other reason. This town is special to her. She's at peace here."

"This town is just another map dot," Geoff said.

"Hardly. She had her reasons for opening the Pleasant Sands store."

"What are you not telling me?"

"Not my story to tell."

A wave of uncertainty tickled inside him. "Is this something I want to know?" Geoff ran a finger under his collar.

Virgil didn't respond.

Mom was always saying, *If it isn't broke, don't fix it.* Especially when he was pitching ideas to improve their processes. But how long had she let this heart problem go without addressing it?

The sick feeling twisted in his gut as he bent to slide behind the wheel of his car.

By the time that feeling of impending doom finally loosened its grip on him enough to allow him to breathe steady, he was almost home. He'd pick up things for his mother in the morning.

The next morning he drove over to his mother's house.

Unlike him, she'd bought a beach house instead of opting for a condo. One of those big, stilted jobs with tons of stairs that overlooked the water and had a cutesy name that he couldn't even recall right now. Probably not the best place to come home and recuperate after a heart attack.

He pulled into her driveway. He hadn't been here since he'd done the walk-through for her when she bought the place. No need to, really. They saw each other every day at work.

Besides, he already knew what the inside of the house would look like. Mom always put the furniture and pictures in the same place. The only thing that changed was the address. Well, and the name. Why did beach houses need more than just an address like every other dwelling?

He glanced up at the colorful weather-blasted wooden sign that had been left behind by the previous owner, a surf shop owner. DUNE OUR THING. Which sounded better suited to a house full of surfers than an aging businesswoman.

He went to her bedroom and opened each dresser drawer until he found the one with her nightgowns stacked neatly in it. He picked out a bright blue one. Her favorite color.

He tucked the nightgown and a few other things into a tote bag hanging from the closet door, then tossed in the novel from her nightstand.

As he walked back out to the living room a steady thump came from the deck. He stepped outside to see what all the racket was.

From up here on the second level he could see clear over the dunes to the water. The seagrass swayed in the breeze, just like the old rocking chair that was hitting the wall. He pulled the chair up a few inches, then sat down.

Why would she keep her health issues from him? Was there a chance he'd inherited a heart problem? It didn't make sense.

He stared out to the water, wishing for clarity.

On the beach a barefoot woman dressed in black tights and a powder-blue jacket caught his attention. Water splashed as she ran along the surf line. She looked so carefree. As she got closer he recognized her. Her hair, the curve of her cheek. Angela Carson. Yeah, Mom would be pissed if she caught wind of that debacle. He hoped there was no television in ICU.

He and his mother, and a steadily increasing staff, had grown the business with a new store each year, but they had reached the point that it was almost too much for him and Mom to handle anymore. They'd been delegating more things to their key talent, but he stayed busy. Christmas Galore was way past the mom-and-pop-shop stage these days.

The workload wouldn't be nearly as difficult to handle with their small team of trusted employees if his mother would let him put the infrastructure in place to automate and delegate the upstart work for each new store, but she was old school and felt every single store needed their personal touch for the entire first year of its opening. With her health in question, he might need to push for those changes.

Chapter Fourteen

DID YOU KNOW?

*Pleasant Sands' population swells to 40–50K in the summer
months when the town is filled with beach vacationers.*

Energized after a run on the beach, Angela tossed her running
gear into the dirty clothes. She showered and changed into work
clothes, but since Emma was opening the store this morning, she
decided to do some much-needed grocery shopping at her favorite store. The upscale grocery market was over near the new condos at the marina. The produce section alone was like a work of
art, the way they purposefully stacked the fruits and blended the
colors to almost kaleidoscope perfection. And the bakery . . .
There was no way you could resist buying something with the
aroma of baked goods in the air. It practically lassoed you and
dragged you over.

This section of Pleasant Sands had a resort-style feel to it now.
When she was a little girl this was an area of messy necessity, filled
with crab pots piled five feet high, and battered boats loosely tied
to an old dock that had seen better days. The old shacks and metal
boat buildings were long gone now.

Even the parking lot was fancy, with white pergolas covering the cart repository, and hedges as neat and tidy as if they were part of the Tryon Palace gardens in New Bern.

She grabbed a cart, a fancy one with a cupholder, and pushed it up to the entrance.

Music filled the store and the baking, cooking and work going on around her felt like a shot of sunshine.

As she passed the bakery she couldn't resist stopping and looking at all the pretty confections.

"Can I help you?" a short woman about as wide as she was tall, all dressed in white, asked from across the glass case.

"You can. I need a loaf of that bread you just took out of the oven, and these pastries are beautiful. Could I get one of those?" She pointed to a petit four with red and green sugar ribbons. "Wait. Oh gosh, it's so hard to pick. Maybe I should take some home too." The bakery case was filled with an assortment of festive holiday treats. Cupcakes with shiny silver dragées and crystallized sugar. Cookies, macarons and even chocolate-dipped pretzels with pretty sprinkles.

"Get one of each," the woman suggested. "That's what I'd do."

"You know what? You're right. Give me twelve different ones. Surprise me. My niece is going to be absolutely delighted! I can't wait to drop in and surprise her. The rest, I'll take to my store."

"You own a store here in town?" the woman asked as she delicately plucked baked goods from the case and placed them in a pretty red box.

"I do." *For now,* she thought. "Heart of Christmas."

"In the lighthouse?" The woman beamed.

"That's the one."

"I've heard of it. I've been wanting to stop in. I collect Christmas bells."

"I have several. Some are tabletop bells, but I also have this beautiful Twelve Days of Christmas bell set too."

"I've got to see that!" The woman's voice rose with excitement.

"You better come soon. Sadly, I'll be closing the doors after the holiday." Angela's nerves tingled. Saying it made her almost light-headed.

"Oh no. I'm sorry," the baker said. "I've been looking for a gift for my mother-in-law. She's so hard to buy for. She collects those nesting dolls, but they aren't easy to find."

"I'm your girl," Angela said, her mood lifting. "I've got a couple in stock. These aren't just the simple curvy-shaped smooth ones either. The artist I buy from actually carves the detail in the largest one. I know I have a Santa set, and I'm pretty sure the nativity set is still there unless we sold it this weekend."

"I'm off tomorrow. You can count on seeing me." She closed the box and taped it. "I tucked in an extra one for you. If you ask me, the baker's dozen should never have gone out of style." She put the price sticker on the side of the box and handed it to Angela. The clear plastic panel made the box look like a snow globe with all the colorful edibles inside. "Thank you, that was so nice of you." Angela walked away with a smile on her face. There was so much good in this town.

She loaded her cart with hot chocolate and marshmallows. She could imagine the warmth of a sweater wrapped around her shoulders and a hot mug out on the deck as she watched the ocean raise a ruckus with the tide. Maybe she'd even roast a few marshmallows over the fire pit.

An instrumental version of "The First Noel" played over the grocery store speakers.

Angela used the automated checkout and bagged her groceries in the heavy paper bags with the handles. The look on Geoff

Paisley's face when she had informed him just how much was wrong with his plastic shopping bags popped into her head.

Calling him an irresponsible oceanfront merchant had been mean. She felt a little bad about that. Momma Grace had raised her better.

Whatever was happening with her store, she had to find a positive path forward. Calling names wasn't a solution, and letting the likes of Christmas Galore get under her skin was a waste of time and energy.

With her grocery bags in tow, she went outside. Next door a new café boasted fresh fish and farm-to-table meals. On the chalkboard sandwich board out front the lunch specials looked tasty, especially the pumpkin fritters.

"I deserve a treat." She put her groceries in her car then straightened her sweater set as she walked across the parking lot.

Inside, the décor had a European feel. The rich burgundy walls gave the space a warm feeling, and the intoxicating savory scent of fresh herbs mingled in the air.

"Just one?" A young woman dressed in black asked her.

"Yes."

"This way," she said, seating her in a booth midway down the left side of the long narrow restaurant.

"Thank you." Angela scooted into the booth facing the door. It was still a little early, but they already had a good crowd.

The waitress ran down the list of specials and Angela settled on a scallop po'boy with the café's signature remoulade and shredded lettuce on a freshly baked garlic toasted bun, and a glass of chardonnay.

The waitress slid Angela's plate onto the table. If she were a social media addict, she'd be posting a picture of her plate right now. She dug in, enjoying the delightful mix of herbs that made the familiar sandwich seem extra special.

Just as she slipped the last bite into her mouth, Geoff Paisley walked into the restaurant with an older, silver-haired man.

She slid down in the seat a little, and grabbed the wine menu tucked between the oil and vinegar cruets, almost choking on her sandwich.

She chugged some water, then leaned out, hoping they wouldn't be seated at the empty table next to her.

Thankfully, the hostess seated them toward the front.

The waitress took the next table's order then stopped by. "How was it?"

"Delicious."

"Excellent. Can I get you dessert or another chardonnay?"

She downed the last sip. "Yes, please, and a large glass of water." There was no way she could leave now.

After giving Geoff a piece of her mind, this was more than just a little awkward, but maybe if she just laid low for a bit, they'd leave and then she could slip out.

Time dragged by, and customers ate and left, but she could still see the two men in the booth up front. Not a big drinker, she'd be drunk if she had another chardonnay, so she ordered dessert and coffee and pretended to be on the phone.

After three glasses of water, wine and a coffee, she couldn't wait any longer. She had to go to the bathroom, so she peeked out to make sure the coast was clear. Geoff and the gray-haired man were talking. She scooted out of the booth and dashed to the back of the restaurant, past the men's room to the ladies' room.

She closed the door behind her and locked it. If she'd thought it out better she'd have left money on the table for her bill and taken the back door out.

After she washed her hands she waited as long as she could, then decided she'd have to suck it up and just hope for the best.

She pushed the button to unlock the door, then grabbed the door handle, one of those weird ones you put your forearm under to resist germs, but the door didn't budge.

Tugging on it again, the door gave just enough to bang against the door frame. "Really?"

Two hands didn't get it open either.

She pulled a credit card out of her wallet and slid it between the frame and the door. All that did was prove the latch seemed to be unlocked, but still the door didn't budge.

"Can someone help me?" She shook the door again. "Hello?"

"Hello?" A man's voice came from the other side of the door.

"The door won't open."

"Oh?" After a brief pause, the man said, "They don't make anything like they used to."

The comment whisked her back to Christmas Galore. Geoff had said that. *Oh no. It couldn't be.* She practically sank to the floor.

"Hang on," he said. "I'll get you out of there."

It *was* his voice. Of all the predicaments to be stuck in, this was absolutely the worst.

"I think I can get it now. You can go away," she said.

There was no other way out. The frosted window on the back wall looked like it was painted shut. Desperate, she turned its lock and tried to lift the window. It only budged a few inches. She was thin, but she was not going to fit through that.

Something banged against the door, which flew open then started to shut.

"Got it!" he said as the door came free.

She ran from the window to the door, putting her foot there to keep him from coming inside. "I'm good. You can go now." At least that's what she tried to say. It had come out more like *Umgoo. Ukago Ow.*

"You're upset. Are you okay?"

She steadied herself before trying to talk this time. "I'm fine."

"Um. Are you coming out?"

"Of course." She tucked her chin and slid out the door with her back to him.

"How long were you in there?" He touched her arm and reflexively she spun toward him.

When she lifted her head, he laughed. "Well, how are you, Angela Carson? How about this?" He extended his hand with another hearty laugh. "We meet again. I guess we should formally introduce ourselves."

She didn't want to shake hands with him. What was the point? "I think I know what I need to know about you already."

"I don't even get a simple thank-you for rescuing you?"

Her pride had already checked out the back door. "Thank you."

"That didn't sound very sincere."

She stepped away. "I told you to go away."

"If I didn't know better, I'd take that personally." He glanced inside the bathroom noticing the half-open window. "What were you going to do? Crawl out the window and run away?"

"Don't be ridiculous." Closing her eyes, she wished she could die and go to heaven with an express ticket right now. No such luck.

"Speaking of running. I think I saw you running this morning. On the beach?"

She felt her nostrils flare. "Are you stalking me now?"

"No," he sputtered. "Were you spying on me when you were in my parking lot on Black Friday in the middle of the night?"

She gulped. "No, I was not. I simply went to see what was going on. And yesterday I just wanted to see if you'd really stolen my idea. I didn't think even someone like you would sink so low to do that. Of course, I was wrong to give you that benefit of the doubt."

"So we've established we're not spying on each other. We're good neighbors, right?"

All she could do was groan.

"It's a small town," he said. "We're going to cross paths. You're clearly upset. Can I buy you a drink?"

"No, you cannot buy me a drink. I'm fine," she said. "I've got to go. I'm late . . . for something." She tried to push her way past him but he stepped in front of her.

"Can't we at least be cordial?" Geoff dipped to get in her line of sight. "After all, we both own businesses in this town." He extended his hand again.

She reluctantly shook his hand. Maybe he'd leave her alone now, but before she could say something he cut her off.

"You're not going to yell at me again, are you?" His sneer was annoying.

Sure, he'd deserved the verbal attack over his stupid snowball fight, but it didn't excuse her for doing it in front of half of the town. And although the television spot had doubled the traffic in her store . . . it didn't change anything.

"I guess I'll see you around." He smiled, but she didn't respond in kind.

Not if she could help it. Their gazes connected. "It is a small town, but I'm sure we won't be traveling in the same circles," she said flatly.

"The tree lighting is coming up," he said like he'd read her mind. "Everyone goes to that, right?"

"Yes. All the merchants close down for it. It's tradition. Everyone gathers in the town square for the annual tree lighting. You don't want to miss that." Or maybe he did. He probably didn't even like Christmas.

"I'm not a fan of closing my business during business hours, but if that's what all the merchants do I'll play along. I guess I'll see you there then. Hopefully you won't get stuck in the bathroom and miss it," he said with a smile. "Merry Christmas."

Easy for him to say. He wasn't closing his business for good. "You're a Mean One, Mr. Grinch" played inside her head.

She walked straight through the restaurant, only stopping long enough to hand a fifty-dollar bill to the hostess and ask her to take care of her check and give the change to the waitress. After commandeering the table during the busy lunch rush, it was the least Angela could do.

By the time she got her groceries home and made her way over to the store it was late afternoon. The parking lot was full, and the store was abuzz with shoppers.

As Angela walked in Emma punched the total on the register, causing the drawer to open with a *ding*. She loved that sound.

She walked into the back room to put some of the treats she'd gotten at the market out for her staff.

Then she sat down and called her sister. No surprise it went straight to voice mail; it was Marie's court day and those were always her busiest, so she left a message: "Hey, Marie, it's me. Why don't y'all come over to the house tonight for hot chocolate on the deck and we can roast marshmallows over the fire pit. Call me."

She hung up and turned to see Emma standing in the doorway.

"How are you doing?" Emma eyed the bakery goods. "Those look delicious." She took a lavender macaron from the plate.

"Thanks." Emma took a bite. "Oh my gosh. This is so good. So, you okay? Or is all this sugar your way of coping?"

"Actually the treats were the best part of the day."

"Uh-oh." Emma pushed the plate toward Angela. "You need one of these."

"I couldn't eat it if I wanted to. I went to that new café by the fresh market."

"I've heard about that. Farm-to-table stuff. Right?"

"Yes, that's the one."

"I bet that was awesome," Emma said. "Good for you for treating yourself, but why do you seem so out of sorts?"

"It was nice, but you'll never believe who came in."

"Who? Wait . . . Someone famous? My brother swore he saw Candace Cameron Bure at the Blue Pelican eating dinner last year. We all thought he was crazy, but then she posted it on Instagram. She was right here in our town!" Emma gasped. "If it was her and you didn't call me, I'm never going to forgive you."

"No. It was nothing as exciting as that." She leaned forward and stage-whispered, "Geoff Paisley from Christmas Galore. I should've known he'd hang out on the swankier side of town."

"You didn't get into another altercation with him, did you?"

"Not exactly." As bad as she felt about the first altercation, another would have been so much better than what happened. It was mortifying. "I hid in the bathroom, but then the door wouldn't open. I waited for a long time. I can't believe he was even still in the restaurant, but when I finally knocked for help—".

"He rescued you?" Emma laughed so hard she snorted.

Angela's face flushed. "Who else would that happen to?"

"So you had to thank him?"

"Barely. I practically ran out the door."

"Maybe you should've suggested coffee to thank him. It's not like you to hold a grudge, and it's a small town. Y'all aren't going to be able to avoid each other."

"I can try." But it didn't make any more sense saying it to Emma than it did thinking it when Geoff had said the same darn thing.

"You offer to show complete strangers around town," Emma said. "What's the big deal?"

"He gets under my skin."

"Well, if I recall you thought he was pretty cute the first time you saw him."

She wished she'd never said anything to Emma about that. "That was a mistake."

Emma said, "Well, you'll have to figure out what you're going to do."

"I know. It's hard. All I've ever thought I'd do is run Heart of Christmas."

"I meant about Geoff." Emma had a quirky grin on her face when she left. "I better get back out there and sell a few things before we close for the day." She stepped toward the door then turned around. "You know they say there's a fine line between love and hate." She lifted her shoulders with a playful smirk.

"Oh stop. I don't even like him!" she yelled as Emma walked out. *I don't. And he's not that cute up close.*

At six o'clock Angela watched the last customer leave, and then flipped the sign from OPEN to CLOSED on the front door.

"Seemed like a good day," she said as she closed out the register. "I'll finish up, Emma. You go on home."

"That would be awesome. That'll give me time to go treat myself to a blowout before my dinner date tonight." Emma grabbed her handbag. "I'll see you in the morning."

"Have fun." Angela tore the tape from the register, then carried the till back to her office to balance the store's sales for the day. Numbers were good, but not compared to other Christmases'. It was just one more reminder that she was making the right decision to close.

Angela's phone chirped. Marie had texted to let her know that Brad had dinner plans with a client, but that she and Chrissy would be over at around seven with pizza.

She walked home and started getting things ready for their visit. She got the big hot chocolate mugs and a Christmassy red tray out of the china cabinet, then went and rounded up a few wire dry cleaner's hangers to straighten out to use for roasting the marshmallows later.

Angela arranged the bakery goodies on the tray then covered them with a glass cake dome. They looked so pretty in the middle of her kitchen island. Almost like one of those pictures in the *Woman's Day* Christmas edition.

Feeling festive, she went to the hall closet and pulled out a box labeled *Christmas*. Inside golden beads, fancy old German glass ornaments that Momma Grace had saved over the years and sparkly hand-tied garlands started getting her in the mood to decorate.

Angela hummed Christmas carols as she swagged the garland around two sides of the island, then delicately laced the gold beads through it.

She took one of the big glass hurricane shades from the mantel to use as a centerpiece in the living room, loading colored glass ornaments inside it, mixing the hues and patterns.

Since Momma Grace had passed away she'd only decorated the store. It had made her sad to decorate the house they'd lived in together without her. This year should be different.

She grabbed a couple of large beach towels, the thick kind, and laid them in the Adirondack chairs on the back deck. Later it would feel good to have those towels to snuggle under near the fire.

Her thoughts drifted back to bumping into Geoff at the market. *Too bad he's such a jerk, because he really is good-looking.*

Chapter Fifteen

Dear Santa,
I hope Mrs. Claus has put you on a diet.
*   My mom says being fat will kill you. I want a race track*
for Christmas. My little brother asked for a bike but he's not
always good. I have been good enough for both of us though.
*   Zeke*

Geoff stopped at Sandy's Florist & Gifts before he headed over to
the hospital. He wanted to take something to his mom, but he
couldn't take his traditional box of her favorite chocolates. He was
pretty sure that would be frowned upon for a heart patient in the
ICU, and she hated cut flowers because they died so quickly. Always had.

He browsed the store then decided on a potted poinsettia in a
tall woven seagrass basket. White baby's breath was tucked between the hardy large flowers. "This should cheer someone up,
don't you think?" he said to the woman behind the counter.

"I couldn't agree more. It really can fit into any décor nicely."

"Hope it goes with hospital green." He was still mad that he'd
been out of the loop on his mother's health concerns.

"A local woman made that basket from seagrass. I just love

that simple art deco look with the beachy vibe. They are very popular."

Sounded like code for "expensive" to him, but could he really put a price cap on a gift to his mother? Especially when she was in the hospital? Hardly.

"I don't know about all that 'beachy vibe' stuff, but I like it," Geoff said. "I'll take it, and can you add one of those little cards with 'Get Well Soon' written on it?" He handed her his credit card.

"Of course." The woman took the tags off of the plant and selected a card from the rack. "If you want to sign it, I'll tuck it in the plant for you." She rang up his purchase, then handed him the card to sign.

He pulled a pen from his pocket. Mom had given it to him when he graduated from college. She'd been so proud of him that day. He hesitated for a moment, not even sure how to sign the card. How did you sign a card to your mother when she was in the hospital for a heart attack that she almost didn't even tell you about? He wanted to be mad at her for keeping the secret, but mostly he was worried.

Should he sign the card with "Son," "Geoff"—or maybe more appropriately, "Don't do this again!"?

Finally, he scribbled his name and handed the card back to the florist. She wove the small card through the tongs of the clear plastic fork then punched the holder down into the dirt.

"There you go," she said.

"Thanks for your help." Satisfied with the gift, he drove over to the hospital.

"I'm here to see my mother, Rebecca Paisley," Geoff said to the volunteer at the reception desk at County General Hospital.

The blue-haired woman leaned in closer to the computer

screen. "Yes sir. She's in our Intensive Care Unit. You'll want to take the elevator to the second floor. Turn right when you get off, then walk down to the next nurses' station. They'll help you."

"Elevator. Second floor. Right. Nurses' station. Got it."

"Yes sir," she said. "The plant is lovely, but you may need to leave it at the nurses' station. Please check with them before taking it into the room."

"Oh," he said. "Okay. Hadn't thought about that."

He followed the directions and stopped at the nurses' station. "I'm Geoff Paisley. My mother—"

"She's in the room right across the hall."

"Can she have this plant?"

"Yes, that'll be fine. The doctor just left."

"How's she doing?"

"She's doing very well. We'll be keeping her here on this floor for at least another day. Her cardiologist has ordered some additional tests."

"How's her mood? She hates sitting still."

The nurse laughed, and glanced over at one of the other nurses, who just shook her head. "Well, she hasn't lost her fight. She's ready to go home."

"Not surprised. Sorry. May I go in?"

"Yes, just make it short. We need her to rest."

"Yes ma'am." He went over to the door and gave a double-knock before walking into the room. "Good morning, Mom."

"Geoff. I'm glad to see you. Can't you get me out of here?"

"I hear the doctor has ordered some more tests."

"So let's get them done and get me home."

"Just relax and enjoy it. Pretend it's a spa. Just press that buzzer and let them wait on you hand and foot."

"This is the furthest thing from a spa."

"Use your imagination." He handed her the bag with her things in it, then placed the plant on the side table.

"At least I can put on a decent nightgown." She tugged at the neckline of the heavy cotton hospital gown. "Thank you for the plant. That was thoughtful."

Geoff pulled a chair closer to the side of the bed and sat down. "You're welcome."

"It's ridiculous to just lay here all day. I could do this at home," she said.

He propped his elbows on the arms of the chair and tented his fingers. "I think we both know that's not true."

She opened her mouth and started to speak, then just laughed. "Okay. Fine. I probably wouldn't."

"That's right. So just relax. I brought a book for you to read too. It was on your nightstand."

"Thank you. That will be great." She tugged the bag closer and withdrew the novel. "This will definitely help." She tucked it between the mattress and the bed rail. "Now tell me how the Dear Santa letters are going." She looked eager to hear.

Only, he really had nothing for her.

"Mom. I'm sorry, but those letters seem so trivial in the midst of all that's going on here. You're scaring me. I sure didn't expect to see you with any health problems."

"Son, I'm more fit and blessed than so many. If it's my time, then I'm ready."

"Mom, stop."

"No, you look around. I didn't want to worry you. That's why I kept this to myself, but I've had a good long run. You're a good son. We've made a great company together. If I go, I'll be with your father again."

"You never talk about him. Where is this coming from?"

"I loved your father. He was my one true love."

"Okay." It seemed a little odd that after thirty-some years she'd choose now to bring that up. "He didn't stick around to help raise me. Never married you. There's something to love about him?"

"I should have told you more. I just couldn't. In the beginning it was too hard. Then, later, too much time had gone by and I didn't know how to tell you. You weren't asking questions so I just let it go. I'm so sorry."

Was there really ever a good excuse for a man to shirk his fatherly duty? He didn't know the story. That much was true. There'd been a time when he'd asked a hundred questions about his father, but his mother got so depressed when he did. Eventually he quit asking, because he hated seeing his mom look sad. Knowing wasn't going to change anything. He wasn't sure he cared to hear any of it now either.

"There's nothing to be sorry about, Mom."

"He lived here."

"Here?" Pleasant Sands was becoming less and less appealing every day. It seemed wrapped in a mile of secrets from the past. And he personally didn't like looking back.

"I met him here in Pleasant Sands. He was a surfer back then. A commercial fisherman for a living, but he surfed every chance he got. He and Virgil were best friends."

"Virgil? Virgil is from here?"

"He was from one of the towns up the coast, but he came down here to surf. He and your dad chased waves from here to Australia one year." She paused, and he wondered what memories were playing in her mind. "Your father died in a boating accident. We'd planned to get married, but he died before we could do that. I was already pregnant, but I didn't want to marry him until after I had you. I didn't want him to feel trapped, but in the end it was me that felt trapped. Trapped in the sorrow of losing him."

"I knew it made you sad whenever I asked about him. It didn't matter anyway. All I needed was you. You were more parent by yourself than most of my friends had with two."

"Thank you. I tried."

"Do I really need to know all this now?"

She reached for his hand. "Listen to me," she said. "If anything should happen to me, I want you to bury me here in Pleasant Sands. His family bought us adjoining plots. The records are in my lockbox. The envelope has a different name on it, but it's called Pleasant Sands Memorial Gardens now."

"Do you know how weird this would've been if you hadn't told me and I was supposed to bury you next to a man I'd never heard about?"

"I'm sorry. There was no money to even put a nice headstone on his grave until after we opened our fourth store. I knew I'd be buried there too. Some day. It's in my will. There's a copy in my lockbox, the combination is your birthday, and of course John has a copy."

John was their lawyer. Geoff wondered how many more people knew about his mother's broken heart besides Virgil and John.

"I should've told you this a long time ago."

"You really did love him. You weren't hurt. You were sad." It was hard to push away the anger he'd carried around for the man he'd never known. All along he hadn't been present because he couldn't be.

Her smile was gentle. "I want to be sure you understand. He would have loved you. You have his drive. His sense of humor."

"Mom, I don't want to talk about this. All I'm worried about right now is you. I'm a grown man. I don't need a father."

"This discussion isn't over, but I'll let it go for now. I'm sure it's a lot for you to take in. So tell me about the letters. Any special ones?"

"You've been in here less than forty-eight hours. I haven't had a chance to even check the Dear Santa log."

"Geoff, it's the only thing I asked you to do."

"It can wait a day or two, Mom. You'll be out of here and anxious to have something to do."

"It's important to me. I need you to answer them," she said. "Promise me."

"Fine. I'll make sure they're answered."

"No. I don't want someone else answering them. I want *you* to address those Dear Santa letters yourself." She held his gaze, and this was her I'm-not-kidding-around face. "Promise me, Geoff." The monitor sped up like a radio station switching from a ballad to a dancing song.

They both looked at the machine.

"Fine."

"Please answer the letters, and don't just rush through them." She paused, and finally the heart monitor slowed back down to where it was. "The Dear Santa letters are special. You'll become part of these children's memories through those letters. Promise me you'll take them seriously. If you do, I guarantee you'll understand why they are so important to me. Wait and see. You're going to want to solve every problem. You can't, but you'll want to."

"I said that I'd take care of it. I will. I promise."

"Thank you." She let out an audible sigh. "You're going to be surprised how fulfilling it is."

He seriously doubted that. "Of course I'll handle it for you." He sure hoped there weren't too many to deal with.

"Tonight." She clasped her hands. The IV in her left hand flopped around like a wild spaghetti noodle trailing to the machine next to the bed. "I need you to answer them tonight."

"All of them?"

"I could be in here another day, or a week. We don't know, but what I do know is that those kids deserve a response. I also know if I get behind I'll never get caught up. So, the short answer is yes. All of them. Tonight." She paused. "Is that really too much to ask?"

"No. I guess it's really not."

"Good." She leaned back against the pillows. "Now maybe I'll be able to relax."

"Can I bring you anything tomorrow?"

"No." She stretched her arms toward him.

He leaned in and hugged her. "I love you, Mom."

"I know you do. I love you too. I'll talk to you tomorrow."

"Call me if the doctor has any updates."

"Of course I will."

But he knew he'd more than likely hear the update from Virgil if he got an update at all.

He walked out of her hospital room wondering how suddenly her following doctor's orders had fallen into his lap, because apparently she'd only relax if he answered the letters like she asked. He really wasn't looking forward to the task, but he'd promised, and he'd never broken a promise to his mother. He had no intention of starting now.

That evening after work Geoff drove home without incident, which was a miracle because he was in such a daze that he'd almost missed the turn to his condo.

He wondered about his parents' courtship. Clearly it was much more special than he ever could have realized.

Knowing that his father had once lived right here in this town had so many questions popping into his mind, and he hated that. That was in the past and he'd wrestled with it then. He didn't like to look back.

But it did make him wonder.

How many people knew that his mother had spent time here before? Did any of the locals know that she'd had a child with a man from here? Were any of the ladies on the committees Mom had suddenly taken a strong interest in from back in those days?

He pulled under the building of his condo and shut down the car.

He'd be lying if he said he hadn't wished for the day he could make the changes to Christmas Galore that he wanted. Mom hated change, and he'd spent plenty of time trying to convince her to let him integrate more high-tech solutions into the company. That was one of those things they just weren't going to agree on. It made him crazy, but he'd figured she'd eventually get tired of the day-to-day business and decide to take a yearlong cruise with girlfriends or just chill somewhere playing bridge with others her age. He never wanted something like this to happen. What if she never came back to Christmas Galore? His heart ached with guilt. Had he somehow wished this on her?

Ridiculous. No. He wouldn't allow himself to think like that.

He ached so much that he felt like an old man as he entered the building. Funny how anxiety and worry could drag you down into a heap so quickly. He pulled himself up straight and forced himself to take the stairs to his eighth-floor penthouse suite.

He punched the code to the front door of his condo, and tossed his keys on the side table as he entered. The place was sparsely decorated, the way he liked it. He didn't have use for anything that caused clutter. He grabbed a beer and went out on the balcony. The waves crashed against the beach below. Clouds had rolled in, eliminating the moon from the equation entirely, making the night inky black. The darkness and low-hanging clouds seemed eerie, or maybe it was just his mood. He stood there staring out at the ocean. The only things visible were a few whitecaps, and the crashing waves.

Finishing off his beer, he went back inside to his desk and turned on the computer. The Christmas Galore logo lit up the screen. With a few clicks he was into the executive portal. He went through his normal routine checking the sales across all of their stores, and comparing actual figures to forecast profits for the quarter. Things were tracking well.

He moved back to the main screen and clicked on the *Dear Santa* icon. A bright blue starry sky with "Dear Santa" in pretty script filled the page. His mother had worked tirelessly on the Dear Santa project. The app was popular; she's received so much mail that there was no way even a team of little elves could answer them all. Last year he'd finally had one small win. He'd gotten his mom to agree to hire a programmer who could build an algorithm that would create a personalized autoresponse to the majority of the letters. She had full control over a list of keywords that would push some letters to her queue. She read each and every one of those, and they received the personal touch only his mother could provide. The rest still got an autogenerated response, albeit one pretty fancy program that made uniquely worded letters.

Plus, letting Mom have her way with the letters had given him the chance to bargain with her to let him add more electronic products to their inventory: televisions, computers, wireless headphones and e-readers. Those items were like shark bait. Put a flat-screen TV or the latest electronic gizmo on sale at a rock-bottom price and customers started circling like it was feeding time. Not to mention that they'd fill their baskets with other items on impulse while they were perusing the sales.

Reluctantly he opened the Dear Santa dashboard. Tens of thousands of letters had already come in, and it was just after Thanksgiving!

Thank goodness only forty-three were in his mother's queue.

He had to read them. He'd promised. There was no getting around it. If nothing else, he was a man of his word.

Geoff got up and got another beer, swigging down half of it before he got back to his desk. He pulled his shirt over his head and tossed it over the arm of the couch nearby, then sat down.

The last Dear Santa letter his mother had responded to had been on Thanksgiving morning.

How hard could this be?

The first letter was from a little girl in Tennessee. He liked that they'd added the location and IP address of each letter.

Dear Santa,

I'm living with my grandma. She's old. Dad got mad and made Mom so scared she left. I miss her. If my grandma dies can I come live with you? I could make toys. I get good grades and I'm not like my dad.

You can pick me up on Christmas while you're here. I don't think grandma would miss me very much. I would like a warm blanket for Christmas. Grandma needs some warm clothes. She is always cold.

Love,
Cassie

What am I supposed to say to that?

"I'll come back to you, Cassie." He moved that one to a folder labeled HOLD, then read the next letter.

> *Dear Santa,*
> *I can't come see you at the mall because my friends will*
> *tease me so much I would die. They don't think you exist,*
> *but I do. I was pretty good except when I caught the ditch*
> *on fire playing with matches.*
> > *Here's my list.*
> > *Fire truck*
> > *B.B. gun*
> > *Remote control racecar*
> > . . .

Geoff kept scrolling through the long list of toys. Kid was a maniac. He scanned the letter again, certain there was something in the letter noteworthy enough to pop it into his mother's personal queue. "Tease." "Die." "Fire." Probably all keywords in his mother's filter.

He clicked on *reroute* and let this one go back through the auto-generated letter process. No way Mom could fault him for kicking this one back.

He'd only read two letters. He glanced at his watch. This was going to take forever.

With a click of a button the next letter populated the screen. It was from right here in North Carolina.

Dear Santa,
There's a bully in town threatening the Heart of Christmas,
and he's using your good reputation to do it.

I've been a very, very good girl, but he's ruining every-
thing, and Christmas may never be the same. I don't know
what to do. How can I fight back? I love Christmas and
Chrissy says you can fix anything. I sure hope she's right.
If not, I'm going to need a year's supply of tissues to get
through all the changes to come. A pony might make me feel
better too.

Merry Christmas to you, Mrs. Claus, the elves and all
of the reindeer.

Yours truly,
Anita C. Miracle

He pulled his hands together and cracked his knuckles. This
one he could answer.

Dear Anita,
I'm sorry to hear you are being bullied. I hope you know
that there's never a good reason for someone to bully
another. Don't worry about the heart of Christmas. It will
remain strong, because it's an important part of each of us.

Don't stoop to the level of that bully. Just keep doing the
right thing. Stay true to yourself, and be the good example.
Trust that everything will work out the way it is supposed
to. Know I'm there with you, in your heart, making sure
you find a happy ending to this situation. Believe anything
is possible.

Be brave. A new approach may make a surprising
difference.

I had you on my nice list even before you wrote me.

Ponies are so hard to fit in the sleigh. Would a bike make you feel better?

Merry Christmas. I'll see you soon.

Ho. Ho. Ho.

Santa

Feeling good about his response to that letter, he continued through them.

Only one out of the next fourteen he read needed to be re-routed to the autoresponder. The letters were thoughtful, some heartbreaking. The last letter he opened wasn't a request at all.

Dear Santa,

Thanks for making people smile. I think your naughty and nice list helps make this world a nicer place.

My daddy is going to help me make cookies for you this year. Mom was talking on the phone while we made them and they burned last year. Sorry about that. It was super nice of you to eat them anyway. I didn't like them.

Love,

Jenna

This letter could've been rerouted, but the note was so cute he didn't mind taking the time to send her a personal response.

Pressing *Send,* he realized he was smiling.

To end on a high note, he closed his laptop.

He'd get up and go into the office extra early in the morning and do a few more so he'd have a positive report for Mom when he saw her.

Chapter Sixteen

Angela sat in a chair by the fire pit. Not because it was cold, it was a pretty nice night, but she loved relaxing near the flickering flames, letting herself be mesmerized by the combination of the fire and the sound of crashing waves.

Growing up here there hadn't been an ordinance against building a fire on the beach. As a kid, they'd done that nearly every weekend the weather permitted.

She opened her laptop to catch up on email while she waited for Marie and Chrissy.

It seemed like there was more junk mail than important emails in her inbox these days. *Click, click, click,* she deleted the obvious junk and spam, and filed the important stuff so she could deal with that later.

The subject line of the next email made her pause.

Re: Dear Santa ~ Ho! Ho! Ho!

Santa?

She clicked on the email, fully expecting a generic response.

Wait a minute. This did not seem like an autogenerated email. Was someone actually answering these letters?

Thank goodness Marie hadn't let her send the first draft she'd written.

"Hey, sis! We're here."

"Aunt Angela?"

Angela laid her laptop on the table next to her and ran inside. "Hey, you two. I was outside by the fire."

Chrissy bounced into the room wearing a red jumpsuit with a candy cane design on it, then came to a stop. "You started having fun without us?"

"No way! You're the most fun part of the night," Angela said. "Now we can get started, and I bought treats!" She grabbed Chrissy's tiny hand and led her into the kitchen.

Chrissy's eyes danced with delight when she spotted the decorations on the island. She ran over to the edge, tippy-toeing to get a better look at the decadent baked goods under the glass dome.

"Wow," she said breathily. "Auntie Angela. Can we really eat those?"

"We can."

"Mom! Come look!"

Marie walked over and shook her head. "I'm going to have to hit the gym an extra time this week."

Angela lifted the dome. "Which one do you want, Chrissy? You get first pick."

Chrissy took her time examining the six goodies.

A cookie decorated like a Christmas ornament. Two cookies stacked with shiny red jelly in the middle, a snowflake intricately cut from the top layer. A chocolate-dipped cake pop that looked like a reindeer with pretzels for antlers. A miniature cake with silver dragées. A red-and-green petit four. A chocolate-layered pastry that was taller than it was wide, with a real-looking red fondant ribbon and bow on top.

Chrissy glanced over toward her mom, looking for approval.

"It's okay," Marie said.

"Can I have the pretty one that looks like a wrapped present?"

"You can. That *is* the prettiest one. Perfect for my pretty niece." Angela slid the parchment cup off of the tray and onto a small plate. "How about you, Marie. What's your pleasure?"

"They all look delicious. I'll take the petit four."

"Deal," Angela said.

Angela chose the cookie in the shape of an ornament.

"Let's sit out back." They all headed to the deck. Angela held Chrissy's plate so she could climb into the large Adirondack chair.

Marie sat down and picked up the laptop. "What is this?"

Angela handed Chrissy her plate, then turned and took the laptop from Marie's hands. "That is not for you, nosey."

"Well, it was sitting right there."

Marie had always been too nosey for her own good. Probably why she was such a good lawyer.

"What are you hiding from me?" Marie asked.

She was about to burst, which made it really hard to not smile. "I got a letter."

"What kind of letter? Like a letter of credit? Sis, you know how I feel about you taking more money out to try to save—"

"No! Not a letter of credit. An email. Not really a letter at all, but you know what I mean."

"What in blazes are you talking about? A love letter?"

Angela shook her head. "No, but it would be funny if Santa was writing me love letters. Would that put me on the 'nice' list forever? Which, by the way, he did say I was on."

"Of course you are. You're the nicest person I know."

"That might be the nicest thing you've ever said to me, but somehow coming from Santa it's way more cool."

"Santa wrote you back already?" Chrissy asked.

"He did."

"My sister is dating Santa?"

"No, but he did write me back."

Marie gave Angela an exaggerated wink, then whispered to her, "See, it didn't kill you, did it?"

"No." She shrugged. "It was way more specific than I'd expected, though."

Chrissy pulled her feet into the chair. "I told you he could help."

"He was very nice," Angela said. Careful to not spoil the magic of Santa for her niece, she added, "But he didn't exactly say he'd help."

"What'd he say?" Marie prodded.

Angela glared at her sister. "I really don't think this is the right audience."

"What's an ahh-de-aunts?" Chrissy asked.

"We'll talk later," Marie said. "Fine. Let me just see that letter."

"Nope." Angela shook her head, kind of enjoying leading her sister along on this chase for information. "I don't think this was an autogenerated letter. It was personal. And thoughtful. Nice."

"Chrissy, go get my phone out of my purse. Okay, honey?"

"Yes ma'am." She sprung from her chair and tugged on the door to go inside.

Marie turned on Angela. "What did Santa say?"

"He said I should be brave, that a new approach may make a surprising difference. I've been mulling that over and I think he's right. I need to do something different. Closing Heart of Christmas is the right thing to do."

Marie's eyes narrowed. "Isn't that exactly what someone else said? Who *was* that? Oh, I think it was me. Someone else says it, and just like that, you're relaxed and ready to face the unknown?"

"Yes. I guess I am."

"Let me see that letter." Marie grabbed for the laptop.

"No, but he does seem like a perfect gentleman."

"Write him back, then," Marie teased.

"I can't do that. This is not online dating. Besides, everyone knows Santa is married."

"True. Maybe you better just let it drop. He could be an ax murderer."

"Santa can't be a bad guy. They'd totally catch him. Who else would be out on Christmas Eve every year?"

"Santa is nice!" Chrissy exclaimed. "He doesn't like bad guys!"

They hadn't heard her slip back onto the porch.

"You're right. He's super-nice, Chrissy. But he'd be easy to profile," Marie agreed. "Are you going to email him back?"

"No way."

"Why not? What other plan do you have?"

"He really can help," Chrissy insisted.

"It was a nice letter," Angela said. "If I met a guy that was thoughtful I'd be thrilled, but I can't decide if it's a very clever autorespond or a person, and I sure don't want to be emailing a computer."

"Hand it over." Marie extended her hand and snapped her fingers.

"It's Santa," Chrissy said. "You have to listen to what he says. That's the way it works."

Angela gave the laptop to Marie and sat quietly for a moment. "Well. What do you think?"

Marie silently read the email again, her lips moving as she did. "Yeah. I think you're right. This doesn't seem like an autoresponder, but it has to be. There is no way people are responding to all those letters." Marie nibbled on her petit four, then said, "I think you should write back. Be a little more specific this time, and challenge this R2D2 responder."

Angela laughed. "We'll probably break the computer."

"No harm in that. It'll be fun to challenge it and see what kind of funny response we get. Come on. Let's do it. And at the very least we can just thank him."

"Okay. Fine. You type this one," Angela said. "I'll make the hot chocolate while you play with Santa."

"Can I help?" Chrissy asked.

Marie said, "You go help Angela in the kitchen."

Angela and Chrissy went into the kitchen. They made hot chocolate and poured it into three big red polka-dotted mugs. "Your turn to decorate with the marshmallows," Angela said to Chrissy.

When Angela carried the tray of mugs back outside, Marie had the laptop closed in her lap.

"Did you write it?"

"Of course," Marie said. "I charge people by the hour. I have to work fast or they get mad."

"Are you going to let me see what you wrote?"

"Nope. You'll just have to wait until you get his response."

"Give me that laptop."

Marie handed her the computer.

Angela pulled up the *sent* folder of her email. "There's nothing here. You didn't send anything." She relaxed into her chair. "You had me there for a minute."

"Actually, a good lawyer knows all about how people cover their tracks. I deleted the copy in your sent mail."

Marie had that sly grin on her face.

Angela rolled her eyes. "I think it's marshmallow-toasting time," she said to Chrissy. "Your mom is up to no good. I can tell by the look in her eyes. Like the time she sprinkled baby powder on my French toast."

"Mom? You wouldn't do that." Chrissy's face screwed up in disgust. "Ewww."

"I might have done that," Marie said, not looking one bit sorry, which only gave Angela more reason to worry.

If things were fair and just in the world, Chrissy would take that bit of knowledge and run with it. Angela hoped French toast was on the menu this week, and Marie would get her just desserts.

Chapter Seventeen

Dear Santa,
I live at the beach. We never get snow. You should live here
in the winter. I have been nice to everyone, even my sister
when she told on me for taking quarters out of the jar on
Dad's dresser. I really want a remote control car and a kite.
Thanks,
Marcus

Geoff took a sip from the cup of coffee sitting to his right on his desk. He forced himself to swallow the cooled coffee. That was the trouble with answering these letters: he kept getting so drawn in that he lost track of time. This was the second cup of coffee he'd had to warm up.

He got up and let out a loud groan as he stretched, then walked down the hall to the break room. The comfortable space looked more like a home kitchen, thanks to his mom's touch. He warmed up his coffee and walked back down to his office. It was still early morning, his favorite time in the office. Virgil hadn't even made it in yet and he'd always been an early bird.

He couldn't control Mom getting well, but he would make sure this business was humming on all cylinders the whole time she was laid up. That, he could do for her.

Geoff sat back down at his desk and leaned forward on his elbows. He was feeling a little melancholy today. Probably because Mom was in the hospital. Maybe from the Dear Santa letters.

Reading the letters made him want to solve these kids' problems. And they made him feel needed.

Or maybe he was suddenly wanting to be more involved because Virgil and Mom had kept information from him. He didn't like the feeling of being out of the loop. He needed to feel connected to something.

Knowing he had some connection to this place made him want to know more about it. Last night he'd even dreamed about what it might be like to put down long-term roots here. A first. And the thought scared him.

"What's going on with me?" He physically shook as if letting that feeling go. "Back to it."

He worked on the letters until he heard Virgil's voice from the doorway.

"You're here early."

Geoff looked up. "Hey. Good morning." He glanced at the time on his computer. "Actually, you're here a little later than normal, aren't you?"

"How would you know? I'm always here before you." Virgil lifted a bushy eyebrow, and laughed that hearty laugh he was known for.

"That's a fact. I just finished working the Dear Santa queue for Mom."

Virgil invited himself in and sat down in one of the chairs on the other side of Geoff's desk. "Just left your mother. She's feeling good this morning."

"That's great."

"Well, probably not so much for the nurses or that doctor. She was raising a fuss about going home when I left."

"I'm sure she was."

"Don't be surprised if she Ubers here from the hospital in her nightgown."

Geoff could picture that. "At least she has her own pajamas and not one of those hospital gowns. That would be a problem."

"Touché." Virgil rubbed a hand across his bushy mustache. "She's headstrong."

Geoff couldn't hold back the need to ask a couple of questions. "Virgil, you've been like a father to me all of these years. You know that. I have to know: Why didn't you ever tell me about my dad? I'd have thought it might at least come up that you'd lived here before, when we were opening the store."

"Your father would've been proud of you. You're so much like him. He didn't live long enough to have a career, but I see a lot of you in him. He was smart, and played hard too. We were best friends. We had some really good times, but we were young when he died." Virgil shifted in his chair. "Younger than you are now. It was hard on everyone. Especially your mom."

Geoff nodded.

"I don't know why things happen. Who does? I didn't tell you out of respect for your mother's decision. What I can tell you is you'd have liked him. Respected him." Virgil leaned back in the chair. "We take the hand we're dealt and we do the best we can with it. Impossible situations aren't impossible; they sure do feel that way at the time, though. I'm sure you're upset, but I'd say this situation has shaped up pretty darn nicely."

"You're right. I'm thankful for the life I've had. Thankful for you being a part of it."

"Thank you, Geoff. I feel the same way."

"I wouldn't change anything."

Virgil's eyes narrowed. "Now, I wouldn't say that."

"No?"

Virgil shook his head. "No. I wish he'd never died and I'd had both of my friends, and I wish I'd been able to break through that wall your mother built after your dad died. She was so determined to never feel that loss again."

Geoff tented his fingers. "Understandable."

"You've picked up those behaviors. Geoff, business is an important part of life. No doubt about it, but I'm here to tell you that finding a woman to share your life with is even bigger. You're missing out on that."

Geoff didn't see that as a problem. He was perfectly happy dedicating his life to this company. He loved the chase of finding the best next location. Loved the competition between the stores to be the best. Loved the challenge of the changing trends.

"Look. You don't have to say a thing. Just keep that tucked away in that noggin of yours. Food for thought."

Geoff nodded. "I'll do that."

"Great." Virgil pushed up from the chair. "Enough of that stuff. Your mother asked me to ask you to water her plants. They are going to keep her in the hospital at least one more day, unless she talks them out of it." He turned to walk out. "You might take earplugs when you go to visit her. I'm sure you'll get an earful, like I did, about what she thinks about that doctor's decision."

"That's good advice," Geoff said. "I'll take care of the plants on my way to see her this afternoon. With earplugs."

"Aisle seven, bin twelve," Virgil said with a laugh.

Geoff printed off the month-to-date report for all of the stores. It was all good news; maybe a few numbers would brighten Mom's day. When he pulled up the Dear Santa dashboard he noticed a letter in a separate inbox labeled RESPONSES REQUIRING FOLLOW-UP. He wondered what letters got rerouted there.

While his report printed, he clicked on that folder.

He smiled as he read the response from Anita C. Miracle.

Dear Santa,

Thank you for the response and advice.

I'm so glad to know that I'm on your nice list. I try to live my life as a good example.

Too bad about the pony. I'm a little too old for a banana bike. The bully that I mentioned isn't a kid. This is a grown-up problem. My business is at risk. A family business that I inherited from my grandmother. Losing her was hard, this is even harder. A scar that won't heal with a bandage, or a shiny new bike. I can't picture my life without my store in it.

What I want is as unlikely as snow in Pleasant Sands, NC. I wish there was someone as thoughtful and kind as you in real life to take my mind off of losing my business and finding a new normal. Someone to jog with on cool winter mornings. Who would, instead of bringing flowers, give me a bucket of shells, or roast marshmallows over the fire pit on the deck overlooking the ocean.

I'm trying to be brave, to believe that this change is meant to be.

My sister and I have a bet that these are autoresponder letters and we're wondering what the keywords in this note will come back with this time.

I hope this doesn't put me on the naughty list for toying with you.

Merry Christmas,
Anita C. Miracle

He reread the original Dear Santa letter that was attached in the email chain. The author had never said she was a kid; he'd just assumed that the bully was a schoolmate. At least his response still applied in this real situation.

It was hard to imagine what she was going through. His business was everything to him too. Should he respond? He hated for her to believe the letter was generated by some kind of fancy auto-responder. Although that was exactly what happened with 99 percent of the letters.

Playing pen pal with someone under the guise of Santa seemed a little weird.

It was pretty weird too that she'd mentioned Pleasant Sands.

Then again, it was no secret that this was where they'd opened their last store, and Christmas Galore did show up as one of the key sponsors of the app, a smart marketing ploy that his mother had come up with. Looking like a sponsor, rather than the owner of the website, the store had made the Dear Santa letters a palatable free service for all children regardless of their location, social status or any other silly little thing that could rub people wrong. His mother had started the project out of love for the holiday, and her love of children. It wasn't important to her if anyone knew that it was she behind that contribution.

He shut down his laptop and put it in his briefcase, then grabbed his coat to leave.

Since he'd spent all morning on Dear Santa letters, he'd better head over and water Mom's plants, then if he had time maybe he'd pick up a fresh-catch lunch from Garvy's restaurant for her. She'd like that a lot better than hospital food.

Driving over to his mom's house, he couldn't keep that letter off of his mind.

What would his life be like had Christmas Galore not worked

out for Mom? This business was their whole life. Even the out-side activities they were involved in always had some tie to the business. With a vendor. Business acquaintances. Conventions. Scouting new locations.

Growing up and all through college he'd always known that he'd work by her side. A family business, just like that of the clever-pen-named writer of the letter, Anita C. Miracle.

If all of that had turned topsy-turvy, what would he have done for a living?

It was hard to imagine.

Inside Mom's house, he got the watering can from under the sink and filled it. Making his way from room to room, he watered and spritzed each plant. There weren't very many personal ear-marks in the décor here with the exception of a dorky high school graduation picture of him, a magazine article about him that she'd had framed, a couple pictures of his mom and Virgil and two store-opening pictures with all three of them at the ribbon-cutting ceremony.

He ran his hand across the old dining-room table. She'd had this table since he was a boy. They'd eaten dinners and done home-work here.

It struck him as funny that she'd never bought a new one. The scratches and dings showed its years of service. If he looked closely he could probably see where he'd traced the Christmas Galore logo from the newspaper when he was nine, marking through the paper into the wood grain. She'd been so angry.

Then there was the dent on the edge from the time they lived in the tiny beach cottage on the Chesapeake Bay in Delaware and he'd run right into the corner of it, breaking his front tooth. Thank goodness it had been a baby tooth. Maybe it was the reason he'd ended up in braces, though.

He walked out on the balcony where a novel and a wineglass sat next to one of the weathered chairs. He picked up the book. The pages were wavy from the humid air and salty spray. He'd take it to her today. She was probably already done with the other one he'd taken earlier.

Was it again a matter of reconnecting dots to the past? They'd vacationed as a family on nearly every beach along the coast from the Florida Keys to Cape Elizabeth, Maine. Had she been trying to recapture something on those trips? Geoff shrugged out of his sport coat and slung it over his shoulder. He hadn't taken the time to really enjoy the beach in years.

He hadn't taken a real vacation since his mom quit planning them when the business had gotten so big.

Chapter Eighteen

Dear Santa,

I like your app. It's so much better than going to the stinky helper Santa at the mall, but how do we tell you our new address? The app only lets me put in my email address, name and age. I live with my mom in Chapman, Kentucky, now. It's really hard to find.

Thanks,
Cole

Geoff drove over to the pier and ate an early lunch at Garvy's at a window table. He couldn't remember the last time he'd taken time to sit and enjoy the view over lunch.

Three local fishermen bragged about their daily hauls at the counter across the way.

Geoff took a last bite of the fresh-caught rockfish. He wondered if this fish had been caught by one of those loud fishermen at the counter.

"Here's your to-go order," the waitress said. "I sure hope your mom is feeling better soon."

"She's feeling pretty good. Giving those nurses a run for their money, I hear."

The waitress laughed. "No doubt. That's a good sign." She tore the check from her pad and laid it down on the table. "Garvy said the fish for your momma is on the house."

"He didn't have to do that."

She smiled. "You know how he is. He loves his customers like family. This is his way of letting her know he cares."

"Thank you. I'll let her know." He placed a twenty on the table, and headed for the hospital.

When he walked into his mother's room, she was sleeping. He laid his jacket over the chair, then placed the lunch bag on her bedside table with the book from her house.

Rather than take a chance on waking her, he walked down the hall to get a bottle of water from the vending machine in the waiting area.

Families huddled together in the waiting room looking tired and worried. The mood was contagious. His dipped immediately. He swiped his card on the vending machine and pressed the button for the four-dollar bottle of water. He noticed a woman crying in the corner of the room. She looked so alone. He turned back to the machine and bought another water.

On his way out, he stopped and handed the woman one of the bottles of water. "Here. Maybe this will help."

She looked up with red-rimmed eyes.

It almost hurt him to look at them.

"Thank you," she said, accepting the small token.

He laid a hand on her shoulder, wishing for the right words to offer comfort. Nothing came to him, though.

He walked out of the room thinking he needed to be counting his blessings.

When he walked back into his mother's room she was awake.

"I saw your jacket. Wondered if I'd slept right through your visit."

"No way." He lifted the bottle of water and took a sip. "You need your rest. I'd have waited."

"All I've done is rest for days now. This is getting old."

"Yeah, yeah." His mom hated sitting still. "It hasn't been that long. Just relax."

"You're right. I should be grateful I feel well enough to complain."

"That's more like it." He pulled the chair over. "I have a question for you."

She muted the television. "I'm a captive audience. Fire away."

"Do you ever regret not taking more time for yourself? I mean, we haven't vacationed in years. We used to when I was a kid. Good vacations."

She didn't hesitate. "A week ago I'd have said no. No regrets. At all. I love spending my time continuing to improve the store and meeting our customers. I like feeling like I'm making a difference in our employees' lives. It's satisfying."

"We do. Our staff always comes first. I'm proud of that."

"As a single mom starting out I know firsthand how important it is to have a place to work where you feel secure, and to be a part of something good."

"I'm glad you taught me that," he said, and he meant it.

"But . . ." She shifted the covers on her lap. "Don't thank me for that. That came with a price, and I do have regrets now. Life suddenly feels very fragile. It can be taken from us at any time. With no notice," she said. Her voice sounded strangely soft. Hesitant.

"Don't say that."

"But it's true. We really need to keep our priorities straight, and that doesn't just mean business. There's so much more. Community. Friends. Family. And you asked about vacations. Yes, absolutely vacations. This country is gorgeous. I should have continued our vacation adventures. Those were fun, and boy, did I appreciate how beautiful our country is when we traveled across it."

"There's a lot to see."

"There is. We need to find balance. I've done a poor job of that, son. I was not a good example. I'm sorry."

Had she and Virgil been discussing this? "Don't ever apologize to me, Mom. You've given me a wonderful life."

She patted his hand. "I'm very proud of you."

"Thank you."

"I don't say that enough. And Virgil's right. I've tainted your image of family. Of love. Seriously, how many men in their early thirties these days have never been married?"

Looking for a way to lighten the mood, he said, "That sounds like a *Family Feud* poll. I have no idea what the answer is, but on the bright side, it's good to be a man who has *never* been divorced."

"Now, that's true." His mother laughed. A good hearty laugh. "That makes me proud too."

He relaxed a little. "Do you know how good it makes me feel to see you smile? To hear you laugh?"

"I'm sorry I scared you. Scared me too, truth be told, but I'm going to be okay."

"You promise?"

"I do. For now. I'll follow the doctor's orders. I don't plan to die anytime soon."

"Good, but can I say something?"

"I'm sure you will no matter what I say." Her eyes twinkled mischievously.

"I just wanted to say that it makes perfect sense to me that you wanted to come back here. Even be buried here, since this is where you met your one true love."

"Your father," she added.

"Yeah, that takes more getting used to. I just wanted to say that it doesn't really matter why you didn't tell me. That's behind us, but I do understand why you wanted to spend more time here in Pleasant Sands."

"Thank you, son."

"I'm interested in learning more about the town. Maybe even my father, down the road." In an odd way, even though she'd withheld important information from him, he felt an even stronger connection to her right now.

"Thank you for understanding."

"No more secrets," he said.

She raised her hand. "I promise."

He'd be happy when she was finally cleared to go home. "Good, and I'll cover those Dear Santa letters as long as you need me to. The top priority is getting you well. Then, a vacation."

"Sounds like a deal."

"Lunch is on Garvy today. I brought you your favorite."

"The rockfish?"

He nodded.

"Thank goodness. A real meal. They could use a better chef at this place."

"Oh!" He tugged the store reports out of his jacket pocket. "I almost forgot. I brought you these, and this book was on your patio."

"Thank you. Oh goodness, the weather did a number on those pages, didn't it?" She fanned the pages. "Still readable. No problem. Thanks for rescuing it for me."

"You're welcome." Geoff turned to leave, then stopped. "One other thing. If you'd lost Christmas Galore, if sales dropped and you were forced to close, what would you have done with your life?"

"Is the store in some kind of trouble?" Her lips pulled into a tight line, creases forming across her forehead.

"No. Not at all." He rushed to explain. "Things are great. You saw the reports. It's just hypothetical."

She glanced down at the numbers again, looking relieved. "In that case, after I had a complete and utter breakdown, because losing it would be like losing me. . . . After that . . ." She raised a finger to her lips. "Gosh, that's not something I ever even considered. I guess I'd have worked in a boutique shop on a beach somewhere. I like people. I love the beach. At least working for someone else we'd have had more time to do other things besides just work."

He nodded. That's what he'd thought.

"Now, don't ever make me think about that again. That's just not nice."

"I promise." He blew her a kiss. "Be kind to the nurses. Be a patient patient."

"I'm trying," she said, raising her hand in a wave.

Geoff walked out of his mother's room to the elevator.

"Excuse me," a woman's voice came from behind him. "Sir?"

He turned to see the woman from the waiting area. The one he'd given the bottle of water to. "Hi. Yes?"

"I just wanted to thank you. For the water." She walked closer. "No. Not the water, really, but for taking a moment to notice. I appreciate your kindness. That was really nice of you."

"Don't mention it."

"I just wanted to let you know that I intend to pay that forward."

"I'm glad it helped."

She nodded, then turned and walked away.

Taking a moment. That's honestly all it was. But how many moments had he really ever taken for others? Selfless acts of kindness: underrated. For sure. He'd do better with that going forward.

On the way home he passed the shopping center near his house. The last time he'd been there he'd been having lunch with Virgil and rescued Angela from the locked bathroom.

That had been a peculiar incident. If he could just stay out of her path things would be a lot easier.

Back at the office, the response to the last Dear Santa letter Anita C. Miracle had written came to him.

He ran up the stairs to his office and pulled up the Dear Santa portal. He had to hunt around for a minute to remember where he'd seen that letter since it wasn't part of the queue. A moment of panic struck. Had he lost it? He should've forwarded it to his personal email.

Finally, he clicked on the dashboard and saw the lonely number 1 with a hyperlink over the folder RESPONSES REQUIRING FOLLOW-UP.

He let out a long breath he hadn't realized he was holding.

What was Anita like? Would his advice even matter? Couldn't hurt.

He drafted the note start to finish without even a pause. Just stream of consciousness, sharing his thoughts with someone he'd never meet.

> *Dear Anita,*
> *You might be surprised to find that this note is not a product*
> *of a fancy autoresponder, although they certainly do exist.*
> *To further prove it, I'm taking this letter off of the*
> *Dear Santa email to a personal one.*

I'm sorry to hear that your business is struggling. If something happened to my family business, I would feel the same way. I'm sorry you're going through that.

Keep believing, and don't be surprised if there is snow in Pleasant Sands this Christmas. Maybe even a bucket of shells under your tree on Christmas morning.

Embrace the magic of the season.

> *Merry Christmas,*
> *from the guy formerly*
> *known as Santa*

He reread the letter, then changed the email from the portal address to one he used for personal correspondence, and hit *send* before he chickened out.

No sooner had he hit that button, a whistle came from his phone.

He jumped and grabbed his phone. It was just a text from Chandler.

"Hey, Chandler," Geoff said when Chandler answered on the first ring.

"I've called you, like, four times."

"Sorry. I forgot to turn the ringer back on my phone when I left the hospital this afternoon. What's up?"

"I wondered what was going on. You had me worried. It's not like you to not answer."

"Sorry."

"Where are you? Did you forget? Tonight is the Pleasant Sands Merchant Group meeting."

Geoff jumped from his chair, closing his laptop and shoving it into his briefcase all in one motion. "Sorry. I haven't even looked at my calendar today. I completely forgot."

"You need to be here," Chandler said. "It's their holiday celebration. It'll look bad for Christmas Galore if you can't even be bothered to make it to the Christmas party. I'm suave, and quite entertaining, but they want you."

"Yeah, that wouldn't be good. Cover me. I'll be there in twenty minutes. Is this the meeting at the miniature golf place across from the pier?"

"Yes. It's casual. Ditch the suit and look like a neighbor."

That irritated Geoff. "Why do you always think you have to give me fashion advice?"

"Because you look like a suit."

"I wear suits. So sue me." He looked at his jacket hung neatly over the chair.

"Golf shirt. Something casual for outside," Chandler said.

"I'm coming." He would have to hurry if he wanted to get home to change clothes. He'd completely forgotten about the meeting being tonight.

He got home and changed in record time, then broke the speed limit getting back over to the meeting.

The parking lot of Animal Kingdom Mini-Golf was crawling with people, several that he recognized. He was glad he'd taken Chandler's advice. He definitely would've been overdressed in a button-down.

Geoff walked across the lot straight to Garvy. "Good to see you again. Lunch was great, and thank you again for calling me after Mom's mishap." Little did Garvy know that had he not called, Geoff may not have known about it.

"Scared me to death." Garvy blanched at the faux pas. "Sorry, didn't mean that the way it came out."

"No worries. I know what you meant. She scared me too."

Garvy dragged his hand through his thinning hair. "How is she?"

"Good." But he really wasn't sure. "She's in good hands over at the hospital. They're keeping an eye on her." Admitting she'd been at risk was something he couldn't give any power. That was too real. And he still wondered if he was getting the whole story. "She's ready to come home."

"Let us know if we can do anything," Garvy said.

"We will. Thank you." Nice of him, but really, what was he going to do? Mom's condition wasn't something that could be cured with food. Her voice echoed in his mind: *Kindness cures everything.*

If only.

"Geoff. Hey. You're here," Chandler called from near the door.

"Excuse me," Geoff said to Garvy, thankful for a reason to get off the topic of Mom's health. He met Chandler near the door and they went inside.

"Grab a plate," Chandler said. "Food's amazing. Most everyone is playing golf right now, and mingling."

Chandler handed Geoff a plate then took one for himself and heaped a mound of macaroni and cheese right in the middle. "This stuff is my kryptonite. I've already had two helpings. And the tomato pie? Who ever heard of tomato pie? Must be a Southern thing. It's my new favorite dish."

Geoff bypassed the cheesy side dish and chose instead a few steamed shrimp, and a slice of mahi-mahi with peppers in three colors that looked a little like confetti had been tossed over it.

"That's all you're having?"

"It's enough."

Geoff followed Chandler out to a table littered with a few empty beer bottles. "Want a beer?" Chandler asked.

"I'm good." He looked at the food on his plate, not really hungry, but after the first bite it was so tasty he regretted not piling up his plate too.

A woman across the way with her back to him looked totally out of place in heels and dress slacks. He should introduce her to Chandler. She could've used the fashion advice memo from him too. Or maybe he should keep her for himself. Good to know there was someone else that felt the same way he did about attire.

He popped the last shrimp in his mouth.

The woman turned, and he almost choked.

"Whoa there, boss." Chandler gave him an exuberant whomp on the back.

Geoff swallowed, and took a sip of water.

"You okay?"

Geoff nodded. "Come on. Let's putt." He walked over to the counter and selected a putter. Chandler's chair screeched as he pushed away from the table and raced to catch up.

With a red golf ball bearing the Pleasant Sands town logo on it in his hand, Geoff headed for the first mat, bouncing it as he walked.

Of all the women in this town, just his luck he'd be attracted to this one.

Chapter Nineteen

DID YOU KNOW?

*Kite Peak Park, one of Pleasant Sands' most visited
attractions, is just 426 acres in area, but features the second
tallest active sand dune system in the Eastern United States,
second only to Jockey's Ridge State Park.*

Angela stood at the one of the tall four-topper tables that had been
set up around the arcade at Animal Kingdom Mini-Golf. Scott
Marshall had offered up his location for the annual holiday party
of the Pleasant Sands Merchant Group this year and it really had
worked out nicely, especially since the weather had cooperated.

Marie sipped a glass of wine, her third since Angela had gotten
there. Angela had a strict no-drinking policy at business-related
events. Although considering the fate of her business, this was only
a borderline business event for her. She felt like a big fat fraud here
tonight, knowing the store was closing. She lifted a highball glass
of tonic with a lime to her lips. Never hurt to look the part, and
she didn't need a drink to have fun.

Marie waved to someone across the way, then leaned in toward
Angela. "I'm glad you decided to come tonight. Just because Heart
of Christmas is closing, which, by the way, you are going to have

to announce eventually, you'll always be a part of this business community. You know that, right?"

"I'm sad that I have to close, but I've decided I'm just going to trust that everything will be all right."

"I'm proud of you, sis." Marie raised her glass of wine toward Angela, then took another sip.

"Thank you." She looked around at the people in the room. Most of them were retailers. Owners of stores, restaurants, hotels and gift shops. "Don't you think it's funny that we're having a holiday mixer night during peak retail hours? You'd think the Merchant Group would know better than to book this the week after Thanksgiving. We're busy. Everyone's probably exhausted after one of the biggest weeks of the year."

"Maybe that's perfect timing. To give all of you a much-needed break before the rest of the season."

Angela knew most of the people in the room, like her they'd lived here all their lives, but tonight she felt awkward. For the most part coworkers and family units clung together, or families talked with other families. Children darted between the arcade machines, while others picked out putters and colorful golf balls to start their round of miniature golf.

"Want to play?" Marie asked.

"I wish I'd changed clothes before I came, now." Rather than go home and change she'd opted to stay at the store as long as possible, so now here she was all dressed up in black slacks, heels, and a bright red holiday sweater with silver and gold ornaments on it. Not quite mini-golf attire. "You should have brought Chrissy with you."

"She's making cookies over at a friend's house tonight."

"That makes me hungry. I'm going to get something to eat," Angela said.

"I'll grab a table outside."

Angela lifted her chin, pasted her ever-present smile back into place and headed to the refreshment table. Garvy, the head chef at Big G's Fish House on the pier, always catered the spread for this meeting. It was his annual contribution, had been since the first year he'd opened his restaurant. Back then it was just fish tacos and nobody thought he'd be open more than a season, but he'd proved everyone wrong.

"It's been too long since I've had your fish tacos," Angela admitted.

"If I'd known that I'd have made some special just for you." Garvy pulled her into a big bear hug. "Don't you do anything but work anymore? I'm not sure I've seen you in my restaurant twice all year."

The familiar darkness settled in her heart. "I know." She gripped the sides of her plate. "I'm sorry. How's the restaurant?"

"Great and we're still seeing steady growth each year. You wouldn't recognize the place. I've redone the whole inside. Has kind of a swanky vibe now."

"You? Swanky?" She glanced down at his cargo shorts, his attire of choice since they were in high school together.

"Oh, don't get me wrong, it's not that swanky. My customers—and I—can all still wear shorts and flip-flops. It's on the pier, for goodness sake. I didn't go crazy."

"Whew. You had me scared there for a minute."

"No. This boy likes to stay in his comfort zone. I don't mind making fancy meals, but I don't want to have to dress up for it. Why should my customers?"

"I hear ya," she said with a giggle. She missed Garvy, but he'd been Jimmy's best friend. He would've been the best man at their wedding, had Jimmy not taken that job in Texas. After Jimmy left it had been awkward, and then so much time went by and she'd gotten busy with the store. She was sorry now that she hadn't kept up their friendship. "The parking lot is packed every time I drive by."

"A good problem to have," he said.

She wished she had that problem. Filling her plate with a little of everything to avoid giving him her update, which would be a big fat downer, she edged around to the other side of the table. "I'm going to dig in before this gets cold. It looks so good."

"Come see me sometime. I was almost your best man once. I still feel like I should be taking care of you."

She hugged him, balancing her plate in one hand high in the air. "You're one of the last few good men."

"Tell Mandy that."

She hadn't even asked about Mandy. It was good to know the two of them were still together. "I promise I will." She gave him a thumbs-up as she made her way over to pour a glass of sweet tea and go outside to find Marie.

Tall gas heat lamps blew warm air across the mild night. With families taking up most of the round tables, she finally spotted Marie leaning against a counter in front of hole 8.

Players had to get their ball around a tricky angle and then through a gator's gaping jaws to the hole on the other side. "That looks hard." She placed her napkin in her lap.

"Must be. No one has made par yet," Marie said.

Angela took a bite. Garvy's food was still as delicious as ever. He was right. She owed him a visit. They'd been so close once.

One by one people took their best shot from the putting green.

Angela's phone signaled new email. Out of habit, she picked up her phone and began flipping through the notifications.

The electric bill.

An email from the artist scheduled to come to the store next week to show her his latest work for an order. She needed to cancel that. No sense wasting his time.

But the next one got her attention.

"'Ho. Ho. Ho. The answer is no'?" She'd read the subject line out loud.

"What?" Marie asked.

"I got an email."

"From who? Santa?" Marie started to laugh and then scooched over to Angela. "Oh gosh. From Santa? Really?"

"Apparently." She clicked on the email.

"What's it say?" Marie hung over her shoulder.

"I don't know." She wiggled away from Marie. "Shh. Stop. Everyone is looking."

"They are not. Read it!"

"He sent it from a private email to prove it's not an autogenerated response." Angela dropped her phone to her side. "What all did you say to him?"

"What? Don't be mad. I was just trying to find out what we wanted to know."

"You mean what you wanted to know." Angela read the rest of the letter. "Marie? What did you say? He knows everything."

"I told him you were going to have to close your business, but if you met a man like him it would be easier."

"You did not!"

"Not verbatim, but something like that."

Angela flipped the phone against her sister's arm. "That is not even funny. Why would you do that?" She lifted the phone and reread the message. "How embarrassing."

"Let me see that." Marie read the note. "It's nice. You can thank me later."

"Or I could kill you now."

Marie scrolled down. "Here's the email I sent. Look, it's not that bad."

Angela read it. "It sounds pitiful, and desperate."

"Well?"

"Stop." She took her phone and shoved it into her purse. "Forget it."

Angela wiggled a finger wave to Scott, the owner of the place, as he took his turn at hole 8. The man teeing up behind Scott was Geoff.

Not again. She scowled.

"What?"

"That's him. The guy from Christmas Galore." He turned and looked right at her. She hoped he hadn't noticed her staring. "His name is Geoff."

"Maybe Santa is already at work. He *is* cute."

"Oh, stop. One has nothing to do with the other. And that would be a pretty cruel joke if Santa sent him to me."

"Remember what Momma Grace used to say?" Marie waved a reprimanding finger in her sister's direction. "If you don't believe you don't receive."

"You're crazy." Angela turned her back on her sister.

As he got ready to putt, she noticed the line of his triceps. He was wearing jeans and a golf shirt, but even dressed down he looked sharp.

Too bad he couldn't have owned any other store in this town.

"Are we going to golf?" Marie asked.

"Sure. Come on." Angela led the way to get putters and balls, then crossed the Astroturf to an open hole.

Across the way a giant elephant sprayed water from his raised trunk up and over a bridge, into a too-blue lagoon. She wondered if the water was that color year-round or if perhaps it was treated with some kind of antifreeze to winterize it.

The business had only opened up for this party. It would remain closed until next May, when the tourists started descending upon the town again.

She made a quick turn to avoid Geoff, who was waiting his turn at the next mat, but just as she stepped up he threw his arm out, throwing her off balance and sending her toppling over a cement lion. Before she could put together what had happened, someone was crouched down by her side.

"Are you okay?" Ali, owner of the hair salon that both Marie and Angela frequented, helped her to her feet.

"Yes. I think so." She swept at her pants, more embarrassed than anything.

Ali looked her over. "That was quite a tumble."

Her anger at the rude maneuver quickly faded as she put together what had happened. Geoff must have caught her with his arm as he launched himself across the green and into the water, because now, across the way, soaking wet, Geoff crouched next to a toddler and a frantic mother. His wet shirt clung tightly to his strong back and muscular biceps as he leaned forward, talking quietly to the child.

Watching him speak gently to the little girl who had slipped into the water tugged at Angela's heart. She hadn't seen that kind of caring in a man in a long time—not since Jimmy, and he'd been gone awhile. Most men were so macho they would've left the comforting to the nearest woman.

Angela shot off toward the building with Marie on her heels. She pushed through the door to the ladies' room, and quickly looked beneath the stall doors to make sure they were the only ones in there.

Marie walked in right behind her. "Are you okay?"

"Yes. I'm fine."

"He's a hero. Did you see him?"

"I did. He was soaking wet. Didn't hesitate one second."

"It's a sign. He literally swept you off your feet." Marie pulled two paper towels out of the machine. "Here. Take these to him so he can dry off."

"I am not doing that. Stop." She crumpled the paper towels and put them in the trash bin. "He's soaking wet. That wouldn't help at all. Besides, he and I are not exactly on friendly terms. Remember?"

"Suit yourself, because he looks pretty fit, and I wouldn't pooh-pooh the idea of helping him dry off if I were you."

"I don't—"

"Ha-ah." Marie waved a finger. "You're a liar if you say you didn't notice."

Angela shrugged then broke out into a smile. "Okay, I may have noticed. His arms are amazing."

"I know. I noticed, and I'm not afraid to admit it." Marie folded her arms across her chest.

"It wasn't exactly a graceful fall." Angela brushed the back of her pants again. She'd definitely have a bruise on her left butt cheek. *Ouch.* "Come on. We've made our appearance. Let's go."

"Fine by me," Marie said.

They walked outside. Half a dozen merchants stood smoking just outside the front door.

"Hey, Angela," Garvy said as he flicked ashes into the flower-bed. "How'd you enjoy the dinner?"

She lifted her hand in a wave. "Dinner was amazing."

"Then why are you leaving so soon?"

"We've got so much to do," she lied.

"You're the hardest-working girl I know. Don't forget to live a little, my friend." Garvy had a concerned look on his face. "And don't forget to come see your old buddy. I miss you."

"I will. I promise," she said.

"I'm holding you to that."

"Okay. Count on it," she said.

Marie had parked right by the door, so Angela hugged her and watched her leave before walking to her car at the far end of the lot, wondering how the man who'd made her skin crawl was suddenly making her tingle.

Chapter Twenty

Dear Santa,
My dad says if I don't believe I won't receive. I'm writing
to tell you I believe even if I tell my friends that I don't.

Thanks,

Mary Elizabeth

The next morning Geoff was in the office on a conference call when Virgil poked his head in the door.

"I'm on mute," Geoff said. "Good morning."

"Hey, just real quick. Your mom wanted me to remind you to send all that stuff over for the Christmas stocking project."

Geoff jotted the note on his desk calendar. "I'll make sure it gets there."

"Good. They aren't sending your mom home today. She's in rare form."

"Oh great."

"Yeah, just wanted to warn you."

"Thank you," he said. Virgil closed the door behind him.

By the time he broke away from the office it was late afternoon. The parking lot at the hospital was nearly empty. He parked in a front spot and headed upstairs. As he passed the nurses' station he stopped. "Has the doctor been in to see Rebecca Paisley this evening?"

"No sir. He won't make rounds again until the morning," she said.

"Too bad. I was hoping maybe my mom had gotten some good news and they'd be sending her home after all."

The nurse just responded with a gentle smile.

He crossed the hall to Rebecca's room. The television was on, but she was fast asleep.

She never seemed tiny, but lying there in bed, she looked different. Less powerful. Less able.

He lowered himself into the chair next to her bed. "Hope you're feeling better tonight," he said, but she didn't stir.

"I'll be glad when you're back to your old self again. The locals like the store. Sales are great, better than we'd even projected. That's the good news."

He paused, looking for any sign of her waking up.

"The bad news is we may experience some whiplash. It turns out the little Christmas store on the point, the one in the old lighthouse building, may go out of business. People are speculating that it's our fault."

He sat there for a moment. She didn't have to respond for him to know what she'd think about that. "I know. It's not a very nice thing to be said about us. In our defense, her store had to already be in trouble, right?"

The machines beeped at a steady pace. Lights blinked and numbers flashed in intervals. "How can you sleep with all this beeping, buzzing and humming going on around you? It would drive me crazy." She laid still, and his heart squeezed.

An older nurse with blued curls and eyeglasses hanging from a beaded chain cleared her throat at the door. Her white shoes squeaked as she walked across the room and began tapping buttons on the machine next to his mother's bed.

He jumped from his chair. "She's sleeping."

"I know. I gave her a little sleeping cocktail in her IV about an hour ago to keep her quiet and calm. She was fussing about missing the Christmas parade. Never heard a grown woman make such a fuss about a parade before." She messed with the machine, pushing buttons, then checking connections. "You know, my momma used to say if you can't get someone off your mind, it's because they are supposed to be there. She'd say, 'The mind can recognize what the heart is trying to deny.'" She quit fussing with the machines, and placed a chubby finger to her chin. "Wait. Maybe it was the other way around. Either way. Don't think too much about it, just let things work out the way they're supposed to." She turned and smiled at him gently. "I'm sure your momma would say the same thing. She told me you haven't given her any grandchildren yet. You might think about that."

Did his mother even want grandchildren? Did this stranger know something he didn't? "How is she doing? I mean, really doing."

The nurse tilted her head. "The same. She's had this heart problem for a long time. She said she was expecting this eventually. She's very peaceful about everything, but Lord, that woman does not know how to take a break. I told her she needs to slow down and let all of this sink in before making any decisions. That's why the doctor suggested the sedative. Maybe some rest will get her thinking more clearly. Or at least just take a minute to think before she makes the decision."

"Decision?"

"She's refusing surgery. Says she's had enough years to think about it."

"She *what?* Why? She didn't tell me about surgery."

"She doesn't have to. I didn't tell you either." She folded her arms across her chest. "Right?"

He nodded slowly. "Right."

"Against the privacy laws and all that. I could get in big trouble." She leaned in close to him. "Since when is it not okay for a family member to know what their momma is going through? Who is the government to tell us when to tell or not? I'm here for my patients. Not the big man on the hill."

"Your secret is safe with me." He hadn't noticed this nurse on his earlier visits. "Thank you. Thank you very much for sharing that with me."

"She'll be awake in a couple of hours. Why don't you come back then?"

"It's hard to leave her."

She smiled wide. "I've been a nurse for more years than you've been on this earth. I know it's the people that come first. Caring is as important as the medicine we treat our patients with. Your momma is good people. Special."

"So are you. Thank you. I guess I'll head on out, and check on her in a couple hours."

"That's a good plan."

"Thank you." He shoved a hand in his pocket and left the room. Was it his place to talk to his mom about surgery? It was her choice. Would he have surgery if faced with the same decision at her age? He wasn't so sure.

Just thinking about it made him tired.

The town parade was this evening. Maybe he'd go and take a

few pictures for Mom. She hadn't mentioned the parade to him, but she loved that stuff. She'd probably like to see the pictures. Wasn't much else he could do for her, and he didn't like feeling helpless.

He ran by the office and finished up what had to be done, then decided to feed his curiosity with a little drive over to the old lighthouse on the point.

He knew about Heart of Christmas, their revenue over the past few years, and footprint. Even their marketing strategies, which were antiquated. Christmas Galore had a team that conducted an in-depth survey on all potential competition in an area before they made a final decision to open a store in a new location.

The only thing Christmas Galore had in common with Heart of Christmas was that they both had "Christmas" in their names. Christmas Galore was so much more. A one-stop shop for everything anyone needed all year round. Heart of Christmas was no different from the other laser-focused Christmas stores in almost every resort town. They only sold Christmas stuff—year-round. Well, Angela Carson's average price point was considerably higher than most of the others'. And she brought art and collectibles into the equation, not just a plethora of Christmas ornaments like the majority of the other stores did. Quite frankly, he wasn't sure how any of them stayed open.

He pulled his car into the parking lot of Heart of Christmas, a shell-sand loop around the building. As he did so, he noticed the historical marker in front of the lighthouse stating its relevancy to the community's history. At least the building was worth something. She had that going for her.

He scanned the cars in the parking lot. There were a few, but not as many as he'd expect the week after Thanksgiving. He didn't see the car she'd been driving at the merchants' holiday party. Then again, she could have more than one. Some people did these days. Or maybe she walked to work. If she grew up in this town it wasn't unlikely that she lived nearby.

He drove around the building to exit onto the beach road.

There she was. Angela. Getting into her car. His heart pounded at a frantic pace, and his palms dampened. Why was he freaking out? Wasn't this why he'd really come? To maybe catch a glimpse of her again?

He idled on by, and then watched in his rearview mirror as she pulled out of the parking space and headed in the opposite direction.

A horn blew, and he slammed on his brakes.

He waved an apology to the man cussing him from the white pickup truck.

"Sorry," he said, motioning to the truck to go on.

The pickup truck blasted past him. He didn't need a translator to know what that guy was screaming at him.

He backed up, then drove around to the front of the building and parked.

Was he really getting ready to go inside? Why? He'd already said they weren't competition. There wasn't one good reason for him to go inside that store.

But he pulled the handle on the door of his car and got out. The shell sand crunched under his feet, leaving dust on the edges of his brown leather shoes. The brick pavers that marked the path to the front door were probably original to the building.

The front door of the old lighthouse was tall and arched. The top half held wavy glass, and in the bottom ocean scenes were carved into the thick wood. The brass handles and hinges had a patina that could only be the result of years of salt water and wear.

He tugged on the heavy door; a soft bell tinkled, announcing his arrival.

Inside he'd expected to see Sheetrock and modern shelving, but surprisingly it appeared to have been kept true to its original design.

"Welcome to Heart of Christmas," a young shaggy-haired man called from across the room. He looked more like he should be hanging ten under the pier than selling Christmas goods.

"Thank you." This wasn't your typical Christmas store. The weathered exterior suggested a lively history, but the old building felt high-end inside.

The display units were all fine wooden pieces. Across the way a cabinet and shelving unit covered an entire wall, at least twenty feet wide, with the most realistic holiday village he'd ever seen. The closer he got the more intricate he could see the details were. The stained glass in the church had lead in the panels. Inside a row of tiny wooden pews complete with hymnals faced an altar. He turned the small red and white tag to see the price, and almost choked.

Wouldn't have to sell too many of those to have a good month.

In this week's circular Christmas Galore had a few Christmas village pieces on sale. Santa's toy shop, a barn and a carousel. Just $19.99 each. The carousel on display in Heart of Christmas put the one they had in his store to shame. Each horse was tacked in unique holiday adornment. The poles appeared to be real brass too. The piece was heirloom quality, with attention given to even the tiniest of details, from the sculpted bells on the harnesses to the texture of the horses' manes and tails.

Then again, it was originally priced as $442. Even at the marked-down price of $150, that would buy a lot of candy canes.

"That's one of our most popular pieces," the salesman said.

"Really? You sell a lot of them?"

"Well . . ." His lips pulled to one side. "A lot of people really like it. The music box inside is handcrafted. It has a beautiful tone." Surfer boy climbed up and twisted the key on the back.

"So you don't sell many."

"Well, these are not mass-produced," he said with a smile.

"Ah. It is nice. Very fine sound." No surprise people liked it. He liked it a lot too, but he'd be hard-pressed to buy something that expensive to only show off a couple of weeks over the Christmas holidays. "Do you have personalized ornaments?" Might as well do some recon while he was here, since his weren't selling.

"Yes. We do. They're over here." He started to walk toward another display near the back. "My name is Jeremy."

"Nice to meet you." Geoff followed Jeremy down a long hall. Several nicely framed articles told of the lighthouse and its history.

"We have sixty-three different ornaments that can all be personalized." Jeremy opened a glass case much like a fine-jewelry case and pulled out samples. "We have wooden, glass, even fourteen-carat-gold ones. We also have some that are occupational- and hobby-focused. What did you have in mind?"

"How about a nice Santa? Something simple."

Jeremy pulled out three different ornaments and laid them on the counter.

Geoff handled each one, noticing the quality of each.

"Just twelve dollars, unless you like the gold one. The fourteen-carat is thirty-eight dollars and that includes the personalization. How many would you like?"

"One. Just one. How about that one?" He pointed to the 14-carat-gold ornament. It was lightweight but unusual. Mom would love it.

"We can engrave it. It won't take long. What would you like on it?"

"Mom?"

"Sure, and how about the year?"

"That would be nice."

"You got it." Jeremy looked pleased with himself for making a sale. "Can I talk you into the carousel? I can wrap it for you. You look like just the kind of guy that would buy something that nice."

He wasn't sure whether to say thank-you or act insulted that this guy thought he was crazy enough to pay that much for a decoration. Didn't matter, because he was about to part with forty bucks for a Christmas decoration. That was a first too. "Not today."

"But you'll be back, won't you? You're our kind of customer. You appreciate nice stuff."

Not in a million years, he thought. But what came out of his mouth was, "Of course I will."

"Good. We're having big sales through the end of the year. Don't miss out."

"What's with all the articles?"

Jeremy looked back down the hall. "The owner. Her great-great-grandfather was the wickie here?"

"What?"

"The wickie. That's what they used to call the dudes who were the lighthouse keepers back then. He and his wife both worked and lived here. When he died, his wife took over. It was very rare for a woman to have that job. But she managed it until the day came that they upgraded with the tall new lighthouse. Too bad this one got decommissioned not too long after that. It's been in the family ever since."

"How did this place become a Christmas shop?"

"When they no longer needed a lighthouse keeper, Angela's great-great-grandmother decorated the lighthouse for Christmas and sold handcrafted ornaments out of the stockpile of wicks that had been left behind to pay the bills. It kind of snowballed from there."

"Interesting."

"Speaking of snowballs, we have a snow room with a real snow machine."

He couldn't have asked for a better lead-in. "Really? Where?"

"Through those doors. It's the first year we've done it."

Just then a group of kids busted through the doors with red cheeks and damp clothes. "That was the coolest thing ever. I love snow," a little boy said, as he high-fived his pal.

"Me too. I want to play in snow every day. We need to move to the North Pole!"

Their father interjected, "It's only fun because you can come out of there and still go without a jacket on your way home. Plus, you don't have to shovel the driveway."

The boys looked stunned for a moment, then started laughing, shouting that it would be totally worth it.

Jeremy led Geoff back to the register. "Will there be anything else?"

"Throw in that sand dollar ornament," Geoff said.

"These are made by Sandy Eversol, a lady who lives in Sand Dollar Cove. She makes a lot of neat stuff for us." Jeremy lifted the delicate sand dollar from the elegant ornament hanger and carefully wrapped it in colorful tissue paper.

"Nice. While you're engraving the ornament, I think I'll check out the snow."

"Snow Valley," Jeremy replied. "Yeah. Enjoy. I'll have this done when you get back."

Geoff went to the back. He could hear squeals and laughter as he opened the door. Wow. Snow Valley was like a miniature theme park. The film-set-type storefronts with benches in the snow were inviting. He swept a handful of snow into his hand—powdery, but moist enough to form a soft fluffy snowball. Totally different from sno-cone ice snowballs. A few groups of people were busy crafting snow art off to one side. A winter castle, a giant ornament, and a team of boys seemed to be building a snowman on a surfboard. Clever.

He hated having to give Angela the score on this one, but she'd totally outdone him. He moved to leave, his wheels already turning on what creativity they could bring to his stores for next holiday season.

When he got back to the register, Jeremy was polishing the engraved ornament with a soft cloth. He tucked it neatly into a shiny red box, then stretched a ribbon of gold around it.

"All set." Jeremy handed the package to Geoff, ready for gift giving.

Jeremy rang up the purchase. "That'll be seventy-seven twenty-eight."

Geoff started to hand over his credit card, then thought better of leaving his name in the pile of receipts for the day. He fumbled for cash in his wallet, and then handed Jeremy a one hundred dollar bill.

Jeremy counted back his change and then placed the ornament box in a cloth bag with the Heart of Christmas logo on the front. "Are you going to the parade tonight?" he asked.

"I'm considering it."

"If you've never been, you shouldn't miss it. Everyone looks forward to it."

"Thanks. Maybe I'll see you there." Geoff noticed the quality of the bag. After that lecture he'd gotten from Angela he shouldn't be surprised that it was made out of some kind of recyclable fabric.

Jeremy raised his hand in a wave as Geoff walked out. "Have a Merry Christmas."

"I intend to." Outside, suddenly feeling nervous that Angela might pull back into the parking lot before he could leave, he couldn't get to his car fast enough.

Chapter Twenty-one

Dear Santa,
Do you have a beard all year? Do your elves live at your
house? Do you get to eat red and green candy all year long?
Did you know peppermint is good for stress? I'm leaving
you candy canes instead of cookies so you won't be stressed
trying to get all the toys to all of us all over the world in
one night.

Thanks,
Bret

Geoff parked behind Christmas Galore.

The annual Pleasant Sands Christmas parade was set to start at six o'clock. He grabbed his jacket and walked outside toward the beach road. Every lamppost along it was decorated with festive wreaths and bows.

Barricades marking off the parade route were already set up at the intersections, and people flowed toward it from every angle.

The banners that normally welcomed people to Pleasant Sands now boasted bright red flags with shimmering snowflakes on them.

Families and friends huddled, talking among themselves as they waited. Some folks had chairs set up along the parade route. Children squealed and bounced around in excitement. It looked like peak tourist season. He took a picture of the crowd to share with his mom. He felt a bit lonely in the crowd. He wished now he'd asked someone from the store to come along.

The *ratta-tat-tat* from the high school band drum line sounded in the distance. Chatter slowed and people edged closer to the street.

The *boom* from a bass drum pounded too, and then the brass section joined in with a blast of horns, and the familiar melody of "Jingle Bells" filled the air. By the time the band was within a few blocks, everyone was singing along.

The shiny instruments bounced from left to right in perfect unison, and cheerleaders wore shiny light-up fingered gloves. Probably bought from his store. They'd had one heckuva run on them recently. After this, more would probably sell. He took out his phone and texted Chandler, saying, "Move the display of those finger LED lights, and the black finger light-up gloves to the front of the store or near the register. They'll be a hit after this parade."

"On it," Chandler texted back.

The band major puffed out a triple-tweet from his whistle and the group started their high-step marching and choreography for about thirty feet before a switch to "Angels We Have Heard on High."

A young woman standing in front of him yelled, "Look! It's Mayor Jessup."

An old '47 Chevrolet pickup truck idled along with its shiny chrome grill making a splashy background for the wreath hanging from the front hood ornament. The sweet cherry-red paint was so glossy that Geoff could practically see his reflection all the way from over here. The mayor waved from the driver's seat. In the back, a blue spruce stood tall and proud with shiny silver garland draped around it, and exaggeratedly large ornaments adorning it in a rainbow of colors. Santa Claus stood in the back, waving and tossing candy canes into the crowd.

Kids scrambled for the candy canes, one of them walking over to offer one to Geoff.

"Thank you," he said to the young red-haired boy.

"You're welcome, mister."

Along the edge of the crowd fancy four-wheel-drive golf carts driven by brightly dressed elves zipped along doing loop the loops as the elves tossed treats into the crowd too.

Geoff laughed at their shenanigans. Mom would have loved this. He snapped off more pictures. It would be fun to share this with her. They hadn't been to a parade together in years.

He sidled closer to the parade route, leaning out to get pictures, when all of the sudden he felt something nudge him. He wobbled then caught his balance and spun around. A big dog stared up at him, drool hanging from one side of his mouth, his tongue lolling as if he had just had a good laugh. "What the—" He brushed his hand across his pants. The dog had left a swath of drool across them. "I just had these dry-cleaned. Man."

"You?"

He lifted his gaze from his lap. Standing right next to the huge dog was Angela.

"Should have known you don't like dogs," she said.

"Everyone loves Rover!" A little girl threw her arms around the big dog's neck. The dog had to weigh 140 pounds. He was huge, and even wearing a silly holiday bandanna he was a bit intimidating.

"This is your dog?" He looked at Angela and then the dog.

"No. It's my sister's dog." Angela rubbed the dog's head.

"He's mine!" Chrissy yelled.

Angela added, "And my niece's dog."

"I love dogs, just not the ones the size of ponies."

"He's a Newfoundland, and he's certified."

"Well, I'm glad he has a job, because Rover can pick up the dry-cleaning tab on these slacks."

"Rover doesn't have a job," Chrissy said. "Who are you?"

"I own Christmas Galore. I know your aunt." He raised his left brow and waited for her to jump in and explain.

"Ohhhhh. You're in trouble, mister, because my aunt wrote a letter to Santa about you. You're a bad man."

"I try to always stay on the 'nice' list," he said.

"Then you need to be nice to dogs," Chrissy insisted.

Geoff couldn't believe he was arguing with a child. "I like dogs."

"Probably about as much as you like Christmas," Angela said with a sneer.

Geoff reached down to pet Rover. "There, there, buddy. I'm sorry if I offended you, but you did make a mess of my pants." Rover took his nose and nudged it under Geoff's hand, then lifted his paw to shake hands.

"You are a smart dog," Geoff said.

"You!" Angela gulped air, then stabbed a finger in the air in his direction. "Quit trying to win over our dog."

The throaty noise that followed sounded more like pain than a sound.

"We are leaving," Angela finally spit out.

Marie, who had arrived at the scene, grabbed her sister's arm.

"That's a good idea." They started to walk, but hadn't gone two steps before Angela spun around to face Geoff again.

"You put me out of business," Angela said.

"I didn't put you out of business. We're totally different."

"My store is special. It's an important part of the history in this town."

He nodded in agreement. "You cover a very nice niche market."

"Don't reduce what I've spent my life doing as some insignificant niche. It's not a niche. It's a whole business."

"I would never call your store insignificant, but clearly it is full of its own virtue." As was she.

"Who do you think you are? You don't know anything about Heart of Christmas, or me." She stepped closer to him and lowered her voice. "I'll have you know . . . the people of Pleasant Sands are very proud of our history. And people love my store."

"Yes. I know, and it's a sweet little shop."

"It's not sweet. It's my business."

"Well, I just meant that it was small. And from the sounds of things it will be not be around for long. I'm sorry to hear that. Maybe we can help by purchasing some of your inventory. You have quite a selection of village pieces. I'm sure they are very popular." He regretted the empty promise as soon as he said it, because there was no use for the type of inventory she carried in any of his Christmas Galore stores.

"You've been in my store?"

Marie tugged Angela by the arm. "We really should get back over here and watch the parade. Come on—"

Angela yanked her arm out of her sister's grip.

"You put me out of business. You and your one-stop, filled-to-the-ceiling warehouse of low-quality junk. No one even cares if what they buy from you lasts through the season."

"And there's something wrong with that?" He shook his head. "It's not my fault that my business model appeals to folks. It's what I do. I'm good at it. Sue me."

"*You* are not appealing at all."

"If you'd been a little flexible in your business model you could have kept your business afloat. It's a charming little store."

"Stop calling my store little, and charming, and sweet. You make it sound like I'm running a lemonade stand."

He wanted to say maybe that was a better idea than what she was doing. At least his merchandise was something people needed at the beach. Who really needed Christmas ornaments in July? That's when most of the customers were in town. But he didn't want to be mean, and his comments had been borderline ugly.

He softened his tone. "I didn't mean to imply that."

"I'll have you know that forty percent of all businesses in Pleasant Sands have only been around an average of three years. Heart of Christmas has enjoyed over ninety years here. We are a cornerstone of this town, and even if it comes to be that I close Heart of Christmas and there is not a store there, that lighthouse will continue to shine on in this town's history."

"You're just a sputtering fountain of local knowledge, aren't you?"

She pressed her hands to her sides. "At least I want what's best for this town. I help bring Christmas magic to this town."

"Yes, well, you won't give anyone else a chance to without starting a war." On that note, he turned to walk away.

There was no sense causing a big scene at the Christmas parade. People were beginning to look.

He wished he were feeling a little Christmas magic right now too. Enough magic to let him disappear.

The last thing he needed was his customers seeing him act like an ass with the town's beloved shopkeeper.

Chapter Twenty-two

DID YOU KNOW?
This year marks the 82nd year since the first Christmas
parade in Pleasant Sands. The first parade consisted
of the local marching band, the fire truck and Santa
riding in a horse-drawn carriage.

"You're just going to walk away?" Angela took a step back as if sizing him up. "Really? Just like that?"

He stopped. "This isn't the place for this discussion. And I've upset you. I'm sorry. That wasn't my intention. I was just here to enjoy the parade."

Her sister stepped in. "Angela, he's right. Come on. People are trying to enjoy the parade." She nodded toward Chrissy, who was staring up at Angela like she'd seen a ghost.

"You're right." Only she didn't walk away. Needing the last word, she turned and leaned in close to Geoff. "I guess you think it's fine to create a tourist trap."

"It's just business."

"That's not the way I do business. I'll remind you too that there are a lot of people that live here year-round. I sell quality items at a fair price. My customers are happy, and so am I."

"You think my customers aren't happy?" Geoff felt his patience slip. "Our customers don't *have* to buy anything. They could easily walk out of my store and drive twenty minutes up the road to the superstore. Or to yours. But they don't. They're buying. From Christmas Galore. Sales are good. Clearly I'm doing something that appeals to the masses. Yes, that even includes your neighbors."

A small grunt escaped her lips. "My store is special. It's unique." She lifted her chin, pressing her lips firmly together in hopes that he wouldn't notice they were trembling.

"It is. I'll give you that." He lifted his chin, mimicking her body language. "Christmas Galore does not need to steal ideas. I was there in your quaint little store because I was curious about the snow after you came and accused me of stealing your idea."

"Oh, and that's supposed to make me feel better? You're stalking me?"

"I'm not stalking you. I was curious, and Snow Valley is very creative. I give it to you, it's way better than our snowball fight. You caught my attention and . . . Oh, forget it."

She crossed her arms and the pulse in her jawline told him she was biting back more she had to say.

"What?" he prodded her. She was cute when she was spun up like this. Her hands balled in fists so tight her fingers looked translucent, and her chest—right there above very nice cleavage—reddened at the pace of a blue crab in a pot of boiling water and Old Bay.

"To you this is a tourist town. To me, to a lot of people . . . this is home. A unique and precious natural resource to be treasured, a string of barrier islands off the coast. Neighbors to the tune of nearly twenty-eight hundred year-rounders who want to help one another. We're just seven feet above sea level here. If I had to guess you probably have plywood stacked to the ceiling back there in hopes of a big storm so you can gouge the locals as they try to protect their properties."

That caught in his throat.

She wasn't wrong.

Every location of Christmas Galore took up precious square footage—a floor-to-ceiling four-by-eight-foot footprint—in their warehouse just for such an event. Plywood and water. "My goal is to sell what our customers need."

Her brown eyes clawed at him like talons. "And riding Christmas just to make a buck." Angela flipped her hair back over her shoulder. "I've heard about your stores. Seen your ads. Your 'Christmas,'" she air quoted, "store in the fall doesn't have anything Christmassy about it. You're as commercial as can be. You're a fraud."

Geoff blinked. "There are Christmas trees set up in our store year-round." Some of them were actually conical-shaped shelves that looked like Christmas trees, but that counted. "And we have one aisle of nothing but snow globes. Over one hundred and fifty different ones across all of our stores." He didn't mention that most were summer and non-Christmas themed, but that wasn't really important at the moment.

"Oh yeah, just to hang random knickknacks, flip-flops, sunglasses and overpriced made-in-China silk-screened items that won't last the length of a vacation, which here in Pleasant Sands is an average of only five days," she shared.

"Didn't your mother ever tell you if you don't have anything nice to say, to not say anything at all?" Geoff asked.

"You're going to talk to me about being nice?" She managed a shrug and said offhandedly, "I can tell you—"

Geoff placed the tips of his fingers against her lips.

She sucked in a breath, craning her neck to avoid his touch, but he'd touched her lips and they were soft. Much softer than the harsh words that had been flying out of them.

"I can see you and I are going to have a lively competitive relationship." He slowly pulled his hand back. "I didn't mean to make you feel second best."

"I do not feel second to you. We are not even in the same space. I own a Christmas shop that has been a part of families' celebrations for generations, and I run it for all the right reasons. You . . . you, Mr. Christmas Galore, are just in it to make money."

"I thought there was room for both of our businesses, but I can tell you if that is not the case, I'm afraid I won't be the one closing my doors."

She turned and stormed off. Don't cry, she told herself. Whenever she got this upset the tears threatened. Heat rushed to her cheeks as she walked by at least ten people who had stepped in closer to get an earful.

Geoff couldn't take his eyes off her as she walked away.

Angela forced a smile toward a burly man with a dark tan and a shock of white hair. "I guess it's not the season for forgiveness after all." She'd never seen him before. Her luck, he probably worked for Geoff.

The white-haired man gave her a little nod and salute as she whisked past him with Marie and Chrissy in her wake. She brushed her fingers across her lips where Geoff's fingers had pressed against them.

"Good heavens, Angela. What the heck was that all about?" Marie said as they practically jogged to the other end of the block. "Hold up. Chrissy can't keep up."

Angela stopped and waited for them.

"I haven't seen you this spun up since the time Momma Grace took your library card after you fell asleep in class for staying up all night reading in your room with a flashlight."

"I loved reading. This is very different." Angela craned her neck, checking to see if she could spot Geoff in the crowd. "He's the enemy."

Marie snorted a laugh. "The enemy? Puh-lease. Angela, you are being way overdramatic. I get it. You're not happy about their store coming to town, but I can assure you there is not a battle plan in their office somewhere. He did not come to the parade to track you down to have words in the middle of this crowd. Which, I might add, is full of customers. Not exactly flattering behavior for either one of you."

Chrissy reached for Angela's hand. "Don't be mad, Aunt Angela."

Angela relaxed a little. "I'm sorry, Chrissy. I'm messing up our fun night." She gave a quick nod toward the corner. "Let's find another perfect spot to watch. I think I see the floats coming."

Marie and Chrissy followed Angela through the crowd, with Rover leading the way.

"Excuse me," Angela said to a man wearing a holiday T-shirt that read, HAVE YOURSELF A SANDY LITTLE CHRISTMAS, across the front, probably from Christmas Galore. "Can we scoot in between you so our little one can see?"

The man stepped back and let them ease in front of him. "Thank you so much."

Marie stepped next to Angela. "You look like you're going to explode. I didn't know you had that in you."

"I didn't either." She looked down the block to see if he was still standing down there.

Chapter Twenty-three

Dear Santa,
I've asked for a pretty pony for six years now and all you
bring me are toy ones. I want the real kind that eat and
poop. Bring me the real one this year or I'm going to have
to go over your head.

Thanks,
Olivia

After the parade Geoff walked back over to Christmas Galore, keeping one eye out for the feisty Christmas shopkeeper. Thankfully he made it back to the store without another altercation.

He walked in the front door and was happy to see that Chandler had already moved the LED finger lights just like he'd asked him to, and at least ten kids were traipsing through the store with them on their hands already. Timing was everything and he always seemed to happen into the next big thing. Like that time in Nantucket when the young pilot whale had beached itself. He'd had two boxes of plush stuffed whales moved to the front of the store and dropped the price. Those whales had wings that day— practically flying off the shelves. What a big week that ended up being.

When Geoff got to his office Virgil was walking down the hall toward him. "Where've you been? I was looking for you."

"I went over to see the parade. Took some pictures for Mom. I thought she'd like that."

"She will. Your mom has always loved that stuff."

"We used to go when I was a kid. I remember the year when I told her I was getting a little too old to go to Christmas parades. She looked so disappointed. I'd wanted to take those words back, but they were already out there."

"It's hard to move backward. Which ties in to what I wanted to talk to you about. When she gets out of the hospital, we need to be sure she takes it easy."

Geoff shook his head. "That *won't* be easy."

"I know. I don't mean to gang up on her but I thought we might be more successful if we were at least on the same page."

"We are," Geoff said. "Maybe we can talk her into taking the whole holiday off. Things are always slower paced in first quarter."

"That's a good thought," Virgil said. "I was going to go over and spend a little time with her tonight. Give you some time off. I'll mention that."

"The nurse said she might sleep for a couple hours, but if she's awake let her know I'll see her in the morning? I'll pick up where you leave off. We'll work this out."

"Sounds good," Virgil said. "I'll tell her."

Suddenly Geoff had a free evening. He went back into his office and gathered his things. Once he got home he downloaded the Christmas parade pictures from his camera onto his computer, then worked on the graphics. Cropping and touching them up. In the one with the old truck, Angela was in the crowd.

He regretted their conversation this evening.

It was bad enough they'd gotten off on the wrong foot. It really hadn't been his intention to put her out of business. Then he'd dug himself into a deeper hole when he gave his opinion on her store. What in the world had he been thinking? He hadn't meant to belittle her store in any way. It really was charming, but clearly she could've done a few things differently and probably saved it from going under.

Why had he gone on the defensive? If he were in her position, losing his company, he'd have been looking for a place to lay blame too. His mother wouldn't be proud of how he'd handled the situation. That hadn't gone well at all.

He printed out the pictures to take to Mom in the morning. Before he closed his computer, he printed one more of the picture with Angela in it.

Carrying the picture with him, he poured a glass of wine and sat down on the couch. Across the way he watched the activity on one of the boats in the marina. A few had Christmas lights strung on them. Another seemed to be getting ready tonight for a day of fishing tomorrow.

It had taken him a while to get used to the boats dieseling out of the marina before sunrise, but now he didn't even hear them leave. After they'd had a good haul he sure did hear them come back and celebrate, though. He fell asleep on the couch holding the picture of Angela.

When he woke up he realized he'd been dreaming of her. Of his mother's desire for grandchildren. Of himself as a father. That wasn't about to happen any time soon.

He shook the remnants of those dreams from his brain and grabbed his laptop. There'd be no going back to sleep for a while.

The Dear Santa portal taunted him. The last thing he needed was his mother coming unglued if more letters had come in while she was away. He'd promised he'd answer them, and he really needed to answer as many as he could for her.

Looking at the dashboard he was happy to see that there weren't too many new ones.

He went through them one by one, then answered the couple that he'd set aside from the other day. He was getting pretty good at this. After he hit *send* on the last one, he printed out the store reports for his mother.

As he flipped from the Dear Santa app over to his email, he noticed an email had been routed from his gotmailnow account to his computer mail. He'd only made that gotmailnow account for one reason: to write back to Anita C. Miracle to prove that he wasn't an autoresponder.

Well, that and to keep up the dialogue.

His heart did a little two-step. He hadn't really expected to ever hear from her again, but he had hoped he would.

He opened her email.

> *Dear Guy Formerly Known as Santa,*
> *Thank you for responding. For being kind. For understanding.*
> *Hearing from you lifted my mood as much as if I'd just received a basket of daisies at just the right time. Daisies are the happiest flowers. I love them. They might be the cheapest bouquet in the store, but they are always full of cheer. Your notes have that effect on me. They make me smile, and I need smiles right now.*
> *It's so funny to me how some people can hide behind "it's just business" when they behave badly. I had a*

miserable confrontation with someone today. I stooped to
his level. I was mean, and I'm never mean.
I'm probably on the naughty list now.
Thank you for spreading joy.

> *Sincerely,*
> *A*

He typed a response.

Dear A,
I wish you all the best. I'm so tempted to say things happen
for a reason, and that something even better is probably
around the corner for you. I believe that. I really do, but
I can imagine it feels like an empty line when you're in the
middle of something like what you are going through.
So instead, I'll say . . . if you were a friend of mine, I'd
bring you a poinsettia and daisy bouquet to cheer you up.
Wishing you a day of smiles, and the most memorable
Christmas of your life,

> *Guy*

He pressed *send*. He felt bad for these people who were losing
their businesses. Especially at the holidays. The economy had been
tough on everyone, but small businesses were the most likely to
get gobbled up in these times. Especially in small towns like the
ones where he had stores.

Before he could even stand to take his glass into the kitchen,
his computer beeped.

A quick glance indicated he had another email routed from his
new gotmailnow account.

She must've been sitting right there when he'd responded to her.

Dear Guy,

Poinsettias and daisies? I can't believe you just said that.
They are both my favorite flowers. I'd never once imagined
them together in the same bouquet. A stunning combination
I'm sure. I have a potted poinsettia on my desk right now.
I'm so tempted to run to the grocery store and buy one of
those little bundles of daisies now. You definitely put a smile
in my day with that thought. And it is the thought that
counts after all. Thank you for that.

Why can't there be more thoughtful men out there like
you?

I've been so focused on my business for all these
years I wouldn't know what to do with myself if I ever
lost it.

All I ever wanted was to run that store. I couldn't bear to
lose it. But now I am.

Running that store is all I know. Okay, well that and a
mind-numbing abundance of history and useless trivia about
the small town I live in. We're a tourist town, but rich in
history. It's a wonderful place to live. And visit. You should
put it on your bucket list. Does Formerly Santa keep a
bucket list? That makes me wonder, can you see the
northern lights from the North Pole? They are on my
bucket list.

Thank you again for the advice. I've decided to close the
doors for good at the end of the day on Christmas Eve.
I hope the big bad Christmas Galore is happy they've
cornered the holiday market in Pleasant Sands.

Merry Christmas,

A

PS—put Pleasant Sands on your bucket list too.

Geoff stalled on the words "big bad Christmas Galore" but when he read Pleasant Sands, he outright lost his breath.

He grabbed for his glass and drained it.

Anita Miracle is Angela?

He looked to the ceiling and rolled his eyes. Why didn't he see that before? It was Angela Carson who needed a miracle. Well, she deserved one. That's all he had to say about that.

And that was the end of any hopes he had about getting a good night's sleep.

He laid in bed, tossing, and then turning. First hot. Then cold. It was a waste of time to try to sleep when all he could think about was those letters. And Angela.

He pulled his pillow over his face, then flung it to the side of the bed.

The next morning, the doctor had released his mother from the hospital, and she was ready to go home. "Are you sure you wouldn't be more comfortable staying with me?" Geoff had never seen her move so slow. "Mom, why don't you let me take you to my house to recover. At least there are no stairs, and if you need anything I could take you wherever you need to go."

"Don't be silly," Mom said. "I've got everything I need here. I can get around just fine. I'm not confined to bed rest, just have to take it a little easier. Maybe I'll get hooked on holiday movies and watch them twenty-four-seven."

"Somehow I can't imagine you sitting in your pajamas in front of the television all day and night."

"True." His mom shuffled through mail that had piled up since she'd been in the hospital. "Half of this is junk mail." She pulled the recycle bin open and started dumping catalogs and circulars into the bag. She started to dismiss the next piece then paused and opened it to take a closer look. "This looks interesting."

"What's that?" He sat down on the couch, crossing his ankle over his opposite knee.

"The town of Pleasant Sands is putting together a new tourism committee. I'm surprised they didn't already have one. This would be something good to get involved with."

"You should do that," he agreed.

She laid the paper aside. "I meant you. Not me!"

"Me? Why would I do that?"

"To be a pillar of the community. Share your knack for coming up with wonderful ideas. It's how you become part of a place. You have to participate."

"What does the tourism committee even do?"

His mother flailed the paper in the air above her head. "I presume they will figure that out together. You'd be perfect. Plus, it would help you get a little balance in your life."

Mom having time on her hands was likely to become a problem for him if she was going to spend it fixing him. "I said we'd both do better, but I'm not sure I want to make a commitment to being on some kind of tourism board. What kind of time would that entail?"

"It'll take whatever time you give it, I suppose."

That was easy for her to say.

She darted around the room checking on her plants, pinching off leaves and twisting the pots toward the sun. "They didn't even miss me."

Finally, she settled down into one of the chairs by the sliding glass window. "It's such a beautiful day."

"You're just happy to be back home."

"You'd have gone crazy in that hospital room too."

She wasn't wrong. He'd have been a worse patient than she'd been. That nurse probably would have kept him doped up to stop him from being a pain in her neck. That'd be one way to get a vacation. Just sleep through it. The truth was, whenever he tried to vacation all he could think about was work. He didn't golf. He didn't boat. He mostly just worked. "I can't argue with you there, Mom."

"So how are we going to slow down?"

"First, we'll delegate some of the things that are easy to take off of our plates," he said.

"If we get that programmer who made my app to put in some exception reporting, that would save me a lot of time on the review of the reporting for each store. I have a very specific set of criteria I look for," she admitted.

"Now you're talking." He'd been begging her to allow him to do some automation for the last two years. He was sorry it took this to get her to budge on the idea, but thankful just the same. It would save him time too. "If you can outline what you're checking, then I can put together the business requirements and get him started on it."

"I can do that. It won't take too long."

"Good. The sooner the better. I was thinking . . . if you need me to continue answering Dear Santa letters, I could do that."

Her face lit up. "You enjoyed it. Didn't you? Admit it."

He nodded slowly. "I actually did."

"I'm delighted to know you enjoyed it. So, now maybe you understand how important those letters are."

"I have to admit I have a very different opinion of them now."

"Excellent. They say everything happens for a reason. Maybe this little episode and my landing in the hospital has offered up some good too."

He had to shake his head. Mom always had a way of turning things her way.

"However, I will take that duty back over. It's almost Christmas. I can handle those, and you all can handle everything else around here until after the holidays."

He stood silent. There was certainly more to this. No way would she back off on everything except those letters so easily. He'd been ready to lay down the law with her. Even call Virgil for backup.

"Why are you just sitting there?" She pulled one balled fist to her hip.

"No reason. Maybe I'm just a little stunned."

"I promised I'd follow doctor's orders. I always make good on my promises."

"Alrighty, then. This is good."

"I'm inviting some ladies over for tea tomorrow afternoon too. Nothing fancy. I'll have Garvy cater it for me. I figure I owe him since I collapsed in the middle of his breakfast rush."

"He's been checking on you. You worried him. You worried all of us."

She waved a hand. "It's going to take more than that to take this old girl down."

"I hope so."

"I've got other things to do. By the way, that nurse of mine has a niece. I told her we'd all do dinner one night."

"Why would you do that? It's the holidays. Our biggest season. I don't have time for—"

"You promised that you were going to cut back too. What better way than to meet someone nice to do things with? You could do a movie or go out to dinner. I heard they have karaoke down at the bar near your condo on Thursdays. Wouldn't that be fun?"

"No!" He didn't like the sound of this at all. "More like funny. I can't sing. You know that."

"That's what makes it fun."

"I'm not sure I'm going to like this side of you."

Chapter Twenty-four

Dear Santa,
If you can't make what I want this year, then you can just
give me tens and ones and I can go shopping online. Or you
could give me a credit card.

Thanks,
Frank

Sales had been strong for the last week, and Chandler had handled every problem with ease. Even with Mom on hiatus, things were going great.

So, the following Friday night Geoff invited Chandler to dinner after work. He and Chandler sat down in a booth toward the back of the Blue Pelican, a nice restaurant that overlooked the water. The blue booths were bright against the whitewashed plank walls. Nautical lights hung from heavy ship ropes, and the windows that overlooked the water looked like portholes. The only pelican in the place was the giant one on the roof of the building. It had to be twenty feet tall, and wore a tiny sailor hat. Geoff had always thought the sailor hat was a weird addition. He hoped that the pelican had found the hat abandoned on the beach, but at twenty feet tall, it wasn't totally unlikely that he'd eaten the poor sailor and kept that hat as a souvenir.

But that was a beach town for you. It had a quirky vibe all its own.

"It's been a while since we've been out to dinner. Thanks for the invite," Chandler said.

"It's been too long."

The waitress brought their drinks to the table and took their order.

"Thank you," Geoff said, then lifted his glass. "To another successful Christmas Galore."

"To many more," Chandler said.

The restaurant was busy, but not packed like a normal Friday night.

The waitress slid by. "Your salads will be up shortly."

"Thank you," Geoff said.

"Everybody must be out Christmas shopping," Chandler remarked.

"I was just thinking the same thing."

"Hopefully in our store." Chandler took another sip of his drink.

The little blue-eyed waitress swung by their table sliding two salad bowls stacked up one arm in front of them, then placed a trio of salad dressings on the table. "Vinaigrette, ranch and Thousand Island. Anything else I can get for y'all right now?"

"One thing," Chandler said.

Geoff rolled his eyes. *Here it comes.*

"Are you an interior decorator?"

The cute waitress looked confused. "No. Why?"

"Because when I saw you, the whole room became beautiful."

Chandler used that tired old line all the time.

She grinned. "You have me confused with someone else. Your

entrées will be right up." She whisked away with a little wiggle in her walk.

Chandler threw his hands up. With a shake of his head, he said, "These girls down here just don't get me."

"Oh . . . I think they get you. But that's a whole other story. I wanted to talk to you about something."

"I wondered what was up with the nice dinner when we're so busy at the store. What's going on? You're not firing me, are you?"

It was hard for Geoff to wrap his head around staying in Pleasant Sands forever, but for his mom he'd do it for a year or two. Then he'd decide if settling down in one place was for him or not, but Chandler shouldn't have to be tied to his decision.

"We're not opening another store next year. We're going to take a year off." He could see the disappointment in Chandler's face.

"But sales are great. So why stay here for longer than the usual?"

"I agree. Sales are terrific, but Mom's ready to call Pleasant Sands her perma-home, and we're going to take one year off opening stores." And surprisingly, saying it out loud, he was feeling good about sticking around too. "I don't want to lose you, though. I know you love the moving around. Being involved in all of the stores."

"I do."

"So, effective January first we're promoting you to sales director. You'll spend your time in all of the stores, however you see fit, keeping them motivated and pushing those sales numbers up."

A smile spread across Chandler's face. "Has my name all over it."

"It does. You can call whatever town you like home. Just let me know where you'd like to land. I'll admit it'll be about seventy-five percent travel."

"You know I'm good with that." Chandler stabbed a forkful of lettuce. "That's great news. Thank you. This is unexpected."

"We've worked together a long time."

"Tell me about it." Chandler groaned.

"Funny."

"That's why you keep me around. Comic relief."

"No. It's because you're great at what you do. You're a pain in the neck. But good. You could use a new pickup line, though."

"Hey, that usually works." Chandler pointed his fork at Geoff. "You wait. She'll be all over this."

"Whatever. We'll announce the promotion at the New Year conference. It'll come with a salary increase and a company car. I thought it might make your holidays brighter knowing what's coming your way."

"You bet."

Chandler paused. "So, I can't believe it. Geoff Paisley settling down in one town."

"Sure. It's a nice little town."

Chandler shook his head. "Never thought I'd see the day you weren't restless for the next place."

"I didn't say I wouldn't be. Just never tried. With Mom recovering I'm trying a lot of new things. I've been answering her Dear Santa queue," he said as he ate.

"*You*? What was she thinking asking you to do that?"

Geoff laughed. "I thought the same thing at first, but don't knock it until you try it."

"Please don't make that part of my new job duties. I *will* quit," Chandler said in a serious tone.

"No worries there. That'll never happen, but I'm going to admit . . . I enjoyed reading and responding to those letters. In fact, I'm a little sorry Mom's taking it back on now that she's

home." Thank goodness he'd routed those letters with Anita—
Angela—to a new gotmail account that he's made just for correspondence with her.

"Well, look at you, Tin Man. Did you pen-pal with Oz to get
a heart?"

"Real funny." But it wasn't so far from the truth; those letters
had softened him in a way he'd never expected. "I have been sort
of writing back and forth with someone else too."

"One of those Dear Santa kids? That's not creepy." Chandler
took a sip of his wine.

"No." *Why did I even mention the letters?* "I've been exchanging
emails with a woman, but I did meet her through the Dear Santa
app."

"Well, sign me up. I haven't found anyone good on my dating
site."

"It wasn't like that." Geoff said. "Anyway, it's a long story, but
we ended up emailing each other. She's nice."

"You're hooking up with someone who sent a letter to Santa?"
Chandler wiped his mouth with his napkin. "Still don't think that's
just a little weird? Does she know you're not, like, a hundred?"

Geoff felt an unfamiliar need to protect his new friend. "It just
so happens Anita is a very nice person. I'm enjoying her letters.
But we haven't met."

"Seriously, Geoff. Come on, man. What kind of woman writes
letters to a Dear Santa app, and then responds to the response?
She's probably a real fruit loop."

"She's perfectly sane."

"Then she's probably a professional con. Hold on to your wallet."

"That's ridiculous."

Chandler hesitated. "Man, I'm just going to say this as a friend.
You need to get out more."

As Geoff watched the hostess walk toward their table, she stopped in the center of the room, just a few tables ahead of theirs.

His heart stalled.

"What's wrong?" Chandler looked around.

"Angela from Heart of Christmas. She just walked in."

Chandler spun around in his chair. "Oh. Let's not have another altercation like the one at the parade, boss. That's all over town. Why can't the two of you be polite to each other?"

Geoff again regretted letting that get out of hand.

Chandler glanced over his shoulder in Angela's direction and turned back nodding. "Very pretty."

"Just because something is beautiful doesn't mean it's good. She was a wildcat the other night. Tore me to shreds." He still couldn't believe that Anita and Angela could be the same person. The two of them seemed so different. Which of them was authentic?

Angela sat at the table alone. Her dark hair hung down her back in soft curls. The way she had it pulled back accentuated her face. She smiled at a couple walking by to another table.

"She is pretty," Geoff said.

"Go make nice with her," Chandler urged.

"I can't do that. Not in another public venue. That could end up catastrophic . . . again."

Chandler leaned forward. "Yes, you can. It's now or never. And if it's never you may as well pack up and head out of town with me."

He had a point. Geoff slid toward the edge of the booth, and then sat back.

"What's the matter now?"

Geoff watched as the waitress brought Angela a glass of tea. "I'm a little nervous."

"You?" Chandler snickered, then pulled his phone out of his pocket.

"What are you doing?" Geoff asked.

"I'm marking this day on my calendar." He exaggerated his typing. "*Geoff. Nervous. With a Woman.*"

Geoff pushed himself out to the edge of the table again. "You're right. She's just like any other woman. I'll walk over, apologize and offer to buy her a drink, or dinner, or—"

"Don't overcomplicate it. Don't bribe her. Just apologize and tell her to have a nice day. Simple."

"Simple." Geoff nodded.

"Right." Chandler sounded like an NBA coach sending his team out after a losing quarter.

"You're right. I'm going to do it. We're done here," Geoff said. He pulled out his wallet and threw down enough cash to cover their dinner with a nice tip for their waitress.

"So done." Chandler rubbed his belly. "Thanks for the dinner, and for the news about the promotion. I appreciate it."

"You earned that, my friend."

"For putting up with you," Chandler teased.

"Shut up." Geoff slid out of the booth and headed for Angela's table, but just as he got ready to stop and apologize he spotted a man with flowers coming toward the table. Geoff slowed, hoping the man would walk on by, but he didn't. Instead the stranger extended the flowers toward Angela.

Geoff turned and gave Chandler the "abort mission" signal, waving his hand up to his throat. They whisked past her table without her ever spotting them.

When they got to the parking lot Chandler started laughing. "Now, that could've gotten awkward real fast."

"You got that right." Geoff clicked his key fob to unlock his car. "At least I won't be apologizing for messing up her date too." He climbed into his car and revved the engine. "Talk to you Monday."

Geoff went straight home.

He couldn't admit to Chandler that Anita and Angela probably really were the same person. It was just all too big of a coincidence to not be the case.

He reread her emails, starting with the very first one. Then he glanced over at the corner of his desk and picked up the parade picture, the one where she was standing off to the side.

He had to apologize, that went without saying, but he was interested too in getting to know more about her. She was passionate about her business, and he'd had a hand in its demise. He couldn't half blame her for hating him.

It was still early. Heavy fog hung over the water like smoke. A dreary day that fit Angela's mood this morning.

It wouldn't take much to just roll over and hide in bed all day. Losing the store was like losing Momma Grace all over again.

For a week now, Angela had put off going public with the announcement about the closing of Heart of Christmas. Subconsciously, maybe she'd hoped that something would turn around, but last night she'd gone over all the numbers again. There was no turning back.

Sweet of Brad to bring them, but the bouquet of flowers mocked her from the side of her table. He was the best brother-in-law in the world. She'd met with him at the Blue Pelican to talk the closing through with him. He'd even offered to renovate the place on his dime if she decided to try to reopen something else in the lighthouse.

The only problem now was she needed to move her inventory; lucky for her everyone was in the mood to buy holiday stuff. If she waited and put the excess up for auction, she'd get pennies on the dollar.

With just twelve shopping days left she was running out of time.

She needed to make that final step forward.

In one quick motion she flung back her sheets and got dressed for a run.

Keep moving, she told herself. *One foot in front of the other.*

Because wasting even one day was a mistake.

Angela raced down the stairs and out onto the beach. The fog was so dense she couldn't even see the pier this morning. It didn't take long before her clothes were soaking wet. She wasn't sure if it was the ocean spray, the fog or tears on her face.

Pushing through the run, which was more difficult than normal with the added weight of her damp clothes, she let out a sigh of relief when she finally got to her backyard. Trudging up the steps, she left her sandy sneakers by the door and went straight to the shower. She was sweaty, but her skin was cold.

She stepped into the shower and allowed herself one last good cry. Promising herself that she'd look forward from this point on, that she'd embrace each tomorrow. Rather than worry, she'd trust that things would be okay, and turn any worry or negative thoughts into moments of gratitude for what she did have. Her health, family, food on her table, home . . . so many things.

She had some money tucked away. Her house was paid for. She could take some time to feel out what made sense for her going forward.

Those letters to Santa had been silly, but they'd also filled a void, and helped her step gracefully over to this mind-set.

She stepped out of the shower and wrapped a towel around herself. Looking in the mirror, she said, "How sad is it that I'm pouring my heart out to Santa? Not even Santa. Some stranger on the internet."

But she couldn't talk to her sister about this. And her best friend, Emma . . . well, it was a shame that they worked together in the store because it was unfair to talk to her about business-related things. On a bright note, she and Emma would surely be even closer friends in the future.

She got dressed, then opened up her computer and sat down to write a thank-you note . . . to Santa.

> *Dear Guy,*
>
> *I just wanted you to know that your notes have brought me strength in a really difficult time of change. What started out as nothing more than trying to appease my niece with a letter to you has been more important to me than you could ever know.*
>
> *I'm at a crossroads. Everything I thought my life was and would be is changing.*
>
> *My store will close. I feel like I've let not only my own grandmother down, she left me that store, but her grand-mother too. It's been in our family that long. My great-great-grandmother handcrafted the first ornaments ever sold there.*
>
> *Running that store is all I've ever known. I'm afraid for the very first time. I have no idea what my future will look like.*
>
> *Thank you for being there—for being a safe place to rest my worries, and for being the daisies in my day.*
>
> *Thankfully yours,*
> *A*

She hit *send*, and went into the kitchen to put on coffee. She tried to imagine a day when she wouldn't go to the store.

A morning run.

A shower.

Coffee.

Then what?

What would she do?

She'd never even interviewed for a job before. She was most definitely not prepared for this.

Fine. So she had a business degree, and she'd run a retail store. If she didn't interview well, who would hire her? And really, why would she want to work retail again? Working for someone else, trying to sell a product that she didn't believe in, didn't seem appealing.

There had to be something else right for her.

She laid across her bed and fell asleep, wishing for a brighter tomorrow.

When she opened her eyes, her hair was mostly dry. She ran her hand through the tangle of waves. She tapped her keyboard, bringing her laptop back to life.

Among the new emails, the one from Formerly Santa sprung her to life.

She pulled her feet underneath her, pulling the computer onto her lap.

> *Dear A,*
>
> *Don't worry. Someone very smart recently reminded me that it's sometimes in the winds of change that we find our true direction. I'm wishing that for you.*
>
> *Be brave, and take that first step to let go of what is dragging you down.*
>
> > *Sincerely,*
> > *Formerly Santa*

She closed her computer and laid her cheek down against the warm cover. Tears fell in a rapid rush. Could she be that brave?

Letting go of the only thing she'd known was scary. Was it true, though, that the longer she held on, the harder it would be to let go? Would another door open? Could she trust the winds of change?

She cursed herself for promising that the time before last would be her last cry. *Don't make promises you can't keep to yourself.*

She changed and pulled her hair into a ponytail, and walked over to the shop.

The front door of Heart of Christmas felt heavier today.

Emma looked up from the cash register with a smile, then a frown.

"Whoa, you don't look so good."

Angela brushed her fingers through her ponytail. "Thanks a lot."

"Are you sick? It's not like you to be late." Emma came around the counter. "Or to look like that."

She shook her head. "No. I'm fine. I just had a couple emails to handle before I came over. How are things going here?"

"Quiet so far. I didn't see you at the parade last night," Emma said. "I was over by the doughnut shop where we were last year. Jeremy came by after he closed up. He said he made a few sales, and thinks he has someone interested in the calliope piece. Wouldn't that be great?"

"Yeah. It would." She looked around the store. "We were at the parade, we just moved a little further up the road to a better spot after I ran into Geoff again."

"Oh no. Is that why you're late?"

"No," she answered with a scowl. "I was responding to another note from Santa."

"Angela, you know Santa's not real. Right?"

"Did you seriously just ask me that?"

"I mean, you're probably talking to some minimum-wage college kid who's working part-time through the holidays to make ends meet. Or someone in another country!"

"I know, but whoever he is . . . he's nice."

"I'm starting to worry about you," Emma said.

"There's nothing to worry about. There's nothing going on with Santa. We're just pen pals. Sort of."

"I guess that'll give you a permanent spot on the 'nice' list."

"That would be nice." Angela helped a customer select a handmade stocking then made her way back over to the register.

"So, Emma. Do you think all this time I've held on to Heart of Christmas I've been keeping myself from seeing or recognizing other opportunities that might be right in front of me?"

A crease formed on Emma's forehead. "You know, they always say when one door closes another opens, so yes, I guess until you put it behind you, you can't move forward."

"I was afraid of that."

"Why?"

"I need to announce the store closing. I had been thinking to close after the holidays, but why not close on Christmas Eve?"

Emma twisted a tag to face forward. "That's just a couple of weeks, but you certainly could do that. Kind of officially end the season on Christmas Eve."

"Yeah, and we'll blow out all the merchandise. We'll mark it all down one time. No haggling, no reducing a little at a time. Whatever I don't sell, I'm going to send over to the church. They can use it, gift it, sell it . . . whatever they want to do with it. I'll just write it all off."

"Wow, you've really been thinking about this."

"Finally, right?"

"I didn't say that, but it's true you haven't really been very vocal about the situation."

"I know. It's not fair to anyone. Or to me. I'm just hanging on to hang on. Wasting time and throwing good money after bad."

"It was not bad money."

"Snow Valley was a waste of time," Angela said.

"But it's fun, and people are making memories. That's important too."

"It is, and that was one of Momma Grace's key questions when we considered something new: Would it be memorable?"

"See. So quit beating yourself up over it."

Angela relaxed a little. Was it talking to Formerly Santa that was making her more at peace with the decision to close, or just that enough time had passed since Black Friday that she was getting used to the idea?

"What will you do, Emma? I mean, after the severance runs out? Do you have any idea?"

Emma nodded. "I'm letting a new door open for me too. My parents offered to help me with tuition to complete nursing school. I've always regretted not finishing. Now that I'm older and more focused, it should be so much easier. I was a little too busy having fun the first time."

"I know what you mean. Although sometimes I swear I feel less grown up now than I did when I was sixteen. Why is that?"

"Because now we know what we *don't* know!"

"True. Now I need to figure out what I will do after I close the doors on this place." Then she picked up a pack of markers from the front desk and walked back to her office, where she drew out several EVERYTHING IN THE STORE ½ PRICE signs.

She then grabbed the chalkboard sign that stayed on the fancy easel next to the front door announcing special events. Carefully she wrote, *We've loved being a part of your Christmas. Christmas Eve will be our last day of service.* In giant letters, across the bottom she wrote, *50% OFF EVERYTHING.*

Angela picked up the phone and called Vonda down at the newspaper, and asked her to work up an ad announcing the store closing.

"That simply can't be," Vonda said. "Heart of Christmas has been a part of this town for as long as I can remember."

"I know. It's time for a change."

"I'll put something lovely together for you. Actually, I think I have a spot for the Sunday paper if I hurry."

"That would be wonderful! I'm putting everything in the store at fifty percent off. What can I do to help us make that deadline?"

"Don't you worry. I'm on it," Vonda said. "It's the least I can do for you. People are going to go crazy for that sale. Fifty percent off. Are you sure?"

"I am."

"Okay, then. We definitely need this in the paper tomorrow."

"Thank you, Vonda." Angela hung up the phone. It was happening. The announcement and ad would run tomorrow. Just eleven shopping days left. She had no doubt the inventory would fly off the shelves. She made a mental calculation of the inventory left. It added up to a tidy sum, even at half price. She picked up her phone and called her sister.

"I won't take but a minute of your time. I know you've got the thing at Chrissy's school tonight."

"What's going on?"

"I'm closing the store on Christmas Eve," she said. A heavy weight hung over her.

"Of course, you are," Marie said. "Three o'clock. That's tradition."

"No. I mean I'm closing the doors for good."

"Oh Angela. I'm sorry, I know this is hard for you, but it'll be better not to drag it out."

"I'm marking everything down. Fifty percent off. It'll be in tomorrow's paper."

"Wow. That's a big sale."

"There's a lot of stuff in the store. Better to get rid of it than to be stuck with it. Can't pay the power bill with a Christmas carving."

"That's true," Marie said with a laugh. "Although I bet the hair salon would take a few decorations in exchange."

Angela smiled through quivering lips. "I'll keep that in mind. Hopefully it won't come to that."

"I'm sorry, sis. You're going to be fine. Better than fine. Something wonderful is coming your way. I just know it."

Angela hung up the phone. At least there would be no more days worrying, or trying to come up with another idea to boost sales. No more wondering *if.*

Now she had a direction, all that was left was to let her team know about the plan. She pulled out the store checkbook and wrote out three checks. She tucked each one into an envelope and wrote the names on the front of each. *Jeremy. Stephanie. Emma.*

Before Jeremy and Stephanie left for the day, Angela brought them together with Emma to discuss the plans to close the store on Christmas Eve.

"Forever?" Stephanie asked.

Angela simply nodded, unable to respond for the lump that seemed lodged in her throat.

Neither Stephanie or Jeremy seemed overly surprised.

She balled her hand into a fist, and swallowed. "I'd planned a severance for you, but since we're not going to work through the end of the year I thought you might like the money for the holidays." She handed each of them an envelope.

"Thank you," Emma said.

Jeremy never looked up.

"I appreciate what each of you has brought to this store and our customers. Please let me know if I can help with a reference or anything."

"We're here for you too," Jeremy said. "I'm going to miss this place."

"Me too," Angela said. She didn't offer anything else. Mostly because she didn't have any other answers, and she was thankful Jeremy hadn't asked her what she planned to do. Because frankly, she had no idea.

Jeremy stood. "I'm not sure I should accept this," he said, turning the envelope over in his hand. "You don't have to do this."

"I know, Jeremy. Y'all have been a big part of this store, though. I want to do this. Really. Please take it."

"Let me know if you need anything. Even after we close," he said.

"We'll all still be neighbors," she reminded them.

Once they left, Angela placed the sale signs around the store, then hung the chalkboard on the front door.

All that was left now was to count down until Christmas Eve.

She wrote one last letter to Santa.

Dear Guy,

Thanks for everything, especially the advice.

Christmas Eve will be the last day my store, Heart of Christmas, will be open. I'll miss it, and miss talking to you.

Wishing you a lovely holiday.

Season's Greetings,
A—

Chapter Twenty-five

DID YOU KNOW?

Pleasant Sands' newspaper, the **PS NEWS,** *started in 1974 as a four-page bimonthly paper. Now it is a daily paper and also offers an online subscription, along with coupons on Sunday.*

Vonda had come through with the Sunday ad and it was so beautiful it had made Angela cry.

The ad had worked. That day the store was so busy, there were times when people were waiting outside for it to empty enough for them to get in. At one point, Angela was worried the fire marshal might be called in.

At the end of the day, Emma counted the till and handed Angela the numbers.

"Wow." Angela sat staring at the register tape. "I didn't trust the tape. I thought for sure we'd overrung something." No mistake. It was a whopper of a sales day.

One day at 50 percent off and she had the best sales of the year. Emma leaned across the table and high-fived her.

Angela heard a familiar knock at the front door of the store. Emma looked surprised. "That's my sister's knock." She jogged from her desk to go open it.

"Surprise!" Marie and Chrissy yelled.

"You two! What are y'all up to?" Angela held the door open for them.

Chrissy skipped inside carrying a tin. "We brought treats."

Marie held up the old Heritage Plaid–patterned jug that Momma Grace used to fill with hot chocolate when they were kids. "Hot chocolate."

Emma rounded the corner.

"Enough for all of us," Marie added.

"I'll get the cups," Emma said.

"Can you believe this?" Angela said. "It looks like we've been robbed."

Emma chimed in, "We had the best sales day of the whole year today."

"That's great news." But Marie looked worried.

"It's okay. I know this isn't sustainable. We're still closing," Angela said. "I'm barely breaking even on some of this merchandise."

Marie winced. "Some of that stuff has been on the same shelf for six years."

"You're right," Angela agreed. "Longer than that. Some of this inventory is from when Great-grandma was still alive."

"Well, it's moving now," Emma announced. "Customers are splurging big-time. It seems like the most expensive stuff is what we sold the most of today."

"That's great news."

"It is." Angela was relieved that there was at least hope that she'd move most of the inventory before Christmas Eve. The more she could liquidate and turn into cash, the better off she'd be.

Emma hugged Angela. "I'm glad it was a good day. I'm going to head out if you don't need me for anything else."

"We're good here."

"Bye, Marie and Chrissy. Merry Christmas." Emma laughed. "Marie. Chrissy. I never noticed that before. *Marie Chrissy.* That kind of sounds like 'Merry Christmas'! How fun." Emma breezed out of the office, and a moment later the heavy arched front door slammed shut.

"She's taking closing the store very well," Marie said.

Angela placed the checks and cash into the bank bag and zipped it up. "They all are. She's going to go back to nursing school."

"I had no idea she'd done that before."

"Yeah. Her parents are going to help her out while she finishes up. Stephanie hasn't said what she's going to do, but Jeremy told me this morning that he's thinking about going to Australia for six weeks to surf with his severance and then figure it out when he gets back."

"Wow. That's exciting."

"It is. Everyone is landing on their feet."

"You will too."

"I hope so. I'm trying to just keep my eyes and heart open to whatever comes my way."

Chrissy tugged on her mom's arm, then whispered in her ear. "Sure," Marie said to Chrissy. She pulled something out of her purse and handed it to Chrissy.

"This is for you, Aunt Angela." Chrissy proudly marched it over to Angela and laid a picture on her desk.

Angela tilted the picture at an angle. The bright blue background had waxy smudges on it, and there was something with a lot of lines on it spreading diagonally across the page. Then it hit her. "Is this a picture of the Dear Santa app?"

"Yes!"

Santa's sleigh and reindeer . . . with a Picasso flair. She reminded herself to never pick Chrissy for a Pictionary partner. "Thank you."

"What's this?" Angela pointed to a wild-haired thing sitting next to Santa. "Is that Santa's elf?"

"No. That's you and Santa riding together in his red sleigh."

"Isn't that fun. I hope I remember to bring a coat."

Chrissy's expression grew serious. "Yes, and earmuffs and gloves too."

"I will. I promise." Angela loved her niece. That kid had one great imagination. "Very good advice. Thank you."

"Can I go make a snow castle in Snow Valley?"

"Sure. We'll be out there in a couple of minutes."

"Thanks!" She ran from the room.

"So you seem to be doing great. I was worried when you didn't take my call today."

Angela pulled her phone out of her pocket. "Sorry, I remember hearing it ring, but I was with a customer. I never even checked my messages."

"That's perfectly fine. I was just worried. I love you, sis. I do understand how much this has all meant to you. I just wanted you to know that I am here for you. I promise things are going to work out for you. I can just feel it."

"Thanks, Marie."

"You want your life to be full. And not just work. Love too."

"That's scarier than being without a job."

"Don't say that. Look at what I have with Brad. He's amazing. You'll find someone just like him."

"What if I find someone like Dad? And he leaves me. That would be more than I could take."

"Angela. Don't think like that. The way he behaved was unacceptable. No question about that. He abandoned us, but I think he really flipped out when Mom died. He couldn't take it."

"I know. I don't know why I brought that up."

"Because you're afraid. There's change coming. That makes everything seem scarier."

"It would be nice to have someone in my life. I envy what you and Brad have. And Chrissy. What a blessing she is."

"Your life will be full. Brad and I are here for you."

"Thank you."

"So, Chrissy and I have a surprise for you too."

"You mean besides the Santa Picasso?"

"Yes."

"Let's go out to Snow Valley with her." Angela led the way.

Marie walked into the snowy space. Chrissy was hard at work building a snowman. Sort of.

"Chrissy, let's tell Aunt Angela about our surprise."

Chrissy came running over to them. "I'm going on a field trip. You get to come!"

"Her school is having a field trip and it's my turn to help chaperone," Marie explained. "I want you to come with us. It's not until they go back to school after Christmas vacation, but you have to come."

"Sure. Why not? Where are we going?"

"The turtle rescue farm," Chrissy exclaimed.

Angela spun toward Marie. "Are you kidding me?"

Marie grinned. "It'll be fun."

"I'm not going to work at a turtle farm."

"I didn't say you were. I just thought it was a great coincidence when Chrissy came home with the permission slip. Perfect timing. Maybe you'll find your Prince Charming there."

"Fine. I guess we'll just have to wait and see how things go. That's still a while off."

"Chrissy, get your things. We need to get home."

Marie held the door open as they all three went back inside.

"Bye, Aunt Angela!"

Marie gave her a hug. "Momma Grace would be proud of how you are handling this." She walked out the door and took Chrissy's hand, turning back to wave.

Angela waved, and then closed the door behind her.

She walked through the store. The place was a mess. Bare spots marked where the merchandise had once sat. Lots of empty spots.

Only ten more shopping days.

It was hard to believe how much merchandise they'd sold today. At this rate, the store would be darn near empty by Christmas Eve. Maybe even sooner.

All that would be left would be the lighthouse. To leave it empty would be a shame, but what could she do here?

What was it that Santa had said? *Well, the guy formerly known as Santa.* He'd said she needed to solve a problem. What did the people of Pleasant Sands lack?

Were there any underserved areas in the business profile of her little town? There were plenty of accommodations, restaurants, bars and souvenir shops. Fishing tours did well year-round. They'd just got the new gym, and that even had spa-related services.

Where did she fit in?

That question made her stomach queasy.

She walked through the store filling in the empty spots where items had been sold with things from the top and bottom shelves, then turning off the twinkle lights on each display. Suddenly the store looked neater and ready for business again.

It was hard to imagine the place any other way.

She grabbed her laptop and started searching the internet for repurposed lighthouses. Some were homes; others had been transformed into bed-and-breakfasts, only she wasn't so sure that was the kind of business she wanted to run. Then again, at the prices some of these were charging she could hire an innkeeper.

But did Pleasant Sands really need another place for tourists to stay? She'd be putting herself in direct competition with people she'd known her whole life.

An alert flashed on her screen. She had a new email.

She smiled as soon as she saw who the most recent email was from.

> *Dear A—*
>
> *I'm quite impressed. That's not an easy decision. See. You are brave. I knew you were.*
>
> *I'm in the middle of a project but as soon as I get things sorted out, would you like to meet for a toast to new beginnings? I'd love to celebrate with you. You said Pleasant Sands is lovely. I hear there's a wonderful Tree Lighting on Christmas Eve. Maybe I'll see you there. I'm easy to spot with the red fur-trimmed stocking cap with the sprig of holly on the side.*
>
> *Maybe we'll even collect shells together as we walk along the beach.*
>
> > *Talk to you soon,*
> > *Formerly Santa*

Meet?

Her heart did a giddy-up. Celebrating sounded exciting, but goodness knows what they'd be celebrating.

I'm losing my business. Hardly something to celebrate.

She'd have to really think about this meeting, and that made her nervous. Her palms were sweating at just the thought. Rather than deal with that she went back to her research. There were several lighthouses that had tours. And if she gave lighthouse tours and acted as the docent she could restrict that to Memorial Day through Labor Day.

She had no idea how much it would cost to keep the lighthouse open without all the hoopla and expense from the holiday lights. They'd been a staple forever. But certainly it would be less expensive without all of that going every day.

She quickly worked up a budget to see what the bare bones would be just to break even on the lighthouse and her own bills.

It wasn't really that much.

Plus she had enough savings to last her a year. A whole year. There was something very comforting about that. Plus liquidating the inventory would provide her with even more of a nest egg.

Tours were always an option, but how many people would want to tour the lighthouse? Especially when there were so many more interesting things to do in Pleasant Sands. It wasn't haunted, and there was no hugely enthralling story tied to it. Didn't even have any historical rescues to speak of, compared to the lighthouses she was reading about online.

There had to be a better solution. All she needed was one good idea.

Chapter Twenty-six

Dear Santa,
How are the reindeer? I'll be asleep when you come, but
my dad gets up real early. You need to bring my toys before
five-thirty in the morning so he doesn't see you. Please bring
him a new pair of gloves. His have a hole in the fingers.

Thanks,

Joe

Sitting at Sunday brunch at his mom's with Virgil felt like old times. Geoff tried to remember the last time all three of them had done this.

It had to have been at least six years ago, but the menu was exactly the same. She'd made omelet croissant boats.

His favorite.

Fresh croissants scalped and gutted, then filled with a mixture of egg, cooked bacon, cheese, seasonings and fresh chives baked in the oven until the eggs fluffed. This was her special brunch recipe. She arranged the boats in a circle on a glass platter like a breakfast regatta next to the bowl of fresh fruit and vanilla yogurt in a cut-glass bowl.

Geoff poured fresh juice for all of them and sat down at the table.

Virgil blessed the food as he always did, with one extra "please, Lord, watch over Rebecca" added in. Geoff noticed Virgil squeeze his mother's hand.

Mom stuck to the fruit, he noticed, but didn't say anything. He was sure it had something to do with doctor's orders, and that made him happy.

After brunch, they adjourned to the living room to help his mother put up her Christmas tree.

The ceiling-scraping pre-lit tree had been a best seller at Christmas Galore a few years back. Virgil had the thing up in less time than it took Geoff to gather the boxes from the attic.

"Almost looks good enough to me with nothing on it," Geoff said.

"No sir. Don't you wimp out on me," his mother said.

"I'm just kidding." He stacked the boxes next to the coffee table. "Just a few more. I'll be right back."

"Tree skirt first," his mother insisted.

Virgil sifted through the boxes. "Here it is."

She unfolded the creamy white fabric and walked out on the deck to give it a good shake and fluff. She slid the door closed behind her, and then spread the skirt out beneath the tree. The silky fabric shimmered. Crystal beads had been hand-stitched into place in the shape of snowflakes, which reflected the twinkle lights from the tree above.

Geoff came back with a stack of three more red-and-green storage boxes. He opened a box of glass balls and handed them to his mother. Then handed Virgil a box of silver stars to hang, saving his favorites, the Twelve Days of Christmas ornaments, for himself. Made of molded mercury glass, each decoration represented a verse of the song, with a small golden number dangling below it. He started at the top with the first-day ornament with the

partridge in a pear tree. Moving around the tree he hung the ornaments in order as he hummed the song, ending with the drummers.

It had been these ornaments that had taught him the order of
those crazy gifts of Christmas in the carol.

His mother peered over her shoulder at him and smiled.

Before long the tree was filled with ornaments, and memories.

"It's perfect." She took a step back, clasping her hands in front
of her.

"Very nice, Rebecca," Virgil said.

Geoff walked around the tree. "No. It's not quite perfect."

"Did we miss a spot?" His mother rushed around to where he
was standing, studying every branch.

"No." He walked over to his jacket on the couch and pulled
out the red box with the gold bow. "For you."

"Oh, I'll put it under the tree. You're so thoughtful."

"No." Geoff touched her arm to stop her. "It's for you today."

"But it's not even Christmas."

"I know that, but I'd like you to enjoy it now too," Geoff said.

She looked like she'd already guessed what it was. "Thank
you." She opened the box. "Geoff, it's beautiful."

"I'm glad you like it."

"This is fourteen-carat gold. Where did you find this?" She
spun the ornament from its fancy hook between her fingers. "It's
absolutely beautiful."

"I bought it at the little shop in the lighthouse."

"Heart of Christmas," she said, exchanging a glance with
Virgil.

"I read in the paper this morning that they're closing shop on
Christmas Eve," Virgil said.

"Goodness. Geoff told me that rumors were going around the
store was in trouble. I'm so sorry to hear that."

"Everything in the store is fifty percent off," Virgil said. "Right off the bat."

Geoff's mouth went dry. He grabbed the newspaper off the counter, and started flipping through it. Virgil had read it right. Heart of Christmas was closing its doors on Christmas Eve. She was really going through with it. Every single thing in stock was marked down half-price. There wasn't even that much of a markup on some of the kinds of things she carried.

"Who's up for dessert?" his mother asked. "I made pumpkin pie."

"With whipped cream on mine," Virgil said.

Geoff closed the paper. "None for me." He'd lost his appetite. Although he knew it wasn't his fault Heart of Christmas was closing, he felt bad for the stress he'd added to Angela's already difficult situation.

Filled with regret he sat down on a bar stool.

Virgil twisted around from the couch. "You worried that going-out-of-business sale is going to throw our sales off?"

Geoff shook his head. "Not really. It'll certainly pull a certain amount of the holiday spend, but what we sell is so different."

"What's the matter, then?"

He could never hide his moods from Virgil. "Just sorry a family business is going under," Geoff said.

His mother walked out of the room and came back carrying two plates. She handed Virgil his, then took a seat in the blue recliner where she always sat. "It is sad. The lighthouse is on the historic places list, so that will still stay on the town's radar. Maybe that new tourism board will think of something to do with it." His mother had a sly grin on her face.

Virgil shoved a forkful of pie into his mouth. "You know, your mother was telling me that you might volunteer for that committee. They are merging the retail merchants group and the business development committee into this new tourism board. They'll be looking at the brand of Pleasant Sands as a whole. You know, coming up with a marketing plan and showcasing the town to optimize tourism."

Geoff hadn't contacted the mayor about it, but the mayor had sent him an email about it too. He wasn't entirely certain that his mother hadn't told them to send that email. He wouldn't put it past her. "I don't know that I have time for all of that."

Virgil's bushy eyebrows rose. "You don't *not* have time for it, boy. That board will drive the demographics and tourism rates for all of us in business in this town. You could do good things as part of that team."

Rebecca smiled gently. "You should share your experience. You're a natural at branding."

Maybe he could offer something of value to that tourism board after all. "Well, it is the season of giving."

His mother sat forward. "Are you thinking about it?"

"Would that make you happy?" he asked.

"Delighted. Absolutely delighted. And proud."

Geoff wasn't sure he'd ever seen his mother look happier.

"I'll contact the mayor in the morning."

Chapter Twenty-seven

Dear Santa,
You are the nicest man in the whole world. I bet Mrs. Claus
loves you a lot. I want to be just as nice as you. Only I
don't think I could give all the toys I made away to people.
But I could give away the ones my elves made. If I could
just have one elf all to myself I'd be happy.
                                              Thanks,
                                              Abigail

Sales had been swift all day on Monday at Christmas Galore. Geoff took packages to the post office for Mom at lunchtime and the parking lot at Heart of Christmas had been full.

There was business enough for all of them. Or maybe he just wanted to believe that.

The post office parking lot was overflowing into the lot of the restaurant next door. He parked and walked across the median, balancing the boxes. The line was long, but the three postal service employees were working with great efficiency in their Santa hats, and it was moving quickly. He listened in as neighbors shared their holiday plans with one another.

By the time he got to the counter he'd heard about the scandal at the Brown family Thanksgiving when Aunt Suzy tried to pass off store-bought Southern pecan pie as her own to Aunt Pat. The cookie swap was being held at the local church tomorrow night. Someone named Gary had a hip replacement. Three women talked about the deals they'd gotten at the closing sale at Heart of Christmas and what a travesty it was that it was closing. Then about a man who had sold his truck to help pay for rebuilding an old lady's kitchen that had gone up in flames in a Thanksgiving Day incident. And how adept the Pleasant Sands Fire Department had been in getting there fast enough to catch it before the whole place went up.

This wasn't just another town where he owned a business. It was a town of caring people. Most of whom seemed to know one another, and wanted to lend a helping hand. It still had that small-town-gossip edge to it too. He wasn't a 100 percent sure if that part was a plus or a minus. He was only happy he hadn't heard anyone talking about his argument with Angela at the parade. That was a relief.

Once he got the packages shipped, he went back to the office. He answered a few emails, signed some checks and contacted a few vendors that required his attention, then he looked at the six o'clock report that had just come in.

Sales were looking good. Not a thing to worry about.

There was no reason he couldn't spend a little bit of time on that tourism committee. He went through his email to find the one from the mayor inviting him to consider being a part of the new tourism board.

He typed a response to the mayor expressing his desire to get together to share a few ideas in person with him at his convenience.

He'd made the effort. It was in the mayor's court now.

And there was still one other thing he could do to help, no matter how that turned out.

Geoff drove over to Heart of Christmas. The ad in the paper had listed closing time as seven o'clock until Christmas Eve, when they would close at three. Forever.

He glanced at his phone to check the time. Fifteen minutes until closing.

A couple came out and got into their pickup truck carrying two large bags. Followed by two other customers, each carrying something.

Only a few cars remained in the parking lot.

He got out of his car and walked toward the building, pausing once. His fingers tingled. *Was this the right thing to do?*

He sucked in a deep breath, then worked his way to the front door.

A woman walked out carrying a flagpole and three colorful holiday flags, juggling them like one of those color guard girls that march with the band at halftime.

"Do you need help with that?" he offered.

"I've got it, but Merry Christmas," she said, clearly pleased with her purchase.

The door opened, sending the string of sleigh bells jingling, announcing his arrival.

Angela stood behind the counter. He didn't see anyone else in the store. She looked like she was straightening up, getting ready to close. She was pretty in a sweater with beaded poinsettias decorating the front, and sharply creased black slacks.

"Hi." Geoff walked over to her.

Her smile fell with the flash of recognition. She looked around almost in a panic. "What are you doing here?"

"I wanted to apologize." He took slow steps, as if afraid she might bolt. "We kind of started off on the wrong foot."

She nodded.

"Your sweater is pretty. Very Christmassy." *How stupid was that?*

"Thank you. Poinsettias symbolize good cheer and success. Not that I'm feeling all that successful these days, but since they are supposed to bring wishes of merriment and celebration . . . it seemed fitting."

Who knew even flowers like poinsettias held certain meaning? Roses, he knew, but this?

She cocked her head. "Are you here to make me an offer on my inventory?"

He shook his head. "No. No, I am not. The truth is, the things you sell here are way too nice to be in one of our stores. You and I both know that."

She stood there staring at him. Then shrugged, as if nudging him to continue.

"I'm sorry," Geoff said. "That day that we had words, and I said I might be able to help by purchasing some of your inventory, I'd like to believe I was offering an olive branch. But the truth is I was trying to be the big dog. That was unkind, and I'm not proud of it. I apologize."

"That's not necessary." She shook her head but didn't make eye contact.

"It is. I'm sorry. I also want you to know that when I said your store was charming, I did mean that as a compliment."

She relaxed a little, giving way to a partial smile. "I was a bit emotional that day. I'm sure I took it out of context. Thank you for the apology. This store is very special to me."

"I'm sure it is. The day I was here in your store, Jeremy told me you had family connections to this place."

"I do." But she didn't offer any further explanation.

The momentary silence was awkward. He cleared his throat. "I bought my mother one of those fourteen-carat-gold ornaments. I gave it to her yesterday when we decorated her tree. She loved it."

Angela looked surprised. Or maybe confused.

"Jeremy is quite a salesman. He would've sold me a lot of things if I hadn't scooted out so quickly."

She smiled, but the way her lip pulled to the left it looked more like a nervous twitch.

Boy, he'd really made a bad first impression.

Talk about something she's interested in. That was always Virgil's advice, for as far back as Geoff's junior prom. "This building is really unique. I can only imagine what it looked like at night when it was a functioning lighthouse."

"Not too much different, once you get rid of all the shelves and inventory. The building is the same." She looked up wistfully. "I bet it was magical back in the day, though. I've seen black-and-white photos, but I'm sure they don't do it justice."

"Yeah. I'm sure you're right." Her eyes lit up when she talked about the lighthouse. "Jeremy said your great-grandparents worked here?"

"My great-great-grandfather. He was the lighthouse keeper here." She looked around, as if seeing things from another perspective. "Back then there wasn't much around here except for this lighthouse. Pleasant Sands wasn't even a town yet."

"That sounds really lonely."

"I don't think so. He and my great-great-grandmother married very young. He was only twenty and she was seventeen at the time. They had two children. I think it was probably a quiet and purposeful existence. When he died, she took over the position as lighthouse keeper."

"The wickie," he said, remembering Jeremy explaining that.

She smiled wide. "Yes. She was the wickie. Not many people even know what that is."

"I have to admit I only know because Jeremy explained it to me. I find it fascinating."

"Yes. It wasn't uncommon back then for a wife to take over after her husband died. It was kind of the only way women happened into those positions. So, she was one of the first women lighthouse keepers working for the coast guard. The first in North Carolina."

"Sounds like a big deal."

"It was, although I'm sure she just thought she was doing the right thing by her husband and for her family. She was a strong woman. Very capable. She had no idea that she'd later be part of lighthouse-keeper history. She finished what her husband had started and loved. They had a purpose in this town's history. I admire that."

He was charmed by the lilt of her voice. The respect for her family's history. "Strong. Capable. Like you," he said.

Her smile was gentle . . . humble. "I don't know about that."

"That was a compliment," he said quietly.

She shifted her gaze back to his. "Thank you."

"So, is that why you bought this lighthouse?" he asked. "Because of your family ties."

"I didn't buy it. I inherited it. My great-grandmother was the one who'd purchased it. When this lighthouse was decommissioned my great-great-grandmother was suddenly out of a job. For four years she watched it sit empty and fall into disrepair. It must've been heartbreaking for her to watch, and she still lived right here in the lighthouse-keeper's house across the way. The same house I live in now. They owned that."

"Your roots do run deep in this town."

"They do. I'm proud of them."

He didn't even have a taproot. Didn't know his father. His mother had no living relatives. Besides Mom, Virgil was the closest thing to family he had, and they weren't even remotely related.

"When the government finally put the lighthouse up for auction, she scraped together every cent she could spare. Her bid was meager, but somehow hers was the winning bid. Folks say she was probably the only bidder. I don't think anyone else could see the lighthouse being good for anything other than its original purpose."

"That's when it came to belong to your family?"

"Yes. It was Christmas and she'd used every bit of her savings to buy that place. She was widowed, trying to raise her children. It had been a risky move, but she hadn't been able to let it go. To her, this place was her husband."

"She was still mourning his loss."

"Yes. I believe so. I think that's why she took such a risk to buy it. In the storage area, there was a stockpile of lanterns, globes and wicks. That Christmas she decorated every square inch of the lighthouse. Not with anything in mind except to honor her late husband. She made handmade holiday ornaments out of the leftover supplies. People raved about them and she ended up selling them. That's when she realized she could earn extra money for food and gifts for her children for Christmas."

"Did it work?"

"Clearly." She raised a hand like *take a look around*. "That's when Heart of Christmas was born."

"Heart of Christmas. I see what she did there."

"Yeah. In her journals she'd said this place kept her sane. I still feel her presence here. I was little when she died, but I can still remember the way her blue eyes danced when we came to see her here."

"So, that's how you know so much. From her journals."

"That and talking to people." She propped her hip against the counter. "Pleasant Sands is rich with history. I like being a part of it."

He nodded. Looked around the store. It looked as if her half-price sale was doing well. There were lots of empty shelves already. "Angela? I was wondering . . ."

"Yes?"

"Can you ever forgive me?" He wanted her to say she could, but he knew now just how much all of this had meant to her.

"You didn't put me out of business. You were just the last shove. I'm sorry I blamed you. It was much easier than taking the blame myself. I let my grandmother down. And her grandmother too." She shook her head and looked away.

"I understand more than you think. Family businesses come with a lot of pressure. Christmas Galore looks like a big corporation, but it's a family business too. My mom started it. I've worked by her side since I was old enough to work. I've learned everything I know from her."

"I guess you do understand." She clutched her heart. "It's a part of who we are."

"Yes. Most definitely."

The clock in the store chimed off the top of the hour. She glanced at the clock, then back at him.

"So why is it that you came?" she asked.

"You're closing. I know. I won't hold you up. I really did come just to apologize."

"That was nice of you." She smiled, not a forced smile, just an easy smile that made her cheeks redden and her eyes sparkle.

"Oh, you know . . . that calliope. The carousel. Do you still have that?"

"I do. It's over here."

He patted his pockets. "Could you take a picture of that and send it to me? I think I know someone who'd be interested in it."

"Sure." She took her phone and snapped a picture of it. "Where should I send it?"

"Here," he said, taking her phone from her hands. He keyed in his phone number and sent the picture to himself. "Thanks. I appreciate that."

"You're welcome," she said, looking a little unsure.

"Goodbye," he said, backing his way to the door. "Good talking to you."

She lifted her hand in a wave.

He stepped outside and let out a breath. He'd managed to get in, apologize and get back out before he pissed her off. That was good. He patted his jacket pocket. Plus, he had her phone number.

Two days later, he was sitting in the Crabby Coffee Pot when she walked in.

Her green sweater would look like a candidate for an ugly

Christmas sweater contest on anyone else, but somehow, on her . . . it looked cute.

She stepped to the counter and ordered.

He felt self-conscious as he watched her. Practically stared. Her smile was genuine. If he didn't know better, he'd think she didn't have a care in the world. She dropped a tip in the big glass jar on the counter, then picked up the cardboard tray with the four whipped-cream-topped coffee drinks and headed for the door.

"Hello," he called from his table.

She spun around. Her face lit up when she saw him. "Hey there."

"How are you?"

"Great," Angela said, walking over to him. "We're so busy. I just ran over to get coffee for everyone."

"Convenient. Right across the street, practically," he said.

She nodded.

"So," he said. "I was wondering, do you have white lights or colored lights on your Christmas tree?"

"Is this some kind of quiz?"

"No. I mean, I've seen your store. It's quite fancy, so I'm wondering what your personal Christmas tree looks like."

"Oh, that." She juggled the carton, then pushed her hair back from her face with her shoulder. "Well, normally, I'd have colored lights, but I didn't put a tree up this year."

"What? Why not?"

"I just didn't feel like it. With everything that's going on with the store and all."

"All the more reason to do it."

"I didn't have time to buy one. Silly. I know. I love Christmas

275

trees. I guess I'm having my own little pity party. I just couldn't get myself geared up to go pick out a tree." She flushed. "Don't tell anyone."

"I bet you like real trees."

"You really have to ask that?" She cocked her head.

"Probably not."

"Yes. Real trees. Always. Even in the store, which I know folks think is a terrible fire hazard, but I don't care. I'm careful and keep them watered, and the real trees make all the difference. When there aren't real trees to be had, I just use the shelving and let the other decorations take a bow."

"'Take a bow.' I like that turn of phrase. So, you don't sell trees in your store?"

"No. We used to have live-tree sales during the season, but the local Rotary Club does a great job, and there wasn't enough profit in it for us all to be doing it, so I let that go a few years back. I know I'll probably regret not having a tree this Christmas next month."

"Why next month? Christmas will be long over."

"Vacuuming random pine needles for months is one of the best parts of having a real Christmas tree." She took a deep breath in, as if she was remembering the smell right now. "That scent. It instantly revives memories."

"Sounds like a big mess to me," Geoff said.

"Why are you looking at me like that?"

"Just . . ." He liked her smile. Her energy. "You're a very neat person."

"I suppose you have a fake tree."

Sheepishly, he said, "Guilty. Pre-lit, even. White lights. And yes, we sell them. I can hook you up," he teased. "I know the owner."

She gave him a wink. "Thanks. Yeah, I'll pass."

"You take care."

"Merry Christmas." She turned and pushed open the door with her butt and headed across the lot toward her shop. He counted every step she took until she crossed its threshold.

Chapter Twenty-eight

DID YOU KNOW?

There were many female lighthouse keepers (the Society
has 80 on file), but most obtained their position when
their husband died or became incapacitated.

"I'm back. Coffee for everyone," Angela said. "Today's special. Mocha Peppermint."

"Whipped cream and sprinkles?" Jeremy asked.

He was such a man-child. "Of course!" She loved these people as much as if they were her own kids.

"What took you so long?" Emma twisted a cup out of the cardboard holder and lifted the top to lick the whipped cream. "So good."

"I ran into Geoff Paisley."

Emma turned her back toward the door. "Christmas Galore?" she stage-whispered.

"Yes," Angela said, as if it was no big deal.

"I'm surprised you made it back with the coffee," Emma said, only half joking.

Jeremy slid past Emma. "Glad you didn't throw it on him. I heard about y'all's run-in at the parade."

Angela blushed. "I may have overreacted that night. We're fine. He stopped in the other night and apologized."

"He did?" Emma looked taken aback. "Here?"

Jeremy walked over. "Look, I know he's the competition and all, but that day he came in . . . I mean, I didn't know it was him at the time . . . but he was really nice. Even bought his mom an ornament. One of the nice ones. Had it engraved and everything."

She remembered him telling her about that. "He, by the way, had glowing things to say about you too, Jeremy."

Jeremy grinned wide. "See. I told you he was a great guy. Must be smart too. Probably a genius."

Emma slid the cardboard sleeve from her coffee cup and hurled it at Jeremy. "You're so full of it."

"Hey now," he said, dodging the projectile. "Just saying the guy has good taste. That's all. He's still the enemy."

"No." Angela shook her head. "No enemies. We are *not* stooping to that kind of behavior around here. We're all neighbors. Things will work out the way they are supposed to. We are all going to land on our feet. We're fine."

"You're right." Jeremy nodded.

Emma shrugged. "Fine."

Angela sneezed.

"Bless you," Emma said.

"Don't you get us sick," Jeremy said as he grabbed the other cup of coffee and took it out to Stephanie, who was still ringing up customers.

"I never get sick," Angela called after him.

"We better get out there and help her." Emma led the way.

Angela was relieved to not have to say anything else about Geoff Paisley.

Customers piled into the store. It was good to see people she hadn't seen in a long while, although so much merchandise was moving that the store didn't look half as beautiful as it usually did.

It was a little like watching someone waste away as they grow old and die. She'd mourn the loss of this store, but she couldn't think about that right now.

People were excited about the sale, but they also seemed to enjoy staying to share their memories of the store and her grandmother.

Angela's heart felt so full from all of the stories. This place had served well for generations.

Friends from high school, and other storeowners who rarely got the chance to shop during normal retail hours, had made a concerted effort to come over and see what kind of keepsake they could grab.

Her demise was their good fortune.

By closing time that night there wasn't a single nativity scene left in the store. From the least expensive one to the thousand-dollar one, on sale for five hundred, every last one had found a home.

She put together the nightly deposit, then spent two hours moving things around in the store to fill in the empty spots. She was able to consolidate things to free up two shelving units, and the back room was now empty except for boxes for items still on sale.

Today she'd sold the train set too. The customers had taken the train with them, since they already had some track, but would come back and get the tracks after the holidays. It was oddly quiet without the *chugga-chugga choo-choo* going on all day. Funny how it had become just part of the background to her.

Angela placed her hands on the edge of the breakfront she'd

just emptied and pulled herself up. Her fingers gently dragged across the dark wood of the wooden counter. These custom pieces of furniture were so big and heavy. There's no way she could use them in her house. There simply wasn't room.

A couple of customers had asked if she'd be selling the furniture.

She'd said yes, but she had no idea how to put a price on these pieces.

Not only did she have no idea what the value was, but also whatever investment there'd been in building the pieces had far been outlived. Did she even really want to part with them? Even if they just sat here collecting dust?

That was just silly.

I'll put the can't-say-no price on them. If someone wants to pay me that much money, I could have a no-regrets price.

So she did. She hopped down and grabbed a piece of card stock and her fat black marker. She cut the card stock in half, making two card tents. With tall thick strokes she put a price tag of $1000 on each one, and the words YOU MOVE IT below.

She could live with selling the pieces at that price with no regrets.

Out in Snow Valley, Jeremy had raked some of the snow back to the edges. The snow machine was shut down for the night, so it was perfectly quiet.

Out here it seemed like a real snowy evening, where sounds were blanketed, and the outlines of everything softened.

She sat down on one of the benches, tucking her hands between her legs to keep them warm.

Across the way the number of snow sculptures had multiplied over the past couple of days. The soft blue LED lighting shone over them, making it seem like a snow palace out here.

She got up and walked through the aisles of sculptures.

A three-foot-tall candy cane.

Santa's sleigh.

She couldn't really figure out what a couple of the sculptures were supposed to be. They sat next to a detailed Santa sculpture. The way the snow was carved, his eyes had that Santa twinkle to them.

A stack of holiday boxes.

And a train.

Some were big. Some were small. Some simplistic, and some looked professional. Some were half-baked messes, while others were quite detailed and worthy of being on display. The staff wrote each contestants' name on one of the surplus of china holiday dessert plates to display next to their entry. After the contest, she'd give each entrant their plate with their name on it as a keep-sake, along with a picture of their sculpture. A way for them to remember Snow Valley and Heart of Christmas forever.

It didn't really matter who won. It was all to bring fun and joy. So really, everyone was a winner.

Her nose began to run, so she went back inside, turned off all of the lights and grabbed the zippered bank bag.

She locked up and walked over the bridge home. The night sky was inky black with what looked to be a million stars twinkling above.

At seven-thirty Angela still had energy to spare, so she hopped in her car and drove to the bank to night-drop her deposit. One less thing to do in the morning.

With just six shopping days until Christmas she headed to the mall to do the rest of her shopping for Marie, Brad and Chrissy. Everyone else she knew would be getting a gift from the store. She'd already tucked favorite items to the side for them.

Chapter Twenty-nine

Dear Santa,
My dad and his girlfriend don't like me to play video
games. I like video games. I'm really good at video games.
Could you bring me video games? I can keep a secret.
                                        Thanks,
                                        Steve

Geoff sat in the parking lot waiting for Sandy's Florist & Gifts to open. He'd had the idea in the middle of the night and hadn't been able to get back to sleep. So here he was, waiting.

Finally, the florist unlocked the door.

He got out of his car and walked inside. The entrance alert didn't have the gentle chime like most stores in town. Instead it had the deep groan of a lovesick humpback whale.

He hadn't even noticed that the last time he was here. "Hello, again," he said to the florist.

"You're back soon."

"I am. I'd like to get a bouquet this time."

"Excellent. I can help you with that." The woman wore an apron that carried the slogan THE EARTH LAUGHS IN FLOWERS. He was pretty sure that was a Ralph Waldo Emerson quote. It was appropriate for his visit, since that's exactly why he was here. To take Angela flowers that might make her smile. They'd look good on the counter next to her register, and she'd said that daisies were the happiest flower in one of her letters to Santa. They'd make her happy. It was the least he could do.

"I've got roses and mixed bouquets already in the chiller over there." She waved her arm across the way. "Each one is marked."

"Yeah, well, I want something special."

"What did you have in mind?"

"Poinsettias and white daisies."

"The poinsettias are on the rack by the window. White daisies are in the bucket right over there, on the front row. How many would you like?"

He looked over at the rack by the window. Those were the potted plants like he'd bought for his mother. "I mean, together. In one bouquet."

"Oh? Well, no one ever asks to do that, but poinsettia is a lovely bouquet flower. I'll have to put it together for you. If you're in a hurry I can do it now, but it will take me a little bit."

"I can wait."

"Excellent! Deep red, pink, salmon or the white poinsettias?"

"Red, of course."

"Of course." She grabbed a potted poinsettia from the rack, then got the bucket of daisies and carried it to the counter too. "Would you like them wrapped in paper or arranged in a vase?"

"Vase."

"Large or small bouquet?"

"The size you put on the counter in a shop. But don't go cheap."

She smiled, and then pulled a big red vase that was as squatty as it was tall out from under the counter. A wad of sticky foam went in next. Then she snipped, dipped the ends of the cut flowers in a solution and arranged the poinsettias first. Then she wired the long stems of the daisies and tucked them in between the poinsettias. "How about that?"

"It's great. Very pretty."

She stepped back. "That's really nice. I'd love it if someone thought to bring me this. Just makes me smile looking at it."

"That's exactly what I'm going for."

She wiped her hands on her apron and rang up the arrangement.

He paid with his credit card then left, anxious to deliver the beautiful bouquet to Angela. He put it in the passenger seat, half tempted to seatbelt the vase to be sure it didn't spill on his leather seats, but the store wasn't that far. He'd just drive carefully.

The front parking space was open at Heart of Christmas so he pulled right into it, then walked inside carrying the arrangement. He felt awkward as heck. It seemed like such a great idea last night, but now he felt kind of like a schmuck. He walked over to the register. "I'm here to see Angela," he said.

The girl at the register grinned. He swore if she started singing "Angela and Geoff, sitting in a tree," he'd pour the flowers over her head and run. But she didn't. Thankfully.

"I'm so sorry," she said. "She's home sick today. She has a terrible cold. Can I help you?" She glanced at the flowers. He hoped she thought he was just the flower deliveryman.

"I'll come back," he said.

Hightailing it back to his car, he was glad no one else seemed to notice he'd been there.

She was sick?

She'd seemed fine yesterday.

He glanced back toward the house over the dune. She'd said she lived there. In the old lighthouse keeper's cottage.

He drove around the block. Her car was in the driveway. If he was going to knock on her door he'd better have a pretty good excuse.

An hour later he was pulling back into her driveway with a Christmas tree overflowing out of the trunk of his sporty red Mercedes.

He wrestled the tree out of the trunk and carried it up to her door. Then he walked quietly back down the stairs to his car and got the tree stand and the flowers. Lord, this was turning into one big production.

He balanced the tree against the porch railing and tightened the bolts on the stand. He could straighten it once he got it inside.

That tree had looked big on the tree lot.

Now, up here on the porch, it looked a little scrawny.

He picked up the flowers and gathered his courage. Balling up his fist, he rapped on her front door.

His muscles twitched, body threatening to run away, but when she opened the door there was no turning back. Her hair was a mess, nose red, and a wad of tissues filled her hand.

Angela looked from him to the flowers to the tree balanced against the deck railing. "What is all of this?"

"Flowers." He thrust the arrangement into her arms. "For you."

"Poinsettias and daisies?" She admired the bouquet. "These are beautiful."

"And a Christmas tree." He held up his hands, which were black with sticky sap. "The real kind."

"Why?"

"Because I heard you were sick, and I thought we could be

friends. You're nice. I enjoyed talking to you. I don't want you to regret not having a Christmas tree next month."

"That's pretty lame in light of bigger matters. Like, what am I going to do for a living now?"

Uh-oh . . . she was snappy. "I don't know. I am sorry for that. It—"

"Don't you dare tell me it was just 'business,'" she said.

"Fair enough." He thrust the tree closer to the door. "Can I bring this thing inside?"

She moved to the side, and he took that as a yes.

As he wiggled the tree through the doorway, she leaned toward him. "It was personal to me. I'm trying so hard to be brave."

"You're very brave." He peeked around the edge of the tree. "Where should we put this?"

Setting the flowers down, she pointed toward the living room.

He said, "You bring this beautiful town to life in a way that no one else can. When you're feeling better I'd love for you to show me more of Pleasant Sands."

"I don't know if that's a good idea."

"Why not? Are you seeing someone? I just assumed. Oh gosh."

"No," she answered quickly. "I'm not seeing anyone. Not really."

"Were you meeting someone that night I saw you at the Blue Pelican? The guy had flowers."

"You were there? No. Well, kind of." She looked like he was forcing her to confess, but all he was doing was standing there.

"So, you're not going to tell me."

"That was my brother-in-law." She shrugged. "The closest thing I've had to a date is exchanging letters with this . . . guy. I don't even really know him. It's silly."

"Are you dating him online? I've never done that myself, but I guess busy people like you and I don't have much time for meeting people other ways. I hear it's pretty popular."

"No, we just haven't met in person yet."

"But you won't show me the town because of *him*?"

"He's special." She walked over to the Christmas tree and tugged on a few of the branches. "Unique."

"You've got a crush."

"I'm not a kid. This is not a crush."

"Mmm-hmm, you've got a crush on someone you've never met."

"That's ridiculous," she said.

"Is it?" he asked.

She looked away.

"He must be very good-looking."

She pushed on the tree to straighten it.

"I'll get that. Hold it there." He climbed under the tree.

She stepped back when he finished. "Yes. That's perfect. Thank you."

"You're welcome."

"I don't know what he looks like."

He put his finger to his lips. "So, you don't know what he looks like, never met, and yet you can't show me around the town . . . because of him? Do I have that right?"

"I—"

Geoff gently placed his fingers on her lips. "Do you think you could just relax?"

She let out a breath.

He held his hand in place. Speaking softly, he said, "I just wanted to do something nice for you. I hope you feel better soon."

"Thank you for the flowers. How did you know I loved daisies?"

"You told me," he said. "I'm going to let you get some rest. I'd love to come decorate that tree with you. And I want to pick out an heirloom piece from your store as a very special gift for someone. Something I can pass down to my daughter someday. Will you help me? When you're feeling better?"

"You have a daughter?"

"No. Not yet." He forced a smile. He'd never said that out loud. Not to anyone. "But someday."

"Yeah. I'll help you." She sneezed, then grabbed another tissue. "Have you ever been married?"

"No. Never."

"Me either. I almost was once. But he had a great job offer, and I didn't want to leave here. Pleasant Sands will always be my home, so I let him go. It was the hardest thing I ever did."

"I bet, but at least you knew what you wanted. Nothing wrong with that." He walked to the door.

"I wish I knew what I wanted now." She shook her head, but didn't continue. "Thanks again."

He opened the storm door. "You're welcome."

She waved from the middle of the living room, so he pulled the door closed behind him and left.

Chapter Thirty

The next morning, Angela was still fuzzy from all of the cold medicine, but she did feel better.

She got dressed and walked over to check on the store. Emma had graciously offered to manage everything while Angela was under the weather, but staying away was harder than it sounded. She walked over, and found the place to be a hive of activity.

So busy, in fact, that neither Emma, Stephanie nor Jeremy even noticed her at first.

Between now and Christmas Eve there'd be a lot of shopping. There always was. Most men wouldn't start shopping until tonight after work.

Emma helped a woman to the cash register. "Merry Christmas," she said to the customer, and then hustled over to where Angela was standing next to the last few tree skirts they had in stock.

"I told you to stay home and get well."

"I know. I couldn't help it."

Emma took Angela by the shoulders and spun her toward the

door. "You look awful. Go walk down to the pier and get some of Garvy's soup. That'll make you feel better."

"That does sound good. The walk on the beach might clear up my head too."

"Exactly," Emma said. "Go on. We've got this."

She knew they could handle it. "You're right. I've got my phone if you need me, though."

"Quit worrying. I'll talk to you later," Emma said as she shooed her out the door.

Angela walked down the side path and over the dune, kicking off her shoes, she carried them as she walked from the edge of the surf to the pier.

She climbed the splintered wooden stairs to the pier, and took a seat in Big G's Fish House at a table near the window.

"Angela? Good to see you. Heard about the store. I'm so sorry." Garvy wrapped her into a bear hug.

He was such a good man. Shame on her for letting her breakup with Jimmy form a wedge between the two of them. Garvy had always been such a good friend.

He finally let go of her. "So after Christmas . . . what are you going to do?"

She was going to have to be able to answer that question at some point. "I don't know. Right now I'm just focused on the sale and getting the inventory out of there."

"Well, don't worry. Something will work out."

"I know."

"You get in a pinch you can always work for me," he said.

Lord, she hoped it didn't come to that. She couldn't imagine working around Garvy's cooking every day. She'd never be able to resist it.

"What can I fix you? Your lunch is on the house."

"You don't have to do that. I'm not flat broke."

"Doesn't matter. It's the only thing I know to do. Let me do it."

"Then, thank you. I came to get a bowl of your homemade soup."

"You got it, girl." Garvy disappeared back into the kitchen.

She sat at the table, feeling thankful for the people in her life. A few minutes later one of the waitresses brought her soup to the table.

She dipped the big round spoon into the broth. It tasted as good as she'd remembered.

Garvy came back out to the front of the restaurant. "Good?"

"It's *so* good. Thanks, Garvy."

"You need anything, please know I'm here for you. One more hug then I've got to get to work on tonight's menu."

She stood and gave him a hug. "Thanks, Garvy. I'm going to be around a lot more. I promise."

"That makes me very happy. I've missed you." He went back into the kitchen, and just as she lifted her soup spoon to her lips, Geoff walked up to her table.

"Hey," she said. "What are you doing here?"

"Are you feeling better?"

She dabbed her napkin to her mouth. "I am feeling better, thank you, and thank you again for coming by yesterday. That was so thoughtful . . . and unexpected."

"Because you expect nothing but bad things from me?"

"I'm sorry. That wasn't fair."

"It's okay. I deserved it. I saw you talking to Garvy when I first came in. He's not your 'guy,' is he?"

"No. We're friends. We go way back. He was almost the best man at my almost wedding. Well, the wedding that didn't happen."

"Oh. Gotcha. I was surprised to see you sitting here. I didn't notice your car in the parking lot."

"That's because I walked down."

"That's a good hike."

"Not that far. I usually jog a lot further than this, and back. When I'm not sick."

"You're a runner?"

"Sort of. I like to run on the beach. Not just run to run."

"Me too. We should jog together sometime."

"Uhh." She put her spoon down, resisting the urge to give him a smarty-pants response. Instead, she said, "Yes. I guess we could do that. I like to run first thing in the morning."

"Count me in. Any time." He nodded to the chair. "Can I sit?"

"Sure. Join me."

"Thanks. My mom lives between here and your house on the beach."

"She does?"

The waitress brought a glass of water for Geoff. "Will you be having something?"

"I'll have what she's having. Thank you," he said, and then turned back to Angela. "Yes. Mom lives in the blue three-story with the white shutters."

"Wait. Does your mother live in the *Dune Our Thing* house?"

"Yes. That's the one. How'd you guess?"

"I know that house. The folks that used to live there were great. They had these dogs. Labs. Those dogs loved running the beach. They were getting so old. I remember when they put the elevator in so the dogs didn't have to go up and down the stairs."

"An elevator?"

"Yeah."

"I don't think my mom even knows there's an elevator."

"It looks like a closet door with another door inside it. If I remember correctly, on the third floor it's off the kitchen hall. Downstairs it's in the closet to the right of the entryway."

"Doesn't that beat all? My mom just got home from the hospital. An elevator would make me feel better about her getting around that big house."

"Nothing serious, I hope."

The waitress brought his soup. He paused. "I'm not sure. It's a heart thing. She's not telling me much. She had an episode here in the restaurant at Thanksgiving."

"I heard about that. They took her in an ambulance."

"Yeah. That was my mom." He tasted the soup. "This is great soup."

"I know. That's why I came. So, I'm so sorry to hear about your mom. Let me know if you need me to come by. I'll show her how the elevator works."

"Thank you." He looked so appreciative.

She spotted the hefty old man Wally, who'd lived here as long as she could remember, walk in the side door. He had long white hair and a beard, with a Willie Nelson–type bandanna around his head. Although he was a longtime staple here in Pleasant Sands, from the look on Geoff's face as Wally walked toward the table, Geoff hadn't encountered him before.

"Hey, Wally," Angela said.

The old man put a hand in the air, then tick-tocked his finger back and forth.

"Oh, I mean *Santa,*" Angela said.

He leaned in and handed her a sticker that read, I MET SANTA. She'd probably collected a hundred of these over the years.

"Thanks, Santa." Angela wondered just how weird it would be if her Santa turned out to be the mute Santa who'd hung around the pier for going on twenty years now. Rumor had it that it was

PTSD. That Wally had been some kind of war hero at one time. Now he lived in a cottage at the far end of the beach.

As Wally moved on to another table, Geoff asked, "Or is *he* your guy?"

"No. He's not. I'll be honest. I've never been much of a Santa fan."

Geoff sat back in his chair. "So let me get this straight. You own a Christmas store and you're not a Santa fan?"

"True. The store is important to me because of my grandmother. The history of the building. The story. If it hadn't been for Momma Grace—she was my grandmother—and for that store I don't know where we'd have ended up."

"We?"

"Me and my sister." Why was she telling him all of this? "My mom died when we were little. I guess my dad kind of flipped out. One day he dropped us off with my grandparents here in Pleasant Sands. He never came back."

"I'm sorry. I never knew my father."

"I'm not sure which is worse, but you must know how I feel. I wrote Santa letters asking him to please bring Daddy back. Of course that never happened. I guess I never forgave Santa."

"Easier than not forgiving your dad."

She'd never really thought of it that way before. "Yeah. I guess so."

They finished their soup, then Geoff asked, "Can I walk you back?"

She placed her napkin on the table. "Sure. Why not?"

They walked down the beach, talking mostly about the weather. Angela gave him a little history lesson about Pleasant Sands, and shared stories about some of the people who lived in houses down this stretch of the beach, until they got to her cottage.

You could just see the lighthouse tower peeking above it.

"This is me," she said.

"I enjoyed today."

"I did too."

He shifted weight to his other leg. "Do you think maybe I could come back over tonight and help decorate your Christmas tree?"

Her mouth dropped open.

"I could bring dinner with me. A bottle of wine, maybe?"

"How about eggnog?" she suggested. Definitely safer than drinking wine with him. "Yes. That would be nice."

He grinned wide. "Good. Thank you. I'll see you tonight."

Chapter Thirty-one

DID YOU KNOW?

Though occupied for several centuries, Pleasant Sands
became an official town in 1953 when it received its
municipal charter, after being purchased by Roger and
Dolly Pleasant for $240,000 several years prior.

Angela watched Geoff walk down the beach toward the pier, where he'd left his car.

How many times had she run that very same track of sand?

He didn't seem to care that the bottom of his pants were dragging in the water. She'd always loved that feeling too. Lots of people rolled up their pant legs or avoided the wet surf line, but that was where she always felt most connected. Where the sea met the sand.

The crushing churn of the water continually changed the coastline by moving rock particles, sea life and skeletal remains onshore, offshore and along the shore, and unearthing delicate shells and colorful sea glass that visitors would collect and cherish along with their memories here in Pleasant Sands.

An unmistakable feeling of glory filled her.

She walked up to the house, kicking her shoes off at the back deck, but standing there watching him.

Was it Geoff making her feel this way, or just relief to be feeling better?

Now that she was saying goodbye to Heart of Christmas, was she so desperate to connect to something that she was imagining Geoff as perfectly wonderful?

Not long ago she thought of him as her mortal enemy.

Now she couldn't take her eyes off him.

Her phone rang, pulling her from the trance.

She rushed from the deck to her kitchen to answer the phone where it sat on its charger.

It was Geoff. Her heart instantly beat out a samba as she lunged for the green button. "Hi! Geoff?"

"I had fun today."

She walked over to the doors that led outside. She could see him. "Me too."

"I'm looking forward to tonight."

"Me too." He waved from down the beach. "See you shortly."

Her heart sang.

Angela felt better, but now that Geoff was coming over she was running through her house tidying up. A heap of tissues were on the floor next to the couch where she'd been parked last night, too tired and snotty to get up and go to bed.

She didn't even know what time he was coming. So, she went ahead and showered and changed into a pair of jeans and a three-quarter-sleeve baseball shirt that said, I'M IN TRAINING FOR A CHRISTMAS MOVIE MARATHON.

Too casual?

She took that T-shirt off and put it back in the drawer, then changed into a white T-shirt with a waist-length red cardigan with pearl buttons. Christmassy. Nice. But not too anything.

She checked the fridge to see what she even had in the house to eat or drink. He said he'd bring dinner, but she needed to at least offer something else to drink. A person could only drink so much eggnog.

Sweet tea would have to do. She put a pot of water on the stove and made the tea, then poured it into a clear glass pitcher with a cranberry handle and brightly colored holly berries painted around the belly of it.

She placed it in the refrigerator to chill.

Excited now to get started, she retrieved all of the Christmas boxes and red plastic holiday storage containers from the storage closet and laid them out in the living room. She opened the box labeled *CHRISTMAS-Colored Lights* in crisp black marker. Each strand of lights was neatly wrapped around a plastic cord handler. She scooted the whole box near the electrical outlet and began plugging them in one by one to test them. To her delight, every single strand lit up perfectly. Was that a first?

She sat on the floor next to the other boxes and started looking through the ornaments. There were so many pretty ones. Some were very fancy. Others one of a kind. But she knew where her very favorite ones were. She spotted the box, ratty and scuffed, but she'd never had the heart to transfer the contents to one of the new storage bins. The box had once been solid red with green wreaths printed on it. Now it was faded to almost pink. The box had probably originally held a wreath. It was square and nearly two feet wide, but only about six inches deep. She lifted the worn lid. Two layers, protected with tissue paper in between, of hand-made ornaments.

These weren't the ones she and her sister had made with Momma Grace over the years. There were plenty of those, and they were special too. But these were from generations ago.

A loud rap at the door startled her. She leapt to her feet and ran to the door.

When she pulled it open, Geoff was standing there wearing a Santa hat and carrying a large paper sack in one arm, and another Santa hat with stuff in it in his other.

"Come on in. You've got your hands full!" She motioned him in and followed behind him.

He put the paper sack on the island in the kitchen. "I hope you like Chinese food. I got a little of everything."

"I love it. Perfect."

"Great. I'm not sure how it will go with eggnog, but a promise is a promise." He held the Santa hat by its white furry trim and pushed it toward her. "This is for you."

Tiny silver bells along the white fur jingled as she pulled it close to her, then dumped the contents on the island.

"This is crazy! What have you done?" There was a bag of mini–candy canes, and four boxes of swirly decorative ornament hooks. Half in silver, the other gold. Which made her start humming the old Girl Scout song in her head.

. Make new friends, but keep the old.

One is silver and the other, gold.

If anyone had told her that she'd feel this kind of friendship toward Geoff Paisley a couple of weeks ago she'd have thought they were nuts.

She pulled the Santa hat onto her head. "I think we're ready!"

He picked up his phone and pulled her closer, extending his arm to take a selfie of them in their matching Santa hats. "The obligatory selfie."

They both grinned, then made a goofy face.

"Good one," she said. "Send that to me."

"Will do." He lifted a carton of eggnog out of the bag. "Right after we get this into the refrigerator?"

"Sure. Should we eat while we decorate, or did you want to eat first?"

"I'm good with eating while we work, if you are," Geoff said.

"Me too." They gathered up the Chinese takeout cartons and carried them into the living room to the coffee table.

Geoff looked around. "I'd have helped you get all these boxes out."

"I know." She shrugged. "I was excited."

He cocked his head. "Good. I am too."

She opened one of the boxes of Chinese food to see what was inside. "Beef and broccoli?"

"Yes. Here." He pulled a menu out of his pocket. "The numbers on the box are from the menu here."

"Yum. I'll have the General Tso's chicken if that's okay."

"Whatever you want. I like it all."

"Ahh. Hedging your bets."

"Well, I'm pretty smart like that." He picked up the box with the number 6 on it and dug in. "So, I'm going to admit. I'm feeling a little anxious about this whole tree-decorating thing after seeing your store. I mean . . . I hope I'm up to the task. The trees in your store are like those in magazines."

"Thank you," Angela said. "I'll take that as a compliment."

"As you should. So where do we start?"

"Lights. No matter what. Lights first," she said. "I already tested all the strands." She picked up the box full of lights and carried it closer to the tree.

"Let me h——" he began, but she was already at the tree.

"I'm quite capable."

"I can see that." He took one of the strands out of the box. "Start at the top, right?"

"Yes. I'll go get us some iced tea, if you want to get started."

He stretched his arms to the top of the tree and began walking around it, letting the cord lay along the branches.

When she walked back into the living room she noticed he was just wrapping the lights around the tree.

"What's that look for?" he asked.

She hadn't realized her expression was painted on her face. "Umm. Well." She sat the glasses down on the table. "You need to kind of tuck them in along each branch so you get a nice three-dimensional shimmer of light and twinkle." To soften the criticism she added, "You know, like they do on the pre-lit ones."

"Light and twinkle." Geoff laughed. "Educate me."

He didn't seem offended. Thank goodness. She pulled the lights back to where he'd started and began tucking them from tip to trunk and then out again. "See? You can open the wires a little and anchor them along the ends too."

"Nice. Very nice," he said. "I think I've got it."

They spent the next hour taking turns eating and placing the lights along the tree branches, coaching each other along the way. Geoff had plugged the lights in midway so they could catch any empty spots, and there'd been a few. Each blaming the other for them, of course. "This is going to take a ton of lights," he said.

"Did you know the average Christmas tree takes one hundred lights for every foot and a half of tree? I'll admit, I use probably three times as many as that."

"There are some advantages to a pre-lit tree," Geoff said.

"That just takes all the fun out of getting it right."

"Clearly one of us is better at it."

"Me!"

"I'm going to have to use the squint method," Geoff said. "Stand back here and squint and we'll see where the gaps are."

"Well, aren't you just clever," Angela teased. "Hope our eyes don't stick like this."

"Yeah, not your best look." He squinched his eyes back at her.

"You realize it's going to take you a day to take all these lights back off this tree," he said.

"You're going to come and help me take them down, aren't you? I mean, you can't just do half the job."

She regretted being so forward as soon as she'd said it.

"Oh, I'll be here." He stopped, looked at the tree and then her again. "I'd like that very much."

It was eight o'clock and all they'd done was get the lights right. That and eat.

"Are you sure you're up for decorating the tree too?" Angela was pretty sure Geoff had no idea what he'd gotten himself into.

"Absolutely. All the way to the point we put the tree topper on. Oh, wait. Star or angel?"

"Oh gosh. Is there a wrong answer?"

"I don't know. You don't have a Surfing Santa or a Billy the Bass or something crazy like that, do you?"

She laughed so hard she had to put her glass of tea down before she dropped it. "We've never sold anything like that in my store."

He got caught up in her laughing. "We have."

"Please tell me that's not true."

He raised his hand. "True story. Okay, it wasn't the real Billy the Bass, which was kind of cool, but it was a singing fish wearing a Santa hat with a candy cane hook in its mouth."

"No way."

"Way."

"I have a couple of Christmas tree toppers. All tasteful. I lean more toward the star or the angel."

"Great. Let's get this tree decorated."

She pointed to a red plastic container labeled GERMAN GLASS CHRISTMAS ORNAMENTS. "Do you want to start with those?"

"Sure." He walked over and slid it near the tree.

As soon as he lifted the lid, she knew which ornaments they were.

"Those are glass ornaments that have to be every bit of eighty years old." She opened the lid on the box in front of her. "These are some of the last original ornaments my great-great-grandmother made. They are what started Heart of Christmas." She lifted a star made from an oil lamp wick, and another in a nautical knot. "They aren't fancy, but they're special. I've never seen anything like them."

"I like them." He carried a bright red glass ornament in the shape of a pointy egg with a silver indention on one side and ribbed in a starry pattern. "I think what makes it special is the story."

"You're right." She hung a wick star on the tree. Then another.

The two of them worked their way up and down and around the tree, spreading out the balls and handmade ornaments to create a perfect collision of textures and colors amid the lights.

"Time for the topper?" she asked.

"I think so. Which will it be?"

She took two wads of taped bubble wrap out of a box. Gently she unwrapped them, uncovering an exquisite Christmas angel tree topper first. Her beautiful dress was made of white peacock feathers, with tiny crystals in a circle for the halo. Going to work on the other one, Angela uncovered a porcelain star that had a place for a light to shine through it, to give it a heavenly glow.

"Which one do you like best?"

"The angel."

"Would you like to do the honors?" She lifted the pretty angel and handed her to him.

"I would." He put the topper on the tree, then pushed the angel with his finger until she was straight.

"We're done."

Angela was a little sad to call it a night.

He took out his phone and took a picture of the tree. "That was fun."

"It was. Thank you for the tree. You're right. I would've regretted not having one." She'd have regretted missing out on this night even more.

"You're welcome. I guess I'd better get going, but I was thinking. Maybe, if you're not too busy tomorrow, you could show me around Pleasant Sands."

"Sure!" She'd answered so quickly. She pressed her lips together, catching her breath. "I know everything to do, and just about everyone in this town. I haven't *done* much of it in years, myself. I've been heads-down with my store, but I can be your tour guide."

"I'd like that."

"What's interesting to you?"

"It doesn't matter. I haven't seen anything except what's out the window of my store or my condo."

"We've got lots of history. How the town got started, pirates and all that stuff. Or, there's always the restaurants, or wait, we could go down to the marina and eat. They cook what's brought in live right from the boats. You won't get fresher seafood. What else? Oh, there's—"

"Whoa. Slow down, Miss Pleasant Sands. Let's start with the marina. But we can't just eat the whole afternoon. Let's do something after we eat too."

"I've got an idea. Can I surprise you?"

"I have no doubt that you can," he said with a laugh.

"What I meant by that was . . . do you *like* surprises?"

"Hmm. You know, I can't say that I've ever been surprised. I don't know if I like being surprised or not, but I'm up for giving it a try."

"Great!" She rubbed her hands together. She loved surprises. At least when she was the one doing the surprising. "I'll take care of everything. Where should we meet?"

"I can pick you up, or you could come to my condo if we're going to eat at the marina. Your choice."

She hesitated. At least if she met him at his condo she'd have her car with her. Plus, she was a little curious to see where he lived. What he surrounded himself with.

"I'll come to you."

"Great. How about noon? I'm at 123 Sailfish. Eighth floor."

"I'll be there," she said, as they walked to the door.

"You've got a date."

The word "date" made her gasp. "I—"

"Don't overthink it. I just meant it's on my calendar."

"Oh. Yeah. Of course. Yes, it will be fun."

Chapter Thirty-two

DID YOU KNOW?
Pleasant Sands has 2.7 miles of beachfront.
Most people say three, but that's not true.

The next morning, Angela woke up in a great mood. She was even happier when she walked into the living room and saw the tree again. She turned on its lights, then got her coffee and sat there looking at the tree, reliving so many wonderful holiday memories. She squinted her eyes, blurring the lights like they had last night.

It had been so much fun. She was looking forward to spending time with Geoff today.

She changed outfits three times before finally settling on "attractive, but not trying too hard."

She drove over to the marina into his gated community and parked in front of his building. She hadn't seen the condos up close before. No one she knew lived here. Mostly they were occupied by older, retired couples, or people who were heading even farther south during the winters and would just lock up their condos and leave until spring.

The place had a resort feel to it. Beautiful, but also somewhat temporary. A little too perfect, with manicured shrubs and grass that looked like sod. Every bit of the landscaping was the same throughout the whole complex.

She parked her car in a visitor spot and took the elevator to the eighth floor.

The mat in front of his door was of an old red woody station wagon with surfboards on the top of it. She rang the bell and waited, wiping her sweating palms on her pants.

This had seemed like such a good idea last night. Now it felt awkward to be showing up at a man's condo.

He answered the door dressed in khakis and a blue button-down. His sunglasses hung around his neck from a black strap. He definitely looked the part of a guy living at the marina. More like one who owned a yacht.

"Come on in," he said.

There was no "excuse the mess" or anything, and it was clear why. Everything was picture-perfect. It looked like she'd just stepped into a model home. The ceilings were higher than the normal eight feet. Probably ten, and the height gave the condo a wide-open feel.

Straight ahead of her was a wall of glass doors opening to a patio with a million-dollar view. "Wow," she said, drawn toward it. "I thought the view from my deck was the best."

"It's pretty awesome. And the people are great here too. Most of the fishing charters go out from here, so that's been kind of neat to get used too. Those boys get started early."

"They sure do." She turned and stepped back inside. "Show me around."

He toured her through the house.

"Did someone decorate for you?"

"Yes. I could never put all this stuff together."

"It's very nice."

"Thank you."

There wasn't anything homey about it, but it was very tastefully done. "I'm going to take you to a little spot that only the locals know for lunch. I made reservations for us. We need to head that way or we'll be late," Angela said.

"I thought we were going to eat here at the marina."

"We are. Sort of. Just on the other side."

"Lead the way," he said. "I'll drive."

"I can drive. I know the way. It'll be easier."

She drove them outside of the fancy gated community, down a road that curved around to the back side of it. There on the water, next to four shrimp trawlers, was a shack. Hand-painted across the front was FRESH FRANK'S in big school-bus-yellow letters.

"Don't judge," she said as they got out of the car.

"I didn't even know this was back here."

"Surprise." She walked through the shell sand and opened the door for him.

He stepped inside, letting his eyes adjust to the dimly lit space.

"Hey, Frank!" she called out. "We're here."

Geoff looked at her with surprise, then lowered his voice as he whispered, "This is where you made our lunch reservations?"

She was enjoying this. She knew the place would catch him off guard, but she also knew it would be the best shrimp he'd ever eaten.

"Come on in. Table in the back is for you two," a man's voice came from beyond where they could see.

"Not just anyone can get a table here," she whispered to Geoff. "Come on."

An hour later Frank was sitting at the table with them, still in his apron, telling stories about his days on the trawler. They had come to an end when he got his leg caught in a winch line. He'd gotten so mangled that he'd lost the bottom half of his leg.

He didn't wear a prosthesis. His empty pant leg just hung next to the other, along for the ride.

"Frank, that was without a doubt the best meal I've ever had, and let me tell you, I've eaten at the finest restaurants up and down the East Coast."

"Thank you, Geoff. I'm so glad Angela brought you over. We don't much let outsiders know about this place."

"This is my favorite seafood restaurant, Frank," Angela said. "And don't tell Garvy or I'll deny it."

"Your secret is safe with me," Frank said.

Geoff agreed. "I'm not going to give you up, unless you say you aren't inviting me back."

Angela pretended to be shocked. "That's bribery."

"That's my ticket to great food." Geoff got up and held the door for her. "Where are we off to next?"

"You'll see," she said.

She drove him through town, pointing out historical homes and sharing the stories behind each one. "We have two-point-seven miles of beachfront in Pleasant Sands. Most people say three, but that's not true. And over here is Kite Peak Park. It's second only to Jockey's Ridge in Nags Head near Kitty Hawk."

"I know about Kitty Hawk. That's where the Wright brothers took their first flight."

Angela gave him a sideward glance and a smirk. "Well, that might be what everyone knows about, but did you know that, in fact, those Wright boys actually came up with the idea that turned into that first air machine while vacationing at their grandmother's house here in Pleasant Sands? That house still stands at the corner of Sunnyside and Dolphin. I'll show you."

The name WRIGHT was engraved in the mortar above the front door. "You weren't kidding."

"I never kid about town history."

She dropped him off at six-thirty, happy for the fulfilling day.

On Sunday morning Angela went to church and then opened the store at noon as usual, but with just three days left until Christmas, things were pretty picked over. Most of the inventory now fit in the front main room of the shop.

She'd be perfectly willing to keep the few high-end items that were left for herself.

Customers trickled in all day long, and no one left without some purchase, even if it was just a small one.

At four o'clock Angela was polishing an ornament she'd just engraved when she heard Jeremy talking to someone. "Good to see you again."

She looked up and saw him talking to Geoff, and her heart fluttered.

"Hey there," Geoff said. "Hope you don't mind me stopping in."

"Hi. No, we'll be closing up here in a little bit."

"This place is nearly empty."

She nodded. It was good, but sad at the same time. "Just a few really nice pieces left."

Jeremy said, "Excuse me, Angela, I'm going to go close down Snow Valley."

"Yeah, that's fine," she said.

Geoff watched Jeremy leave, then said, "It looks really different in here. This place is a lot bigger than it seemed when it was full of inventory."

"Did you need something?"

"No. Not really. I was just thinking about you."

"That's nice."

He walked down the hallway that Jeremy had taken him down to get to the special ornaments the day he'd been here. He took the time today to read the framed newspaper articles.

"You told me about some of these things," he said. "I remember you showing me this house yesterday."

She nodded. "Everything on this wall is from the town's history."

"Your face . . ."

"What?" She swept at her cheek, suddenly self-conscious.

"No. It's perfect. It lights up when you talk about these." He looked back at the framed history on the walls. "It's not really the Christmas stuff at all, is it?"

"What do you mean?"

Geoff turned and leaned against the wall, standing between an article about Angela's great-great-grandmother being the state's first woman lighthouse keeper, and one about the Wright family house. "It's this place. The history that you love. And not only the history, but sharing it with others."

"I do love that."

Geoff stepped closer to her. "This wasn't a store. It was almost a museum."

"I've thought about other ways I could let the lighthouse earn its keep, but there's not anything so special about it that it would draw people in, and I don't see myself as the bed-and-breakfast type." Angela walked down the hallway. "I'll figure something out."

"I know you will," Geoff said.

Jeremy came back inside and stomped the snow from his boots on the mat. "All done!" he called out.

Angela tried to hide her laugh. It was as if he was trying to be sure he wasn't going to walk in on them in an awkward situation.

"Tomorrow night my niece is a mouse in *The Nutcracker* over at the auditorium. Would you by chance like to join me?" Angela had thought about it the other day, but it wasn't until now that she'd gotten up the courage to ask him.

"I'd love that. What time should I pick you up?"

"Six-thirty?" Angela was looking forward to going to the show with someone. A first in a long, long time. "It's casual."

"I'll see you tomorrow night, then."

When he walked out the door she was standing there still staring when Jeremy came up behind her.

"He kind of likes you."

"No. We're just friends," Angela said.

"That was not a friendly look in that man's eyes. He likes you." Jeremy pulled on his coat. "I'll see you tomorrow."

"Good night. Thanks for everything," she said. Including that last little bit of information. Was it possible Mr. Christmas Galore really did like her?

Chapter Thirty-three

DID YOU KNOW?
Pleasant Sands is the birthplace of Danielle Shelton.
A student at Pleasant Sands High School, in 1987 she
played the Nutcracker, and won the chance to play a
walk-on role in a soap opera in 1990. Since then,
she has gone on to appear in more than ten movies.

Angela and Geoff sat in the middle of the auditorium waiting for *The Nutcracker* to begin. Children zipped back and forth between the back of the stage and sneaking last-minute moments with their parents.

"There's my sister and her husband," Angela pointed out. "In the second row."

He recognized her sister. Then two little girls raced out from behind the curtain to the second row, hand in hand; one was dressed as an angel and the other was a Christmas mouse.

"It's like watching a Ping-Pong match," Geoff mused. "They are going back and forth, and back and forth. That's crazy."

"They are moving as fast as giddy greyhounds," she said.

"Now, that's a graphic." He placed his hand on her leg.

She glanced at it and for a moment she thought he was going to pull his hand back, but then she gently placed hers atop his.

"Speaking of greyhounds," she said.

He held back a snicker. She had trivia about everything. "Did you know the owner of the most winning greyhound in 2011 was from right here in Pleasant Sands?"

"I can honestly say that I did not."

"It's true. Oh, and my sister called me earlier today. She offered me a position as a secretary in her law office."

"Is that what you want to do?"

"I haven't really done anything else other than work at Heart of Christmas. My sister always said that was a big mistake. I thought she only said that because she was jealous of the relationship Momma Grace and I had."

"What do you think now?"

Angela's mouth turned down. "I'm thinking maybe she was right. I don't have a great fallback plan. My life has been very focused."

"Well, everyone's path is different. There's not a right or wrong way." Geoff thought about all the places she'd shown him over the past week. "You know all of those places you showed me over the past few days? I'd have never known about any of those if it hadn't been for you."

"It's been fun for me." She sat back, offering a gentle smile. "I'm glad we've been able to put our business differences behind us."

"Me too. You're very nice. And smart. You know everything about this town. So tell me, why are all the brochures only about the beach?"

"That's easy. It's why people come to Pleasant Sands."

"It's what gets them here, but what keeps them coming back?"

Her wheels were turning. He could tell that much.

He pushed further. "What do the visitors and tourists in this town do on a rainy day, or after they get their Northern pasty-white skins so fried in the sun that they can't go back out on the beach?"

She laughed so hard she snorted. "It's so easy to pick out the tourists. They always look like steamed crabs. Is there a point to all of this commentary?"

"Maybe. I'm just thinking you need to give yourself a break. Your store isn't even closed yet. You don't really have to take the first job that's offered to you. Trust me, you have a lot to offer. The right thing will happen for you."

"You seem so sure," she said.

"It's the night before the night before Christmas. Christmas magic is in the air."

And he couldn't have planned that comment better, because the curtain rose and the music began as the lights dimmed in the auditorium.

It was Christmas Eve morning, and Geoff was standing on the front porch steps of the Pleasant Sands Town Hall building, freezing.

Across the way in the middle of a green grassy field, the town's Christmas tree stood in the center of the story-and-a-half-tall gazebo. It was as big as a carousel. Maybe it had been one once. He should ask Angela about that.

Town Hall wasn't actually one building but a row of buildings that had been gutted and converted into space for all of the offices the town needed: Zoning, Planning, even the courthouse were all on this one block. There were also several lawyers, bail bondsmen and accountants along here.

All the buildings were sea green with white trim. Scrolling gingerbread with seashells in the corners had been added sometime along the way. It was kind of a 1950s-meets-cottage-style mishmash of architecture.

The mayor walked up, huddled in a heavy wool coat. "It's colder than a . . . a . . ." The rest was just a grumble. "You must be Mr. Paisley." He extended his hand.

"I am." Geoff shook his hand. "Nice to meet you, Mayor. Call me Geoff."

The mayor gave him the once-over and a nod. "Nice to meet you."

"Thanks for meeting me here on such short notice and on Christmas Eve, but I have an idea . . . well, a proposition really . . . that I think you're going to really like."

"I hope so. I've still got Christmas shopping to do."

"I know the guy who owns Christmas Galore," he teased. "I can get you a discount."

The mayor unlocked the door and invited Geoff to follow him in. "So I'm guessing that you're considering our request to have you on the new tourism board. This has been something we've been talking about doing for a few years now. The recent growth in our town has been wonderful, but we're not leveraging it to its full potential. I think having some forward thinkers like you added to our local team can help us make strides toward our goals. I'm looking forward to hearing what you have on tap."

Geoff entered the meeting room at Mayor Jessup's side. The room held a few familiar faces—people he'd seen at the merchant meeting, the local bank branch manager—as well as several people he hadn't yet met.

An hour and a half later the meeting concluded.

He'd not only satisfied his mother by accepting the position on the tourism board, but he'd got exactly what he wanted, right out of the gate.

The group dispersed and the mayor and Geoff were the last in the room. "Thank you for pulling everyone together. I know it was poor timing."

The mayor laughed. "You know, sometimes things have to come in their own time. All of us want what's best for Pleasant Sands. I do believe you will fit right in. I'll contact Angela this evening and talk to her. If she accepts, there's no reason to open the position up for general applicants."

"I agree. She is the most qualified for this position. She knows the history of this town like the back of her hand. She can make the connections so easily, and people trust her around here."

"I don't think there's anyone that disagrees," the mayor said. "With your generous donation, how could we object?"

"You couldn't," Geoff said. He shook the mayor's hand. "Please don't mention that part to her."

"I don't mean to look a gift horse in the mouth, but why are you doing this?"

"I've come to really like this town. My mother loves this town. She has old ties to it."

The mayor lifted his head in surprise. "Really? We had no idea."

"My father was from this town. I never knew him, but now I understand why he loved it."

"He was from Pleasant Sands? I've lived here all my life. I probably knew him."

"He died the summer before I was born. A drowning accident. He was only twenty at the time."

The mayor settled back on his heels. "You would have been Robbie's son. I should've known when Virgil came back to town there was something up. They were best friends. Virgil left and never came back after that summer. That accident hit this whole town hard. Robbie was a good young man."

Something unexpected ran through Geoff. Hearing the void that Robbie's death left behind, even to this day, not only in his mother's heart but in this town made him feel more complete. Like part of something bigger. Connected to something, some place, for the first time.

"I'd really love to talk to you in more detail after the holidays about my father, if you don't mind."

"I'd like that," the mayor said. "I have some great memories from our younger days."

Geoff said, "My mother's health is beginning to fail. She wanted the connection with this place. I just learned of all this recently." He looked around. "But, this place, all of you, the people . . . I can understand why."

"Thank you, and welcome to Pleasant Sands. We hope you plan to make this a permanent home."

"I do."

The mayor patted him on the back. "That Angela is just as enchanting as her grandmother was."

Geoff tried to hide his smile. She was definitely that.

The mayor lifted his fingers to his lip and turned the invisible key, pretending to toss it away.

Geoff gave him a nod and headed outside. There was a certain lift in his step as he came out of the building and headed to his car.

"Geoff?"

He turned. "Yes?" The woman who'd called out to him . . . It took him a minute to place her face as Angela's lawyer sister. "Hi, Marie. It's good to see you again."

"Has to be better than last time. That was ugly."

"It was a bit . . . uncomfortable."

"My sister can be a bit passionate about things."

"That's nothing to apologize for," he said. Although he'd admit, that day he'd thought she was bordering on nutjob. But that was before he really knew her.

"I just came back to pick up a couple gifts from my office. That little girl of mine is quite a snoop. What are you doing here at Town Hall on Christmas Eve?" she asked.

"Well, it's still morning, technically, but I just came from a meeting." He didn't want to tell her what meeting, because the last thing he wanted was for Angela to misconstrue his motives. If she knew he was on that board, she might not stay open to what he hoped would be a happy ending. He hoped too Marie wouldn't ask for more details.

"Oh, well good to see you."

He turned to leave, but Marie's voice carried.

"I know this isn't any of my business, but I hope you'll move carefully around my sister. If you're being nice to her out of some sense of guilt for putting her out of business . . . just stop. She's hurting right now. Grieving the loss of that business. She doesn't need a heartbreak on top of it."

"I can respect your concern," he said. "I assure you my motives are sincere."

"I hope so. Y'all have had a tumultuous start, and I'm just a little wary of the two of you together."

"Afraid we'll combust?"

"Possibly," she said with a smile.

He spoke mindfully, hoping to put her at ease. "I can promise you that I wish we'd opened our store at a different time. I didn't set out to put her out of business. We always scout where we feel like there's enough market share for everyone. The timing was horrible, and I don't like that we had any impact on that outcome."

"Thank you for saying that. My sister is very dedicated, and she wanted to keep things the way they'd always been. Hang on to the past. I'm sure most of her problems came from not adjusting her business approach to the current times, but that really doesn't matter now. I just want to know that you'll consider that when you cross her path."

She clearly didn't know that they'd been doing a lot more than crossing paths lately. They'd been walking paths, together. "You're sort of her guardian angel, aren't you?"

"Sisters are like that. My mom used to say that sisters were angels-in-waiting. I remember Angela's face the first time Mom said that. She looked at her, so wide-eyed and innocent, and asked if she'd grow wings."

"Cute."

"Yeah, but Mom was sick by that time. We didn't know it, though. She'd said, *You girls are my angels, and I know you'll always take care of each other, because sisters are angels-in-waiting. You'll do lots of good things before you become real angels. Make me proud, okay?* I'll never forget her saying that."

"I bet. It's nice you have each other. As an only child, I can just imagine how it would be to know you always had someone beside you."

"Yeah. That doesn't mean we've always seen eye to eye, though. I was the oldest. I was always trying to take care of her. Losing my grandmother was really hard on her. She was so little when we lost my mom, and then Dad ran off and abandoned us with Momma Grace. Don't get me wrong. We had a wonderful life with Momma Grace, but Angela really clung to her for that stability. Always did. It's why the lighthouse and Heart of Christmas are so important to her."

"I'm glad you shared that with me."

"Probably sharing way too much, but I wanted you to understand why she reacted the way she did that night at the parade. She really is the most kind and generous person I know. That was really out of character for her."

"I realize that."

"Good. Well, I'm sure we'll see you around."

"I hope so," he said. And more than that he hoped Angela would give him a chance to prove that his interests were in her happiness. Both business and pleasure.

Chapter Thirty-four

DID YOU KNOW?

The poem "Twas the Night Before Christmas" was
originally titled "A Visit from St. Nicholas." It was
anonymously published in 1823. It has been attributed to,
and claimed by, Clement Clarke Moore but there is
some controversy as to whether he actually wrote it.
Clement is a distant relative of Zane Moore,
owner of Moore Lumber on Shore Drive.

It was almost three o'clock on Christmas Eve.

The last customers had left. Jeremy had officially closed down Snow Valley two hours ago and packed up the equipment to return to Angela's friend in Boone on his way to go skiing, and both Stephanie and Emma had left at noon. There hadn't been enough inventory to even really bother staying open until three, but Angela hadn't wanted to let down even a single customer all the way to the end.

She boxed up the last few ornaments and placed them on the counter. The bigger items could wait until the new year.

She'd be taking some time to figure out what her next steps were going to be anyway. Working for her sister wasn't the answer.

Sure, it was now, and it was convenient, but that wouldn't keep her satisfied for long.

The sleigh bells jingled from the front door. She half expected to see Geoff walk in. He'd been nearly a fixture around here the last couple of weeks.

"Mayor Jessup?"

"Hello, Angela." He unwrapped the long scarf around his thick neck. "It's bitter cold out there today. Dare I say we might actually get a white Christmas this year?"

"I wouldn't. The warm ocean water will keep anything more than a little flurry at bay. You know that." She thought of her note to Santa. The one where she said what she wanted was as unlikely as snow in Pleasant Sands. "Don't tell me you're still doing Christmas shopping at the last minute?"

"Guilty. I've been your last customer the last seven years. Why stop today?" He lifted his chin in a smile, his red cheeks as rosy as if he were Santa Claus himself.

"I'm afraid I'm not going to be of much help this year. With the close-out sale, just about everything is gone."

"A good problem to have."

"Indeed. What was it you were shopping for?"

"Something extra-special. What's the nicest thing you have left? If you were going to be gifted one thing that you have left in the store today, what would that be?"

"Easy. I'd want the calliope. It's been my favorite piece for a long time. Maybe that's why it hasn't sold. I never really was sincere about selling it." She walked over and took it down from the shelf.

"Well, then, you should keep that. What's your second favorite?"

"This piece." She carried a hand-carved Santa from the shelf to the counter. "This is a one-of-a-kind. It's funny, because all of the Jim Shore pieces fly off the shelves, but this one is just as beautiful. And more unique. It's carved out of an old wooden rolling pin."

"You know my Patsy loves to bake."

"I do know that. It's actually kind of the perfect gift for her. The colors are brilliant. The details so refined. Look at it."

He stooped to eye level. "That is really interesting. And unique. I'll take it."

"Excellent. I even have a box that will be perfect for it. Would you like it wrapped?"

"You spoil me so."

"Well, we have done this for seven years running."

He gave her a wink. "Thank you, my dear. You are one of the good ones."

She went to the back room and retrieved the box for the carved rolling-pin Santa. She tucked twisted lengths of tissue paper around the rolling pin to keep it from moving. "She'll never guess what this is."

Angela made quick work of wrapping the gift, finishing it off with a fluffy bow from the gold wire ribbon. "All set."

"It's beautiful. Thank you, Angela."

"You're so welcome."

He handed her his credit card. She rang him up and slid the receipt his way to sign it. "Perfect. Now that my Christmas shopping is done, I do have one other piece of business to settle with you."

"Business? What is that?" She was confused by his comment.

"We are looking to create a town brand, and bring more tourists to the area while evaluating our plan to attract new businesses to our town. We are collapsing the Merchant Group and a couple other committees into one."

"That makes sense." Angela nodded. "What does that have to do with me?"

"We need a tourism director who can lead all of that while retaining the small-town charm of Pleasant Sands."

"You certainly don't want to sacrifice the small-town feel. That is what people love so much about this place. Both the residents and the tourists."

"I agree. Which is why we'd like for you to fill that position."

"Me?"

"You," Mayor Jessup said. "It's a salaried position. Now, there is a hitch. The position is guaranteed with funding from an outside source for the first eighteen months, but we'll count on you to hit targeted goals to ensure that funding of the position is ongoing."

"I don't have that kind of experience," she said.

"You have everything you need. You know this town. You know the people. You will have the support of the tourism board we've put together to help."

"I'm overwhelmed. This is so unexpected." She pushed her hair behind her ear. "I'll put my résumé together, but frankly all I have is this job and a degree. That's it. Not very impressive."

"We don't need your résumé. We need you."

She'd just lost her business. Why was this happening? And why was it happening on Christmas Eve to boot?

But it did sound like a dream job. She'd be able to incorporate the history of the town into things to attract tourists and help them get the most out of their visit there. "We might even be able to create small collectibles to keep them coming back year after year to add to their collections, not so unlike those national park pins or state quarters. People love collecting things. Maybe even town Christmas ornaments. The people that didn't make it back might even be willing to buy those online." Her wheels were turning.

"See. You know exactly what we need. Just say yes. The position won't start until the first full week of January."

It was a lot to process.

"I tell you what. Give it a try. If you're not happy with it after sixty days, then you can resign. All you're wasting is two months of your time. You'll be paid handsomely and you'll contribute with just the ideas you rattled off without even really having time to think about it."

She thrust her hand forward, and shook the mayor's. "I accept. I'll give it a trial run. If either of us is not happy with the progress, on March first we can just walk away."

"That's fair. Now, I must really go before the missus prefers to hit me over the head with the very gift I'm bringing her. Merry Christmas, Angela."

"Merry Christmas."

It was almost too good to be true. Marie would never believe it. She walked with the mayor to the door, and sure as they were standing there, it was snowing.

"I think we'll have a white Christmas in Pleasant Sands after all." The mayor threw his scarf around his neck and rushed to his car, with his shoulder to the wind.

She stood there in the doorway, letting the snowflakes fall over her. She'd thought there was nothing more unlikely than snow for Christmas in Pleasant Sands, but here it was. Had Santa, or the guy formerly known as Santa, somehow had something to do with this? Was it some kind of sign?

Maybe they *should* meet.

Chapter Thirty-five

DID YOU KNOW?
It's rare for Pleasant Sands to have snow, given
its proximity to the Atlantic Ocean and the wind
blowing over the warmer (than air temperature) water.

Angela walked through the falling snow toward the town square. She pulled the fur-edged hood of her jacket up closer around her face. She'd been here hundreds of times. Her sister's office was right next door, but it always felt like the first time she'd ever been here on Christmas-tree-lighting night. She breathed it all in: the buzz in the air. The joy in the tiny faces. The appreciation of the elders who shuffled down the walk to join in the festive evening.

Her breath made smoke in the air. It was one of the coldest nights she remembered around here.

The crowd was thick despite the cold temperatures, and she was thankful for the windbreak as people crowded closer.

The town tree stood tall and proud in the center of the white gazebo. A shiny black piano was the only other thing on the platform. A man in a Santa hat walked by. Her heart hitched. Could it be her guy formerly known as Santa? She craned her neck to see him, but his hat was one like the kids and the other folks were wearing tonight. No holly on the side.

She nodded hellos to people she recognized from her store.

A glorious ruckus rose around the tree as people talked and laughed, waiting for the big moment.

Suddenly, everything went black, and a hush came over the crowd.

Then those familiar chords on the piano under the gazebo sounded. The first chords of "O Christmas Tree."

The high school band joined in, and the chorus began to sing. Then everyone joined in. All five verses and one last round of the first verse.

Then all was quiet and *three* . . . *two* . . . *one* . . . The tree lit in a burst of glorious light. Big lights. Little lights. LEDs and good old-fashioned bulbs too.

The piano keys sounded, followed by the dynamic accompaniment of the band and choir as "We Wish You a Merry Christmas" filled the air.

As Angela sang the words her heart was so full of memories and thankfulness that her eyes teared.

"There you are." Geoff's voice came from over her right shoulder. "I've been looking for you. I knew you'd be here."

"Hi."

"You're crying?"

She smiled through the gentle tears. He was dressed in a black overcoat and that silly Santa hat.

"Are you okay?" He placed his hands on her shoulders.

She shook her head, but said, "Yes. I'm fine. It's beautiful, and it's snowing."

"What are the chances of that?"

"Believe me, I thought they were zero, but today is very special in so many ways." She hadn't even had a chance to tell anyone about the job yet. Not even her sister. "I was offered a position as the tourism director. Here. In Pleasant Sands."

"You're perfect for that job."

"Thank you for everything you've done for me. I'm glad we're friends now."

"You deserve that job. No one knows more about this town than you."

She froze. The mayor had said the position was being funded by an outside source for the first eighteen months. Had Geoff done it, out of guilt? She'd have to turn the position down if he had, and she didn't want that either.

"Thanks. I'm really excited." She said, "It's almost too good to be true."

"No such thing. I'm happy for you."

"Me too. I'm glad we put our business differences behind us."

She looked away, scanning the crowd. Now would be a good time for her guy formerly known as Santa to show himself—to take her out of this situation.

"Who are you looking for?"

"No one."

"Wait a minute," Geoff said. "Is that formerly Santa guy supposed to be here?"

Her lips pulled tight. "Yes. Maybe. He'd mentioned the tree lighting."

"Well, I'll leave you to that, then." He pulled off his hat. She hadn't even looked for the holly on his. "He's very lucky."

"Thank you," she said quietly.

At least now she knew how to take a compliment. He turned to leave, then turned back. "But before I go I want you to know that

I regret the hostility at the beginning of our relationship. Timing really is everything, isn't it?"

She stared at him. Wide-eyed.

"I have to know. If it hadn't been for our businesses colliding, if we'd met at a different time or place, do you think we might have been able to honor and cherish through all our years, and in all that life may bring us?"

"Don't do this . . ." She closed her eyes and sucked in a breath. "I've got to go." She turned to leave with tears in her eyes.

He watched her walk away.

Geoff trudged toward the parking lot. He'd even parked right next to her. His heart hurt. Maybe this was exactly why he never got serious with anyone. Hurt too darn much when it didn't go his way.

When he got ready to get in his car, the flowers on the front seat made him want her even more.

No. He wasn't willing to give up so easily. This was for the rest of his life.

He put his hat back on, and unlocked the car and got the flowers out. A dozen long-stemmed roses and a white daisy nestled next to each perfect bud, wrapped like they were ready for a beauty queen.

He stood there holding the bouquet.

No, too desperate. Cliché.

He leaned against his passenger door, right across from her driver's door, and crossed one leg over the other. She wouldn't be able to miss him.

No, too suave.

But when he looked up she was less than ten feet away. She was walking with her head down and she hadn't even seen him, but even if he wasn't ready, he was going to make this happen.

He held the flowers behind his back and smiled. His lip twitched. He rubbed his hand across his mouth, hoping the tic would stop before she got close.

The expression on her face didn't give him any indication of what she was thinking.

He wanted to pull her into his arms, but he just stood there. Waiting.

She swept a hand through her hair. "You were behind it all. The job offer, I mean." Her left eyebrow raised, just a tad, as if challenging him to do anything but tell the truth.

He smiled, hoping she'd give one in return.

"Angela, some things in business are personal. I realize that's okay now. Like what was important to my mother—so important that she even put it in her will."

"I don't know what you're talking about, and what does it even have to do with me?"

"Answering Dear Santa letters."

Her jaw went slack. Realization written all over her face.

He rushed to explain before she could get mad. "I didn't take Mom seriously. The Dear Santa letters project has been hers since the day we opened the first store. I thought it was silly. It was always a priority for her. She used to answer every single one she got. I thought she was compromising what was important for our business with her personal preferences, especially when she had to start hiring people to help her get the job done."

Her brows pulled together.

"But I was wrong. Angela, those letters, they were good. Maybe not directly for business, but where it counts. In the heart." He held his hand to his heart. The flowers felt heavy in the hand behind his back. "When my mother was in ICU she asked only one thing of me."

"What was that?"

"To answer the Dear Santa letters that were routed to her. No matter how personal the motivation had been I'm thankful for those letters, because I'd have never met you if it hadn't been for her demanding I personally respond to them."

She looked scared.

"I know that you're Anita C. Miracle. I think you've been realizing that I'm your guy, but you didn't want to admit it. I'm so lucky I found you."

"I never expected a personal response. Maybe that's why when I received one I felt so connected to what was said."

"I hope you were feeling as connected to me as I was to you."

"When did you know?" She swallowed hard. "That it was me?"

"Not for a long time. I'd already fallen for you, before I knew you were you." He handed her the flowers.

She held them in her arms. "Daisies and roses," she said quietly as tears streamed down her face. "My business was waning before Christmas Galore moved into town, you were just the last punch. If it hadn't been you it would've been some other store . . . or some other time. Don't feel guilty."

"That's one thing I don't feel."

"Well, then, why are you funding that position for the town to have a tourism director?"

"Because you're perfect for that job, and I have ties to this town now too."

"The store."

"More than the store. My mom met my dad here. He was from

here. I never knew him. He died here before I was born. I'm glad she finally shared this little piece of her past with me. In a way, I guess I inherited something else from her too."

"What do you mean?"

He touched his hand to her cheek. "We both fell in love in Pleasant Sands."

"You mean *with* Pleasant Sands," she corrected him.

"No, Angela. I mean I fell in love here."

Her brown eyes sparkled. Her head slightly tilted.

"With you."

Angela said, "I so wanted to believe that. I was afraid . . ." The words seemed to catch in her throat.

"I want to jog on the beach with you—" He had almost forgotten. "Hang on." He ran to the trunk of his car and came back with a bucket in hand. "To collect shells along the shore together. I want to buy you flowers just because it's Tuesday, wake up to your smile and go to sleep knowing you're nearby. I look forward to every tiny piece of trivia you tell me."

She slapped his arm playfully.

"I'm not kidding." He took her hands into his. "You light up when you talk about this town. The new job . . . it suits you, and that makes me happy. Your eyes dance, and you get this little dimple right there on the right side of your chin when you're really excited. It's cute. I want to be the reason for those smiles."

"You are."

He pulled her into an embrace, a bit awkwardly at first. "Angela Carson, will you spend Christmas with me?"

"Yes."

"And can I be your Santa every Christmas to come?"

She looked up at the hat, clearly recognizing the holly. "Dear Santa. Most definitely."

Epilogue

DID YOU KNOW?

This museum resides in the original Pleasant Sands
Lighthouse built in 1823. Decommissioned in 1921,
it's remained a town landmark ever since.

THE FOLLOWING JULY

It was hard to believe just last December this place was a Christmas store. The historical lighthouse may have been decommissioned long ago, but now it was restored to its original beauty. Gone were the heavy wooden displays filled with Christmas decorations that used to be Heart of Christmas, and the train that chugged along the ceiling entertaining the tiny tots while their parents shopped.

The only Christmas ornaments in the store now carried the new brand for Pleasant Sands—an eye-catching logo on a porcelain sand dollar or glass ball.

Where the Heart of Christmas sign once stood, now a sand-blasted wooden sign read, PLEASANT SANDS VISITOR CENTER. A free tour through the original lighthouse, including climbing to the top of the harlequin-diamond-daymarked tower, was open to visitors four days a week. From the top one could see the original lighthouse lens and view the ocean and whole town. The tour also included a walk through the history of the town, with interactive displays and framed articles and pictures of Pleasant Sands a hundred years ago.

The only thing that remained from Heart of Christmas was the trivia Angela posted out front. Posting that was still her favorite part of each day.

Angela sat at her desk talking to the owner of Akaw! on the phone about the opportunities and tax breaks for new businesses coming into Pleasant Sands. She'd learned from him that "Akaw!" was something surfers yelled when they spotted the perfect wave. Fitting for a surfboard company, and they were looking for an East Coast location. Pleasant Sands seemed like a good fit.

"Yes sir. I look forward to talking to you next week. We have your reservation all set. See you then." She hung up feeling satisfied with the progress her small team had already made in the past short six months.

Just as she hung up the phone, the new blue-and-white trolley dropped off a load of tourists in front of the lighthouse. Stephanie met them out front, greeting them and taking their tickets for the next tour.

The season was starting out great, and tomorrow there was the huge Fourth of July celebration. A parade, a new gourmet-burger cook-off and the best fireworks display they'd ever had in this town.

Pictures lined the bookshelf across from her desk. One was of her with the most important people in her life at the ribbon-cutting ceremony for the new visitor center: Marie, Brad and Chrissy, and, of course, Geoff. Beside that stood a picture of her with Momma Grace at the register in Heart of Christmas when she was seven.

She glanced down at the diamond ring on her finger. Everything had moved so fast, but she'd never been happier.

Marie walked in with a smile so bright Angela was almost afraid to ask what was going on. "What are you doing here in the middle of a workday?"

"I couldn't wait." She flailed a priority mailer in the air overhead. "The sample is here! It's even prettier than I thought it would be."

Angela jumped up from her desk. "You're kidding. That was so fast. Let me see."

Marie opened the envelope and slid out the invitation.

Each corner had been folded in, with laser-cut daisies around a poinsettia meeting in the middle, where a small silver bow held the invitation together.

"I love how the intricate cuts soften the square shape. You were right, Angela."

Angela carefully pulled the silver bow and opened the invitation into an even larger square.

Inside, the message was simple.

Geoff Paisley
AND
Angela Carson

INVITE YOU *to* JOIN THEIR
WEDDING CELEBRATION

DECEMBER 24TH ~ AT 5PM
AT THE TOWN SQUARE GAZEBO
PLEASANT SANDS, NC

Nuptials will be followed by the Annual Holiday Tree
Lighting. Celebrate with cupcakes, punch and a holiday

band with the happy couple as they begin their life as husband and wife in Pleasant Sands.

No RSVP Required.
In lieu of gifts, bring a canned good
for the food pantry.

"Do you love them?" Marie asked.

Angela looked again at the collage of special moments on the shelf. A picture of her standing between her sister and Emma on the last day of Heart of Christmas. The ribbon-cutting when she reopened the lighthouse. The first elementary school tour of the lighthouse. And the picture of Geoff on bended knee proposing to her on Valentine's Day.

Angela smiled as a warm glow flowed through her.

"I do."